KYLA
THE HIGHLAND CLAN BOOK 9
Published by Keira Montclair
Copyright © 2017 by Keira Montclair

Cover Design and Interior Format

Kyla

THE HIGHLAND CLAN BOOK NINE

KEIRA
MONTCLAIR

TO THE READER

EACH OF THE NOVELS IN The Highland Clan is a stand-alone novel. However, for the richest experience, I would recommend starting with the first novel: Loki.

You'll see there is an extensive list of characters, ones you will grow to love if you start at the beginning.

The Clan Grant Series is the series in which the parents were introduced.

The series can be read separately, but many characters appear in both.

THE GRANTS AND RAMSAYS IN 1280S

GRANTS

LAIRD ALEXANDER GRANT and wife, MADDIE
John (Jake) and wife, Aline
James (Jamie) and wife, Gracie
Kyla
Connor
Elizabeth
Maeve

BRENNA GRANT and husband, QUADE RAMSAY
Torrian (Quade's son from his first marriage) and wife, Heather—
Nellie and son, Lachlan
Lily (Quade's daughter from his first marriage) and husband,
Kyle—twin daughters, Lise and Liliana
Bethia
Gregor
Jennet

ROBBIE GRANT and wife, CARALYN
Ashlyn (Caralyn's daughter from a previous relationship) and hus-
band, Magnus
Gracie (Caralyn's daughter from a previous relationship) and hus-
band, Jamie
Rodric (Roddy)
Padraig

BRODIE GRANT and wife, CELESTINA
Loki (adopted) and wife, Arabella—sons, Kenzie and Lucas
Braden
Catriona
Alison

JENNIE GRANT and husband, AEDAN CAMERON
Riley
Tara
Brin

RAMSAYS

QUADE RAMSAY and wife, BRENNA GRANT (see above)

LOGAN RAMSAY and wife, GWYNETH
Molly (adopted) and husband, Tormod
Maggie (adopted)
Sorcha
Gavin
Brigid

MICHEIL RAMSAY and wife, DIANA
David
Daniel

AVELINA RAMSAY and DREW MENZIE
Elyse
Tad
Tomag
Maitland

CHAPTER ONE

Summer in Grant land,
the Highlands of Scotland,
late 13ᵗʰ century

JAKE GRANT STOOD ON THE dais of the great hall filled with Grants and Ramsays. The majority of the Ramsays, who were considered family by marriage, were still at Grant castle after joining them for Sorcha Ramsay's wedding.

A messenger had arrived not long ago, and the man had immediately been led to the solar. Kyla Grant had watched it happen, and she now trembled in anticipation of the words that were about to come from her brother's mouth. Something dangerous was afoot; she just knew it. As acting laird of the Grant clan—along with his twin, Jamie—it was her brother's duty to pass on the news.

"Prepare for battle," Jake said, not attempting to soften the directive. "Word has reached us that Glenn of Buchan has a band of mercenaries who plan on attacking our castle within the fortnight with the intent of killing our sire, Alex Grant." Kyla sucked in a gasp as Jake nodded to their father, seated at the front of the dais. Alex had passed on the lairdship to Kyla's brothers after he was injured in a recent battle. "Buchan's plan is to make his move while my sire is still in a weakened state."

Jamie added, "He also still voices vengeance against the Ramsays, so we are all targets."

Gracie Grant, Jamie's wife, reached over to clasp Kyla's hand. "We have a verra strong clan, Kyla. Never forget that." Was her mood so easy to read?

"But how much more can we endure?" The clans' shared enemy, Ranulf MacNiven, had finally been defeated. Still, it had not put a stop to their troubles. Baron Crichton of Duncrub had attacked the Grants, wounding Kyla's father, and though they'd defeated him, his second, Simon de La Porte, remained free. And Bearchun, a former guard with the Ramsays, had escaped after making an attack on Sorcha. If all these enemies had banded together with Glenn of Buchan, they were in trouble indeed.

Logan Ramsay, Sorcha's sire, stood at the end of the dais. "We've discussed this at length. Quade and I will not put any lives at risk by traveling through the Highlands with English mercenaries running wild under the bastard Simon de La Porte. We assume he is with Buchan, but we really know naught about him yet. The Ramsays and Grants are stronger together."

A hush fell across the group at Logan's announcement.

Kyla's father slowly got to his feet to address the small crowd. He didn't need to silence anyone. They all anxiously awaited his announcement. "I know you have many questions, but this is all we shall reveal for now. Rumors are rampant throughout the Highlands at present, including talk of my death. We felt it necessary to address them. The details of what happens next will be up to your lairds and our warriors, but know that we are prepared to defend Grant land. We may even decide to go on the offensive—if our king is willing to support such a movement. Molly and Tormod will travel to Edinburgh to meet with King Alexander. Until then, we wait.

"I ask you to be patient, and for everyone to stay close to the safety of our castle walls. We welcome the Ramsays. Their warriors will join our ranks, and I believe we have the best minds in all of the land working on our strategy."

The gathering broke up, but all Kyla could do was sit and stare, entranced by what had taken place in front of her. Her mother, Maddie, helped her sire back to their new chamber on the first floor. Logan, Jake, Jamie, and a few others headed into the solar with Molly and Tormod. The few warriors who'd been allowed to join the gathering headed out the door, their voices loud and boisterous as they discussed the possible battles ahead.

Why must men love to fight so?

Finally, when Kyla could get herself to move again, she hustled into the kitchens to speak to Cook and make sure there were no problems with the supper menu. They'd been preparing extra since Sorcha's wedding.

When she returned, she leaned against a post, uncertain of what to do next. She needed to do something, and while she had an idea of what she wished to do, it was a foolish plan at best.

Or was it?

She found Sorcha in the still-crowded great hall—an easy task given her cousin's bright hair—clasped her hand, and led her up the stairs and into the new woman's solar that had been created from her parents' old chamber. Peeking inside, she noted they were alone, which was exactly as she'd hoped. Closing the door behind her, she put her finger to her lips.

"Hush, Sorcha."

"What is it?"

"We must do something." Kyla squeezed her cousin's hand. "We cannot stand by and watch our beloved Grant castle be ruined or taken over by the infidels. I have a plan, but we must make haste to Buchan land to carry it out."

"How are we to do aught?" Sorcha asked, clearly alarmed. "True, I can use my bow, but one archer cannot do much alone, and I am certain Cailean would not approve of it. 'Tis not safe."

"Bring Cailean along. 'Tis a mission of peace. Buchan would not dare attack us under those conditions or the king would take his castle. If we can speak to them, mayhap we can convince them to stop this madness before any more blood is spilled."

"My father would never allow it."

"Why not? Molly and Tormod travel alone all the time."

"Aye, but only after they were trained. Molly has told me a wee bit about what they were asked to do, and 'tis not for me." She motioned for Kyla to keep her voice down.

Kyla led her to the hearth on the outer wall, away from the door. "Sorcha, I'll ride there alone if I must. If I can put an end to this for our clans, I will."

"Did you not hear what they said about the mercenaries? They could be approaching our land as we speak! Can you not guess what they would do to a beautiful lass? You'd be kidnapped like so many others have been. You must stay here." Sorcha's voice shook with passion, and Kyla knew why: she'd been kidnapped not long ago by three unsavory characters. If it hadn't been for her husband, she might have been raped.

The door swung open, and Gracie stepped into the solar. She halted as soon as she saw the two of them huddled near the hearth. "I knew it. I could tell by the glimmer in your eyes, Kyla Grant. You're planning something. I knew for certes as soon as you hurried out of the hall."

Sorcha spun around and said, "Nay. She was trying to, but I'll not allow it. Gracie, talk some sense into her. She aims to ride to Buchan land. Alone, if need be—amidst the mercenaries. Tell her 'tis mad!"

"Nay, Kyla," Gracie cried out. "Please do not do it. I could not tolerate aught happening to you."

There were tears in Gracie's eyes, and Kyla rushed over to kiss her cheek. She'd chosen not to include her sister-in-law for this very reason. While she loved Gracie dearly, she'd known the other lass would not approve of her plan. "Rest easy. I'd not *really* go alone—I was carried away by the moment. But I must do something." She cast a hopeful glance at Sorcha, who was more impetuous than Gracie, still hoping she might agree to help. Given her talent with a bow, she'd definitely be an asset.

Sorcha sighed. "I meant what I said, Kyla. 'Tis too dangerous. The men in our clan are different from the ones you'd encounter on the road. There are men who take what they want, regardless of whether you're willing, and I'll not put any of us in a position to be kidnapped. Look at Jake's wife! Poor Aline was kidnapped and kept against her will for years." She visibly shuddered at the thought.

"Mayhap so, but we have so much to celebrate. You both had beautiful weddings, and my sire survived his wounds. Now we are all together. We should be happy; we should be celebrating. I won't allow those louts to ruin all we've worked for because of greed and treachery…" Would they be agreeable if she told them more about her plan? She would only know if she tried. "I recall tales of Davina well," she continued, "and I think she would help me."

"What makes you believe Buchan's daughter would help you?" Gracie asked, clearly surprised by the suggestion. "And even if she does, how could two women hope to stop a battle?"

"Mayhap women should become the peacemakers. I believe we

could settle all sorts of foolishness in a rational way. Davina has softened. Do not forget that she helped Molly and Tormod catch MacNiven in the end. She loved him, but she realized he'd turned evil. If I could find a way to get to her, mayhap I can convince her to talk to her sire, to get him to see reason. If nothing else, she can tell me about what he intends to do. We'd be able to stop this nonsense if we knew more about his intentions."

But a quick look at them told her that they both thought her plan was mad. "If you do not wish to assist me, I'll find my own way," she said quietly. "But I do promise I'll not go alone."

She headed for the door, struggling with disappointment, when Sorcha called out to her. "Molly and Tormod are heading that way. If you insist on traveling to Buchan land, at least go with them." Sorcha pulled her into an embrace.

"Can you not see that I must do something?" Kyla asked, needing them to understand. "My mother has run this keep beautifully for years, and now her time is devoted to my ailing sire. This could worsen my sire's condition…it could cause my mother to fall ill. 'Tis too much for them. I must take some of their concerns on my shoulders." She could not stand by and watch the people dearest to her, her *clann*, torn apart.

"Aye, I understand your concern, but your parents are stronger than you think," Sorcha said.

Kyla rested her chin on Sorcha's shoulders as tears trailed wetly down her cheeks. She and Gracie locked eyes, and her sister-in-law came closer.

"I'll help in any way I can," she said softly, running a hand down Kyla's hair, "but I'll not leave Grant land. Please don't do aught without telling us. We can help you decide what is best."

Kyla looked back and forth between her dear friends. "Will you promise not to tell my sire until I'm well off Grant land? I know he would never allow me to seek out Davina, but I need to try… If there's any way I can stop this, I have to do it."

Sorcha replied, "I'll not tell unless something untoward happens, but then I'll be forced to tell all. Before you decide on anything, we need to find out what is being decided in the solar. Come. We'll return to the hall."

"But who will tell us what they've discussed?" Gracie asked. "I'll ask Jamie, but I'm not sure if he'll tell me all."

"I saw who went inside," Sorcha said. "Jake and Magnus—" She nodded to Gracie, whose sister was married to Magnus, Jake's second, "—my sire, Uncle Quade, Jamie, Finlay, and Connor."

Connor. Kyla's hope began to sprout wings. She and her younger brother were extremely close. He would help her find a way to Davina.

Sorcha frowned. "What is it? Your expression has changed."

Kyla smiled. "Connor. He's been left out of most everything, and he wishes to take an active role in protecting our clan. He'll help me for certes." She spun around and headed out the door.

Gracie called out from behind her. "But Connor has never been involved in any of the clan's battles yet. How can he help you?"

Kyla raced down the passageway, lifting her skirts to give her speed, and hurried down the staircase to wait by the hearth. She'd catch Connor as soon as he came out. Gasping for breath, she did her best to calm her racing heart.

Her sire would rage if he knew what she was thinking, but she could not sit by while her wonderful, strong clan was pushed into another war. She'd find a way to fix things. She'd find a bloodless way to win them peace.

The door to the solar opened and she strolled over casually just as Gracie and Sorcha came hurrying down the stairs behind her. The men strolled past her, tension in their shoulders as they moved out to the lists. Only Quade and Logan stayed behind in the solar.

One of the warriors winked when he passed her, she knew she had another accomplice should she need him.

Finlay MacNicol, her brother Jamie's second.

ℭ

Finlay strode out the door and almost stopped in his tracks. Three lasses stood there waiting for someone, but only one drew his attention—the dark-haired beauty with bright blue eyes. When had Kyla Grant become so attractive? Each time he saw her, she was prettier, if that were possible. Something had changed in the way he saw Kyla after he escorted her to Cameron land to see her injured sire. At the time, Alex's survival had not been a sure thing, and Kyla's bravery had astonished Finlay. He'd learned to appreciate her as a person instead of Jamie's wee sister.

He hurried to catch up with Jamie Grant, who'd already made

his way out the door and down the steps. Alex and Logan had decided to send a group of warriors out to the Buchans to see if Glenn would speak to them. He'd allowed them in before, and if they could get inside the curtain wall, they'd learn more about the rumors traversing the Highlands. Upon their return, they'd scout the area around the Grants to see if they could locate Simon de La Porte and his men. Molly and Tormod would travel with the group, and they'd head to Edinburgh when the rest of the guards returned to Grant land.

Jamie had asked Finlay to join them—an honor befitting his role as the laird's second in command.

"We leave on the morrow. Are you certain you're willing to leave your mother?" Jamie asked.

Finlay nodded. "I'll go because you need me. I am your second, if you've forgotten."

"If her time is near, you are to remain behind," Jamie said, "and that's an order. You'll not forgive yourself if she passes while you're gone. Aye, and I see that look on your face. Save your sharp tongue for another time."

His friend knew him too well. Humor had always been his way of dealing with life's challenges. In truth, he was conflicted about leaving at such a time.

"Check on her and meet me in the lists," Jamie continued. "You can assist Jake and me in choosing our guards."

Finlay nodded and headed toward his family cottage, tucked inside the bailey. His heart ached each time he stepped through the door. He and his brother Fergus had been assigned to Loki Grant, but they'd returned to the main Grant castle because their dear mother, Inga, had taken ill.

Several healers had told them there was naught she could do. His mother had been ill for a while now, and they all knew her time was coming soon.

Finlay opened the door with a sigh, knowing what he would find. Voices carried through the stone walls, telling him they had company, something he was not fond of because visitors tired his mother out.

This time was different. Lady Brenna and Lady Jennie, Alex Grant's sisters, both talented healers, were at Inga's bedside in his parents' chamber. Lady Brenna was the one who'd told them his mother had a woman's growth inside her belly that they could not stop. His mother had deteriorated quite a bit since then.

He stood in the doorway to the chamber. "Greetings, Lady Brenna, Lady Jennie." He nodded to each of the healers. His sire was not far from his mother's bedside, as usual. "Papa, could I speak to you outside?"

Nicol turned to him. "I'll be right there. I'm going to change your mother's position so she rests better."

"Papa, I'll do it." He did not bend on this. True, his sire was still a strong guard, but his lower back troubled him at times. Finlay moved to his mother's side, bent his knees, and scooped her up with ease. She'd lost so much weight that it saddened him. "Mama, tell me which way you'd like to settle."

A weak, raspy voice answered him. "I'll answer if you speak to your sire here. No secrets, if you remember, Finlay. Please?"

"All right, Mama," he said. As usual, he could never refuse his mother. A sweeter woman had never walked the Highlands. He and Fergus were only a year apart and his mother had never had another child, much to her dismay. She'd begged for a daughter, but the good Lord had never blessed her with one. However, she was not one to complain.

Brenna and Jennie stepped back and said, "We shall stop by later." Lady Brenna glanced at his sire and said, "Nicol, if you need us, please call. We'll be here as quickly as we can. You have more of the primrose root to help her sleep?"

"Aye, many thanks to you both." He escorted the two women to the door.

Finlay reached down and carefully smoothed his mother's hair. "I'll wait until Papa returns and tell you my thoughts. Now, which direction?"

"On my left side, please." Once he had her comfortable, he sat down on a nearby stool.

His mother took his hand. "I understand what goes on in your heart, you know. You are my son. Papa has told me of the situation in the Highlands. 'Tis your duty to go."

"Mama, 'tis also my duty to stay at your side when your time is near." His mother's skin had taken on a yellow hue, which he did not take for a good sign. "I could stay and take you to the waterfall again. You know how you love the heather in the fields nearby and the other wildflowers."

He felt his sire's presence behind him just as his mother attempted to lift her hand to cup his cheek. "Finlay, I'd prefer to stay inside. We are blessed that your sire was such a good friend to the Grants, and they gave us this cottage inside the bailey. I care not to go anywhere that could risk…" She paused to gain the strength to continue. Her hand went to her chest before it fell back on the pallet. A great, rattling cough issued from her chest, and Finlay helped her sit and held her goblet of water to her lips.

How he hated to see her in such a condition. He clung to the memories of his childhood—his mother taking them to the loch for a swim or cooking the best stew in the Highlands at their hearth. That was how he wished to remember her.

"I'll not go outside again. Go…do what you must. Fergus will stay if he has not been chosen to join you. And if I am not here when you return, do not suffer any guilt. I am ready. You know I love you, and I'll always watch over you."

Her eyes closed for a scant moment. In a broken voice, she whispered, "Please, just a moment to rest my eyes."

Finlay leaned in to kiss her cheek and then covered her up with a plaid. She'd fought so hard and continued with her chores at home for so long. Now he almost prayed for her time to come soon. Watching her endure the pain was too much for all of them. He could see how much it had worn on his father.

He and his sire exchanged a look before leaving the cottage together. The healers awaited them. "What is it?"

"She'll not last much longer, I'm afraid," Lady Brenna said as she wrapped an arm around Finlay's shoulder. "It would be best for you to stay."

Finlay wanted as much information as possible. "How long is not much longer?"

Lady Jennie shrugged. "Could be a day, but probably less than a sennight. Her belly continues to grow from what's inside her, and it will take her last breath eventually. I'm so sorry."

The healers hugged him and his sire and then took their leave. Finlay stared at his sire for a long moment. "Jamie asked me to go, but he said only if Mama is well enough. What do you think, Papa?"

His brother Fergus came along the path. After greeting them, he said, "Och. I know you were chosen for the scouting mission, Finlay, but you need to stay here. I overheard most of your conversation with the healers."

Finlay nodded at his brother. "Agreed." Then he turned to his father, clasping his shoulder, and said, "I'll stay, Papa."

"Many thanks," Nicol said. "I could use your support when the time comes. But if aught changes, you both may need to leave. You can skip a scouting mission, but not a battle."

He sighed and moved back inside to grab a flagon of ale before he made his way to the lists. His mother's voice carried to him. "Finlay?"

He hurried to her side. "Aye, Mama?"

"You must go."

He knelt next to her bed. "Mama, I'm going to stay here with you and Papa and Fergus. 'Tis only a scouting mission."

"Nay, you do not understand." She reached for his hand, tears misting her eyes. "Listen to me. Go. You *must* join them."

"But why, Mama? I don't understand." He tucked the blanket around her shoulders and reached for another to calm her shivering.

"Have I not taught you the importance of honoring a dying person's final request? Well, this is your mother's. I wish for you to go on this journey. 'Tis a journey that will affect your life more than any other."

"Final request?" Aye, everyone knew a dying person's final request was to be heeded if at all possible. However, the rest of his clan believed he belonged here by her side. "And what do you mean by affect my life?"

"Please, Finlay. I cannot explain, but don't tell your brother. You know he'd feel slighted if he knew my final wish was for you." She paused to gather air to speak. "Just do as your mama asks. Do not listen to the others. They know not what I know." She closed her eyes and fell into a deep sleep. How he wished she would explain her reasoning, but it did not matter.

He would honor his mother's final request, no matter what anyone else said.

He had to go on this mission.

CHAPTER TWO

AFTER A LONG CONVERSATION WITH Sorcha and Gracie the previous night, Kyla had finally settled on a plan. They all felt confident that she could travel safely with the group Uncle Logan had chosen to go to Buchan land.

They were just as confident that Sorcha's sire would refuse to take her, so the only way Kyla could join the group was if she snuck along behind them, keeping hidden until they were far enough from home that her uncle wouldn't be willing to turn around. It was unlikely she'd be sent back. After all, this was a peaceful mission, and Kyla believed she could be an asset to the group. The lasses had promised Kyla they'd explain the situation to her mother…but not until much later that evening.

There was only one more step to her plan. She intended to cajole her youngest brother into joining her so she would not need to make the initial ride alone.

On the way to the stables the following day, Kyla caught up with her brother Connor. "I have a proposal for you."

"What kind of proposal?" Connor's gaze narrowed. "This cannot be something you wish for our parents to know."

"Nay, I don't wish them to know about any of it." She grabbed him by the elbow and tugged him behind the armory where they could speak in private. "Listen to me. I'm planning to follow the scouting group. Will you come with me?"

"Have you lost your mind?" Connor asked, his eyes wide. "Why would you do something so foolish?"

"Because I want to put an end to this. I'm tired of all this battling. I wish to speak with Davina Buchan. Glenn of Buchan seems to have lost his mind over the deaths of his two sons, but mayhap Davina and I can convince him to step down. I can speak with her much better than Uncle Logan or Jamie could. 'Tis true that Molly will be there, but she killed MacNiven, so I doubt Davina would tell her anything."

"And you think the man will listen to you, a Grant?" Connor paced, rubbing the whiskers that he hadn't shaved in a while. Over the years, his coloring had darkened so much that he was almost the image of their sire. He and Kyla bore a strong likeness, but while Kyla had their mother's blue eyes, Connor had the gray eyes of their father.

"Please, Connor? I can no longer stand back and wait for our clan to be destroyed. Have they agreed to send you with the group, or are they leaving you behind as though you're a bairn?" She knew she was prodding Connor's greatest weakness, but these were desperate circumstances in her mind. She could goad her brother into listening to her.

Connor's eyes danced with the same fire she often saw in her sire's gaze. "Nay, I'm to be left behind again. Jake is staying at the keep, so I asked to go, but our sire refused. I'm tired of being ignored. I'm almost ten and nine. Jake and Jamie had traveled half the Highlands by the time they were my age." His eyes narrowed as he stared at her, a firm set to his jaw.

She quirked her brow and waited, hoping he would come to the right conclusion.

A moment later, he said, "Aye, I'll go with you. They leave at midday."

"We can follow at a distance and catch up to them as soon as we're off Grant land. Jamie will not send us back then, nor will Uncle Logan."

He thought for a moment, then grinned, but a split second later concern crossed his features again. "What about Mama?"

"I've arranged for Gracie and Sorcha to talk to Mama this eve, tell her we've gone with Uncle Logan. I do not want Mama and Papa worrying about us. They trust Uncle Logan, so at least they'll know we're safe."

"You already told them I was going along?"

She smirked. "Aye, I thought I could convince you. 'Tis a journey for peace. I know not why there should be trouble." She patted his arm. "We have to keep Jake ignorant of our plans before we leave."

"I've been assigned to train in the lists with Jake. I'll claim illness midday and head to the keep. I can hide a couple of horses near the cluster of oaks. I'll meet you there."

Kyla was so pleased, she clasped her hands to her chest before throwing her arms around Connor's neck. "My thanks, Connor. We shall be successful."

"Aye, we better be…because if we're unsuccessful, we'll never be allowed to leave the castle again."

Kyla had no doubt he was correct.

☾

Midday arrived, and Kyla huddled behind the two horses waiting under the oak trees, praying Connor would be along soon. A short time later she heard someone approaching, and she held her breath until her brother broke through the trees.

"You made it." She threw her arms around her brother's neck. "Many thanks. I promise you'll not regret it."

His face lit up. "Jake pays me no mind, thinks of me as the wee one. By the time he discovers I'm gone, we'll be halfway to the Buchans."

Connor helped her mount and they headed out, trailing the scouting group down the main path to the south of Grant land. When they finally caught up with the band, they were off Grant land and well on their way to the Buchans.

The two guards at the periphery rode back to intercept them and then sent them up to ride alongside Jamie's horse. He immediately held up his hand to stop the group's progression before turning to his sister and brother. "Has something happened to Papa?" he asked, his face turning pale.

"Nay," Kyla hurried to reassure him. "Everything is fine."

"Then why are you here?" He tipped his head to the side, that movement he often made when he was wise to her trickery.

"We wish to assist you in your mission." Kyla glanced around at the others in the group, noticing the slight smirk on Finlay MacNicol's face. She lifted her chin another notch, though she was unnerved by something she had just noticed. "Where is Uncle Logan?"

"He's gone ahead scouting as he oft does." Jamie dismounted

and pointed to a spot off to the side of the path. He said to the others, "Take care of your needs. We'll be moving on in ten minutes."

Connor reached for Kyla after dismounting, but she managed on her own, not wanting to show any weakness in front of the others. She'd not allow Jamie to talk her out of this. It was actually a good thing Uncle Logan was not nearby. He might be harder to convince than her elder brother.

"You're not going along. Neither of you were part of the group we selected." Jamie crossed his arms in front of his body, glaring at both of them.

"I don't care that we weren't chosen," Kyla shot back. "I'm sure we were *never* considered for this mission."

"Which is the reason we have joined you," Connor added with a scowl. "We're never considered."

Jamie nodded his head. "Connor, I understand your frustration. I could be convinced to allow you stay." Then he pivoted to face Kyla. "You, nay. You're going home. And I'll say no more on the matter. If I don't stop you, Uncle Logan will. He'll send you back for certes."

"But why? Jamie, listen to me. I believe I can be an asset to this group. Your plan is to speak with Glenn of Buchan in the hopes that he'll agree to a peaceful resolution. But he's not likely to speak the truth. We'd be much better off appealing to Davina. I can talk to her woman to woman, better than any man could, and I can convince her to talk to her sire." She believed in her plan, and she'd plead her case again and again until they allowed her on this journey.

"And what is Davina to do? She'll not convince her sire of aught. Buchan has no respect for women."

"Jamie, please. She is the only child Glenn of Buchan has left. I think she could convince him to act more honorably. You heard about the way she acted with Molly." She noticed Molly was listening to the conversation, so she pointed to her. "Ask her. She'll tell you how the woman has changed."

Jamie turned around and lifted his chin, giving Molly the chance to speak. "She has changed, I'll not disagree with you, Kyla. She is more soft-hearted than she was before. I'm sure Tormod would agree that she was truly sympathetic toward the bairns."

Tormod, not one to speak up, just nodded and said, "Aye, I'd agree she's changed."

"If 'tis true, then Molly can speak with her," Jamie immediately replied.

Molly shrugged. "I could speak with her, but since I killed her betrothed, I doubt she'll have much interest in speaking to me." It was the same conclusion Kyla had reached, but she was glad she didn't have to make the argument.

Kyla's head spun back to Jamie. He couldn't have any argument with that reasoning.

"But she didn't care about MacNiven anymore at the end," he objected.

Molly said, "Forgive me for disagreeing, but she did still love him, or she would never have left her sire's clan to join him. Ranulf rejected her for trying to do what was right. She knew his mind was addled. I'll not have much luck with her. Kyla could."

Hope blossomed in her heart. She could kiss Molly at this moment, but she restrained herself.

Jamie's gaze narrowed and he paced in a small circle. "Finlay, join us."

While they waited for Finlay to move, Jamie said, "Does Mama know you're here, Kyla? Or Papa?"

"I left a message with Gracie and Sorcha. They'll tell Mama this eve. I do not wish to add to her worries, Jamie—I wish to lift them from her. If we're successful, 'twill be the best possible thing for both of our parents. Papa can't go into battle before he's ready."

He nodded to Connor. "And you?"

"I left the lists. Told Jake I wasn't feeling well. He'll not look for me until the morrow either. Kyla included my name in the message for Mama and Papa."

Jamie turned to Finlay. "I'm assigning you as Kyla's protector."

Finlay grinned in response. "Aye, my laird. I'd surely be pleased to protect Kyla."

"Nay," Kyla said. "Why must you assign me a protector?" She followed Jamie back to his horse. "Why, Jamie? Does Connor have a protector?"

He mounted his horse and said, "Don't be surprised. We did the same for Ashlyn, and she's an expert archer. Connor can fight for himself. Can you? If you wish to travel with us, you'll not leave

Finlay's side, and you'll promise to do what he says and whatever I say. Connor, you'll be by my side. I'm sending a messenger back so Mama will not worry. I want to be certain they know you reached us safely. If you do not agree to the terms, I'll send you both back to Grant land with him. You have less than a minute to decide. And understand 'tis against my best judgment, but I understand how it feels to be overlooked." He nodded at Connor. "To my mind, you should have been allowed to travel on scouting missions long ago."

Connor grinned and glanced at Kyla. "I accept the terms."

She groaned before she ground out, "I accept. Finlay, you better be kind."

Finlay chuckled. "I've never been aught but kind. Surely you can see the angel's halo over my head, lass."

Jamie choked down laughter.

"This is no time for jesting, Finlay." She opened her mouth to blast Finlay, but Connor whispered in her ear, "We're going. Be silent."

Finlay winked and held his arm out to her, as if to escort her to her horse.

Kyla couldn't argue with Connor, so she sighed and took Finlay's arm. Against all odds, she and her brother had been allowed to stay. She was now on her first scouting mission for the Grants.

What could possibly go wrong?

☾

It was just past dark when they made camp at the outskirts of Buchan land the following night. Uncle Logan had ridden back to join them, and his first comment was about Kyla.

"When did Kyla and Connor join us?" he asked, looking as taken aback as she'd ever seen him.

"They followed us undetected until we were well off Grant land," Jamie replied. "You know I've often fought for Connor to join us. He needs to learn, so I allowed him to come along. Kyla gave me good reason to believe she could assist us by speaking with Davina, so I've given her permission to travel with us since this is intended as a peaceful mission. I've assigned Finlay as her protector."

Uncle Logan gave a slow nod. "I'll not argue with you, laird. I agree your sire has kept his youngest son back for too long, and he's becoming one of your best swordsmen. But Kyla? 'Tis your decision. Did you send a messenger back to inform your sire?"

"Aye."

Uncle Logan peered at Finlay. "You have been given one of the most significant jobs of all—guarding Alex Grant's eldest daughter. Do you understand the importance of your assignment?"

Finlay swallowed hard and his usual wry smile left his face. "Aye, my lord. I will protect her with my life."

"Good. See that you do." He turned to Jamie. "When we arrive, we shall tell Buchan we come in peace. I scouted the area but couldn't determine who else is inside. While we're calling attention to ourselves at the gate, Molly and Tormod will climb over the curtain wall in back to see if they can determine if Simon de La Porte is inside. I wish to know for certes if he's joined arms with Buchan. 'Tis my primary goal for this mission. I don't expect Buchan to reveal anything to us willingly. Since I have our king's ear, he'll hide everything."

Jamie asked, "And your secondary goals?"

"Look for that bastard Bearchun. No one touches my daughters and lives."

"Understood," Jamie said.

"When I find that bastard, I'm going to rip him into tiny pieces, saving his black heart for last."

Kyla noticed a couple of the guards paled at her uncle's graphic description.

Jamie nodded. He turned to the group. "Take care of your needs and get some rest. We'll head out before dawn."

Uncle Logan walked away from the group with Molly and Tormod, no doubt to seek the best path up the curtain wall.

Kyla moved in the opposite direction, toward the forest, to take care of her needs, only to find Finlay directly behind her. She stopped, her hands on her hips. "Where are you going?"

Finlay gave her a wide grin. "With you."

"Nay. I need my privacy."

"But have you forgotten that my laird gave me strict instructions to stay by your side?"

Finlay asked, a supreme look of innocence in his gaze.

Kyla swung her hand and connected with him square in his chest, though he never flinched. "You'll not go with me." She glared at him, daring him to contradict her.

Jamie chuckled at his friend's antics, but then called out, "Finlay, you can allow her to pish on her own."

"But I wished to see what special technique it takes for a lass to find the right space."

"Jamie, he's even cruder than you are. Must I tolerate him?"

"Me?" Jamie stopped to give her a look of exasperation. "What have I done? Never mind. Do not answer that question. Aye, you must tolerate him. I have Connor to watch and 'tis enough for me. Finlay, leave her be." He stalked off into the trees.

Finlay waggled his eyebrows at her, smirking, and she stomped off into the bushes.

"Do let me know if you need any assistance, lass," he called out. "I'd be happy to find you a nice broad leaf or two."

She spun around and glared at him, her hands clenched into fists, before she continued on her way. True, she'd always liked Finlay, but sometimes he just pushed things too far… And yet she knew his dear mother's condition weighed heavily on him. Perhaps, in an odd way, his jests were his way of handling the situation.

She chastised herself and promised to be more forgiving of him.

When she finished and found a stream to wash her hands, she strode back to the center of their small camp, reminding herself that at least she'd made it this far. Buchan castle was nearby. She settled on a log across from Finlay, who smiled at her when she sat down. The other guards settled in a separate place.

"So if you do not mind my question, what is it you think you bring to this mission?" Finlay asked as he chewed his way through an oatcake.

"A sense of reason others clearly do not have." She tugged her plait over her shoulder and twirled the ends with her finger.

"Your brother? You say your reasoning skills are better than your laird? Hmmm. Have you told him that, lass?"

"Nay. And what makes you think I cannot help?" Kyla stared at Finlay. It struck her that he looked particularly handsome in the dark of the camp—at least when he wasn't talking. He hadn't shaved in a couple of days and the mix of red and brown gave his beard a glorious color. His hair had been bright red when he was younger, just like his brother's hair, but it had darkened over the past few years into a rich auburn. It was also the length she preferred—just to his shoulders. His brown eyes glittered at her, as if there was naught he'd rather do than tease her.

His husky voice brought her out of her trance. "I did not say you couldn't, but there have not been many instances of a lass helping in a battle. Och, but I forget how you've trained hard with your sword, and your bow is said to be mightier than many..."

"You speak ridiculous tales and enjoy teasing me. Say what you will. I stand by the fact that a woman can do as much as a man. We just operate differently."

"That you do, lass. I'll not argue that point." His chuckle told her his thoughts had taken a different turn.

"Being so close to Jamie, I thought you knew about the Ramsay women, or have you forgotten their names? Gwyneth, Molly, and Sorcha are all experts with the bow, and do not forget our own Ashlyn. Or will you continue to insist that only men have skills that are helpful in a battle?" As she waited for his answer, heat settled in her belly and traveled to places she didn't care to think about at the moment. His gaze didn't shift from hers, and it felt like those warm brown eyes were pinning her in place. Before she knew it, she found herself focusing on the way the muscles in his arms flexed every time he moved. Was she losing all sense?

His voice caught her, sending chills down her spine. "Oh, I remember them well. Just as I remember *you*, Kyla." He stood up to throw something into the woods, but not before his gaze raked up and down her body.

Her stomach flipped one way and then flopped another. What was the fool doing to her?

She didn't know, but it scared her how much she liked it.

CHAPTER THREE

E ARLY THE NEXT MORN, THEIR group sat at the gates of
    the Buchan Castle, requesting entrance. Molly and Tormod
had split from them a while ago and would find their own way in.
Finlay pulled his horse as close to Kyla's as possible as they made
their approach.

"What's your purpose?" one guard yelled.

Jamie Grant said, "We are from Clan Grant, and we come in
peace. I wish to speak with your laird."

"Wait here."

While they sat their horses in silence, Finlay glanced at Kyla—
her back straight, her expression proud. When he'd first learned
he was to protect her, he hadn't expected it to be such a pleasant
experience, but the duty had morphed into something delicious.
True, he'd purposefully goaded her with all his comments about
lasses, but he'd enjoyed every moment of their talk. Teasing Kyla
had kept his mind off his mother. He prayed twice a day that she
would still be there on his return. If not, the shame would likely
crush him. Even though she'd made it her dying wish that he join
this mission, he couldn't reveal that to anyone else lest his brother
discover the truth. He couldn't allow that to happen. They'd always
been too competitive, even when it came to approval from their
parents. Fergus had often had trouble accepting that Finlay would
be chosen over him for anything, strictly because he felt it was his
due to be first. Finlay had understood it when they were laddies,
but now they were both grown men—what did it matter if Fergus
was the elder?

He'd abide by his mother's last wish, come what may.

Kyla drew his gaze again. If he had to admit the truth, he had nothing but admiration for the lass. Her father had been seriously injured, and here she was trying to protect him, her actions driven by sheer love and loyalty. Her strength had struck him before, but he'd never spent much time alone with her until now. She continued to surprise him.

He moved his horse closer to hers, and she jerked her head toward him. "You hale, lass?" he whispered. He could see the fine tremors in her hand whenever she reached up to twirl a piece of hair that had escaped her plait, a move belying her outer display of calm.

She nodded, giving him a glare that told him to hold his tongue. He shrugged, thinking it would be fine with him if he sat and watched her for the next hour. But it wasn't to be. The guard returned with haste, followed by Glenn of Buchan on horseback. Four warriors rode at the laird's side.

Buchan had a cold expression on his face, so Finlay doubted they'd be welcomed inside. His men looked no more welcoming—hatred practically seethed from them. Buchan's gaze traveled across the entire group, stopping on Logan Ramsay for just a moment before returning to Jamie. A flash of fury crossed his face, but he covered it quickly.

Everyone in the Highlands knew the hatred between the Ramsay and Buchan clans. Two of the laird's sons had died in skirmishes with Ramsays, the eldest in a direct attack on the Ramsay clan. The second had lost his life when he'd kidnapped Logan's dear niece, Lily.

Glenn of Buchan uttered one word only, "Grant."

Jamie spoke, "Buchan. I come in peace, wishing for a meal at your table. I would like to discuss the present situation in the Highlands with you."

Glenn chuckled. "You would, would you? Why is that? Because your sire is near death and you wish to gain more allies?"

"My sire is not near death. Aye, he took an injury, but he improves daily. Why can we not be on friendly terms? Do we not wish for the same? For both of our clans to flourish in peace?"

"Aye, 'twas what I wished for when my two sons were alive. I wished to flourish, watch my grandsons grow and take over my castle, but 'tis not to be, is it? You and your Ramsay allies have put an end to all my wishes."

"We seek to make amends."

Glenn of Buchan said, "I see no good reason to allow you in, especially with Logan Ramsay at your side. You know my opinion of all Ramsays. I have naught to bring me joy thanks to you and yours. Go home. All of you."

A silence settled between the clans as they each took the other's measure.

Kyla broke the silence, pleading her case. "Davina, your daughter…" she stammered. "How does Davina fare?"

Finlay thought the man's gaze softened for a moment, but it immediately returned to its hardened state. "Who are you? And why would you care about my daughter?"

"I am Alex and Madeline Grant's daughter." Kyla's voice carried across the warriors, strong and clear. "I-I asked to come with my brother because I know she's had little female companionship. I wished to offer my own to her. We are of like age. I am twenty summers. I would be honored if you would allow me to speak with her."

Again, Finlay saw the older man soften. Kyla had been able to get more of a reaction out of him than anyone else had. "I fear Davina is turning daft. The loss of her brothers and that fool MacNiven have proven too much for her. Again, who may I thank for that, Ramsay?" he snapped, his gaze flashing at Logan.

"Please?" Kyla asked, her voice soft and warm and urgent. "Mayhap talking to another lass would be helpful."

To Finlay's great surprise, Glenn dropped his head before lifting his gaze to hers. "I'll allow you to speak to my daughter. The others will wait in the great hall. I offer you ale only. And you are to be gone before nightfall. I do this for Davina."

Uncle Logan glanced at Kyla with new respect before replying, "Accepted."

"I speak to the Grants, not you, Ramsay."

Jamie nodded. "Accepted with appreciation."

They followed Glenn into his inner bailey to the stables, and Finlay followed Kyla as closely as he possibly could. After they dismounted, he was tempted to haul her up against him and not leave her side. Her bravery was beyond impressive—she'd ridden out here with the express purpose of speaking with Davina, and she had ensured it would happen. But he worried that same bravery would get her into trouble.

As they traveled across the courtyard, Finlay couldn't help but notice the difference between this castle and the one he saw every day. Grant Castle stood tall and had grown over the years, the laird adding towers and chambers. Their people worked the land, herded sheep, and produced goods for the clan, and the clan was always growing. Every year, new cottages were added outside the walls.

This castle showed signs of wear—deterioration was visible in the curtain wall, in the crumbling steps to the keep. There were few fields that showed any evidence of being ready to harvest, and only a few livestock outside the walls. How did they feed their people?

He'd counted around fifty men in the lists, and a few more hustled inside the bailey, but where were the women? On Grant land, you'd see them washing laundry, caring for bairns, tending gardens.

If Buchan was planning an attack on anyone, the evidence was well hidden.

They followed Glenn into the great hall, where he gave instructions to his serving maid and then motioned for Kyla to follow him. He stopped as soon as he saw Finlay trailing after her.

"Your name, lass?"

"Kyla Grant."

Glenn turned to Jamie. "Kyla goes alone."

"Nay," Jamie said without hesitation. "My sister goes nowhere without my second as an escort."

The two lairds stared at each other for a long moment. Kyla finally cleared her throat and offered, "He can wait for me outside Davina's door."

The old laird sighed and nodded his head. "Aye. Only one."

Together, Kyla and Finlay followed the man down a passageway. When they reached the door at the end, which appeared to lead to a tower, he turned to Kyla. "I am only allowing this because I truly fear my daughter has addled her brain, and I have no woman I trust to speak with her. Even our healer says she is lost. I…I hope she will talk with you. Her chamber is at the top of the stairs, two levels up. She never leaves it."

"Is there some reason you feel she's addled?" Kyla stopped and folded her hands in front of her before ascending the stairway.

"Aye," his voice gained strength and purpose. "Convince her she's to do as her father wishes. I only want what's best for her. I love her, she's my only bairn left, but she refuses me repeatedly." He stopped and dipped his head, running his hands through the grizzled strands of hair that remained on his head. When he looked back up at her, he let out a deep sigh. "I shall return for you in one hour. If she sends you away before then, I'll have a guard waiting here to bring you to me."

The sadness in the man's eyes was undeniable, and Finlay couldn't help but wonder what it would do to the great Alex Grant if *his* daughter lost her mind. "I promise to do my best."

"Lass, I allow you this only because of your mother's reputation," the Buchan continued. "Madeline Grant is a woman I admire."

He turned and left.

Kyla headed up the stairs as soon as they stepped through the tower door, but Finlay tugged her back up against him. Oddly enough, she did not push away. "Lass, please wait. I believe he is genuine, but I would prefer to go up first. You may follow behind me."

The shove he expected came next, straight to his chest, so he took a step back. "Nay, you cannot go with me," she whispered. "She'll not talk to me if you are there. You must wait here. Did you not hear what I said earlier?"

"Of course, I'll do whatever you say," he said. Then he rolled his eyes and added, "Did you forget that I'm meant to be your pro-tector? I'll go in first to make sure no one else is there. Otherwise I will have failed in my job. Once I've determined it's safe, I'll step back out and guard the door."

"Can you not be serious for once?" She brought her face close to his and all he could think of was tasting her.

The fire in her eyes excited something in him. He'd always thought her a stunning beauty—what man wouldn't?—with her dark-as-night black hair and blue eyes the color of a glittering sapphire, but he hadn't expected to have such a carnal reaction to her. This close to her, he had a good vantage point of every single curve of her body, and it looked as if they would fit him perfectly. She was almost as tall as he was, very tall for a lass, but her sweet arse had curves that he wished to sink his teeth into. Now her lips were tipped up to him, begging to be ravished.

Hellfire, but being this close to her was akin to torture, and keeping his cock under control was going to prove to be his biggest challenge.

"Are you ready?" he asked, trying to shield himself against her allure.

"Aye."

Just then, a loud sound of crashing metal echoed in the passageway, but he guessed it to be the soldier assigned to guard the door they'd just come through.

He listened for another moment but heard nothing beyond a distant drip of water. No other sounds echoed through the quiet of the hollow tower, but he waited anyway, just to be sure. She turned to him, but he whispered, "Let's stand here another minute." He needed to be sure she was safe before they moved forward. She nodded and leaned against him, resting her head on his shoulder in a silent plea for support.

How the hell was he supposed to handle *that*? She smelled of some flower, but he had no idea which one. He didn't care. He only knew that he wished to carry that scent around with him through the day and into the night—and then wake up to it in the morn. The swell of her breast met his chest and he stifled a groan, forcing himself to focus on the task ahead instead of the luscious woman now in his arms.

Damn, he'd lain with women before, but this—this closeness—was something far more intimate than those experiences.

What was happening to him?

He leaned forward to gently push her away from him, then took the lead and unsheathed his sword as he headed up the staircase. It was a wide stone staircase with no railing, and he forced himself to look up as they ascended since he was not overly fond of heights. When they reached the top, he let go of Kyla's hand to open the door and then led the way inside.

Davina of Buchan stood in the middle of the chamber.

⟨₆

Kyla peered around Finlay and saw Davina. They had startled her, but the dark-haired beauty did not scream, something that puzzled Kyla.

"Davina? 'Tis Kyla Grant. I came here to talk with you."

The sadness in the woman's eyes almost broke Kyla's heart, but it turned to coldness in a matter of seconds. "Of course I remember the Grants. You are allies with Clan Ramsay, our enemies, the clan that killed my brothers. Why are you here?"

"I'm here to talk about bringing peace to our lands." She stepped out from behind Finlay and motioned for him to leave. There was no one else in the chamber, so there was no need for him to be there. While it had comforted her to have him close outside of the chamber, where unknown harms could befall them, he had to leave. She'd never gain Davina's acceptance with a warrior next to her.

While she waited for him to leave, she glanced around the chamber, noting the beauty and care with which the tower room had been decorated. There were actually two chambers because a wooden wall had been built through the center of the space, presumably to house a bedchamber on the other side. The door to that chamber was presently closed. She nodded toward the door after Finlay took his leave. "Are we alone? May we talk, please?"

Davina closed her eyes and sank into one of the cushioned chairs arranged around a table. The walls were covered in thick, gold-threaded tapestries. There was a thick rug on the cold stone floor, and an area at one end of the expansive room held a hearth and a large black kettle. Two more chairs were arranged in front of it.

"Aye, we are alone, but I am most weary. Please be quick about it."

Kyla sat across the table from Davina, not waiting for an invitation. "Our clans are about to do battle again, or so we are told. Is there not some way we can stop this? My sire has already been hurt in battle and you lost your two brothers. We must try to put an end to this cycle of death and destruction."

Davina chuckled. "And you think I can help you? Have you not heard? I am the lowly woman in my clan; my opinions matter naught to my father."

"'Tis not what I observed. Your sire is most concerned about you."

"Aye, you speak true—" she hesitated but then added, "—but only because he fears I will no longer do his bidding. I have followed his every instruction my entire life. Ever since I reached six and ten, he has forced me to attend to the men of his choosing. And you? Has your sire forced you into the bed of the men from whom he wishes to gain something?"

Kyla frowned, unable to believe the lass's own sire, the man who had seemed so concerned for her, had forced her to do such a thing. "I…I'm so sorry." It was the only thing she knew to say. She couldn't help but think of how determined Uncle Logan was to catch and punish Bearchun for daring to frighten his daughters. And her own sire…she knew he would never allow anything to happen to her.

"I see I've surprised you. My father uses me to get what he wishes. He says my beauty will turn the head of any man, so he promises me to anyone who asks. My problem was I fell in love…" Tears had started falling down her cheeks, and she swiped at them angrily.

"With Ranulf?"

"Aye, with Ranulf. But between my sire's greed and his own, he went mad. Now he's dead, and I'm left with nothing. I've requested to be left alone, but my sire cannot understand. He thinks me daft. I'm not daft; *he* is."

Kyla reached for the other woman's hand, cocooning it in her own. "How terrible. I cannot imagine how difficult all of this has been for you." The sight of this woman's pain was almost too much to bear, and she found tears falling down her own cheeks. How could anyone be treated so horribly?

"Now he tells me of his latest plan to use me as a bargaining tool, a plan that I want no part of…" She brushed the tears still sliding furiously down her cheeks. "It makes me wish I could run away and never see my sire again."

"We could arrange that, if you wish it. You can join our clan and you'll never be forced again." It was not an offer she'd intended to make, but she would do anything to soothe this woman. To save her from the father who had done her wrong.

Davina snatched her hand away.

"So another man could force me to do his bidding? Have you ever been forced to go to the bed of a man who disgusts you? Have you?"

Kyla did not know what to say to her. "Nay. I'm sorry, but nay. Come to Grant land. I'll see that you are not forced. I promise. Or do you have a relative in another clan? If so, I'll make sure you get there safely."

Davina dropped her face into her hands and sobbed.

"Why do you cry? What is your sire planning this time? Is he preparing to go to war with us? To fight against the Ramsays? Help me and I'll help you," Kyla implored.

Davina shook her head forcefully. "I cannot. I will never leave here, but I must make him stop. Help me, please. What can I do?" She leapt to her feet and continued to sob inconsolably as she paced the room.

Kyla stood also, wishing she could wrap her arms around the poor girl and comfort her, but Davina made no move to stop. Finally, not knowing what else to do, she held her arms open. The other girl flew into them, sobbing on her shoulder—gut-wrenching sobs that ate at Kyla's soul and made her vow to help no matter what the cost.

"Come home with me," Kyla whispered again. "I promise to help you. We'll put an end to your torture, help you find your own husband, someone you can love."

She lifted her head and stepped back, not stopping until she reached the door in the wooden wall. Before she opened it, she whispered, "I cannot. I'll never leave this place, but I'll help you if I can. You're the only one who has listened to me." She swiped at her tears. "How can I be of assistance? As upset as I am with my sire, I do not wish to lose him. I do not wish for a war any more than you do."

"Do you know what he plans? Have you heard of a man called Simon de La Porte?"

"Aye, I have heard of him. Before I tell you what I know, I would like you to come with me. I have something I wish to show you."

Kyla's heart leapt in her chest. Would she find out where Simon de La Porte was concealing himself? She nodded, agreeing to follow her into the next chamber.

Davina opened the door and found a candle inside the chamber. Kyla followed her to a large basket set atop a table and held the candle close. She peeked inside and saw dark curls around a tiny face. The wee bairn lay on her belly, her face turned toward them, her tiny bottom sticking in the air because her knees were tucked underneath her. She had two fingers in her mouth and she sucked on them in her sleep.

Kyla gazed into Davina's eyes. "She's beautiful. Is she yours?"

Davina nodded. "She's the only thing I have left of Ranulf, and I'll never leave her." The woman's face had lit up at the sight of her daughter. A small smile crept across her lips whenever the bairn sucked her fingers. Kyla understood now. The woman would never leave her daughter behind.

Davina's face hardened when she turned back to her. "I wish to spend my time raising my daughter. 'Tis all I've asked of my sire. Instead, he wishes to make me mistress to another man.

"He plans to give me to his new partner, Simon de La Porte."

CHAPTER FOUR

FINLAY HEARD NOTHING FROM WITHIN the chamber. Kyla had been inside for quite some time now. He bent his ear to the door, but there were still no sounds from within. Worried for her, he turned the knob and opened it, only to find the chamber inside empty. He stepped into the room before noticing the open door leading to the next chamber. His pulse sped up. Was there a guard inside that room? Was Kyla in trouble?

"Kyla?" he called out, moving toward the inner door.

Just as he reached it, Kyla stepped out from the other chamber, acting in complete control. Davina followed her. Both lasses ignored him. Kyla turned to her new acquaintance and said, "I promise to talk to your sire, see if I can do anything to help. My thanks for your hospitality."

Davina nodded. "And I promise to send you a message if I learn aught about his intentions for Clan Grant."

Finlay placed his hand on Kyla's back, urging her toward the door. "I suspect our laird is awaiting your return."

Kyla glanced back over her shoulder, her expression a bit wistful, and he couldn't help but wonder what she'd spoken of with the lass. Had she succeeded in her mission? The apparent friendship between the lasses made him suspect she had.

Glenn of Buchan met them outside the door to the tower as promised, his guard standing at the ready with his sword. "Did she share aught with you?" the older man asked. "Did you explain to her that I only want what's best for her and for me?"

"She did share with me, my lord," Kyla said. "She showed me her daughter. You have a beautiful grandbairn." The words sent a little jolt through Finlay. Davina had a child? Kyla twirled her hair—a sure sign of nerves—and he kept his reassuring hand on her back.

What did the man expect of his daughter? Wouldn't she be busy enough with her new babe? She was of noble blood, a daughter of the laird. It would be unusual for her to be put to work.

"Aye, 'tis true, she is a beauty." A quick look of joy passed over his face, but his eyes soon narrowed. "Can you not see how daft she is? Did you convince her to do her sire's bidding, as any good daughter should?"

Kyla lifted her gaze and squared her shoulders. "I could see that she is not daft at all. She only requests to be left alone to raise her daughter."

The Buchan laird exploded, yanking his sword from its scabbard and slamming the blade down hard on a stone bench nearby, the noise echoing down the passageway, an act of uncontrolled anger.

Finlay instantly stepped in front of Kyla to protect her, one hand shoving her behind him and the other yanking on the hilt of his sword. "Stand back," he bellowed to Buchan. "Laird or not, you'll not lay a hand on her."

Glenn's lips curled as he spoke. "I'll not hurt her, but she must understand what should be happening."

"You'll mind your tone with her, as well. She's the Grant's daughter and offered to help out of the goodness of her heart. I'll remind you of that. See if you can find a morsel of your Highland honor buried inside you." Finlay was furious, but he reminded himself to maintain his control. The Buchan had failed to do so, and the situation could quickly become dangerous if he were not careful.

Glenn's voice came out in a near growl. "My daughter is to do what I bid her to do. That is not too much to ask. I need her for an important task." He re-sheathed his sword, wiping the sweat from his brow with his sleeve. "Go. Go from my castle and never return." His voice turned into a growl that caught Finlay's attention. "Gather your kin and get off my land."

As soon as Buchan put his sword away, Finlay did the same, but he would not let Kyla move out from behind him. "We'll leave now," he said. "This was meant to be a peaceful visit. Do not change it into something you do not wish to bring down on yourself."

Buchan snorted, his face turning a deep shade of red. "You

Grants are all the same. Guard, lead them back to the hall and escort the rest of the pigs off my land."

They followed the guard and Finlay hauled Kyla behind him, her steps struggling to keep up with his fast pace. She grabbed his elbow and whispered, "I'd like to speak to him again."

He glanced over his shoulder, his jaw clenched. He admired her courage and tenacity, but there were men who would not listen to the truth, no matter how it was delivered. Buchan was beyond the point of reason. "It'll not bring aught good to this. We leave now. This man is ready to lose his patience with you, Kyla. We'll leave their land. I promised to return you to your sire, and I intend to keep my word."

Once they knew their way, Finlay rushed her down the passageway and into the great hall. He stopped at the trestle table full of Grant guards and said, "We've been ordered off Buchan land."

The two guards behind Finlay barked in unison, "Now." One of them added, "We will see you off."

Logan Ramsay shot Kyla a curious glance, but he must have decided questions could wait because he fell in on one side of his niece while Finlay continued to guard the other. They headed to the stables like that, Jamie leading the way.

"Do not stop until we are off their land," Finlay whispered to his friend. "Kyla, you'll be riding with me."

She opened her mouth to argue, but he held his hand up. "You'll not win in this. I'm charged to protect you, and a man drew his sword on you. You'll ride with me."

Logan eyes narrowed, and he said, "You ride with him or me, lass. Take your pick."

Kyla followed Finlay to his horse, making her choice. "Must you be so demanding?"

"Do not argue until we're off this land, or I may have to throttle you. That man back there is ready to slice both of us in two. At least he'll have to go through me to get to you."

Fortunately, she held her tongue. Once all of the Grant warriors had mounted their horses and moved out through the gate, they were able to speak. The Buchan guards followed them at too great a distance for their voices to be overheard.

Kyla turned her head back to him. "If you had heard all Davina said, you'd understand why 'twas important for me to try to gain the Buchan's agreement to leave his daughter be to care for her child."

"I'll not argue with you, but safety comes first. Dead bodies don't do much convincing that I've ever seen. He had lost control."

She reached for his hand and squeezed it, away from the view of her brothers and uncle. "Forgive me. I was unable to think with a clear head. I'm still shocked by what I learned from Davina."

His voice softened. "Your heart is as big as your mother's. Everyone knows it, even Glenn of Buchan did. 'Tis a fine quality to have." He slipped his hand away from hers and wrapped it around her waist, pulling her closer. Hell, if she didn't feel just fine where she was.

His laird's voice brought him back to their present circumstances, so he dropped his hand, only to have Kyla find it and put it back on her waist. He concealed his smirk and gave his full attention to Jamie.

"Care to expand on your instructions, Finlay?" Jamie asked. "What happened?"

Finlay replied over his shoulder, "I will when we're off their land. Glenn of Buchan seems eager to use his sword on someone, and it'll not be Kyla or me."

"Just ride," Logan shouted to Jamie.

Two hours later, the guards trailing them disappeared and headed back to Buchan land. Logan gave the sign for their group to keep riding, then motioned for them to stop at the next clearing they reached. Finlay dismounted and helped Kyla down, but she immediately stalked off into the forest.

Logan gave him a questioning look—one he didn't quite know how to answer—then indicated they were to gather on a group of logs. "Over there. Tell me what happened before you head into the woods so I know what to do with the guards."

Jamie sent Connor off. "Keep an eye out for Kyla."

The rest sought to take care of their needs.

"What in the hell happened?" Logan said, pacing around the clearing. "I trusted Kyla to make the situation better, not worse."

Jamie said, "Let's wait for her. I'd like to hear her explanation."

She joined them a few moments later, an answer to her uncle's question already on her lips. "Uncle Logan, I did naught wrong."

"Nay, she didn't," Finlay cut in.

Logan held his hand up to Finlay, his gaze on Kyla. "Continue. I wish to hear your entire tale."

Kyla sighed and replied, "Glenn allowed me to speak to Davina alone. He thinks she's gone daft, and asked me to convince her that he has her best interests in mind."

Jamie barked, "Where the hell were you, MacNicol?"

"Outside the door," Finlay said. "I checked the chamber. Davina was alone, so I chose to guard from just outside the door."

"You do recall 'tis my sister you guard?" Jamie asked. "Aye 'twas what we agreed to with the Buchan, but I trusted you to know better."

"I said I'd guard her with my life and I did." He crossed his arms as if to add emphasis to his words.

"Continue, Kyla," Logan said in a tone that brooked no refusal.

She glanced at Jamie and Finlay before speaking. "Once I was inside, Davina introduced me to her daughter."

"Daughter?" Connor blurted out as soon as he joined them. Logan's glare silenced him.

"Aye, she has a daughter by Ranulf. She adores the bairn, and her dearest wish is to be left to care for her daughter."

Logan began to pace, his hands behind his back. "But?"

"Her sire chooses her men, and he's chosen a new one for her."

Logan stopped his pacing, apparently as shocked by this revelation as the others were. "He chooses her men?" he repeated.

No wonder Kyla had been so desperate to push Glenn of Buchan. Unfortunately, the grizzled laird was not the kind of man who would listen to reason. This was why she was still angry; why her eyes kept darting back toward Buchan Castle as they rode even further away.

"Aye, and he has been doing so since she turned ten and six. Do you have any idea what that would be like for a lass? Imagine Papa sending Elizabeth off with a man to gain that man's favor in battle."

Her words fell like a heavy stone in the middle of the clearing. Finlay had difficulty understanding how a father could treat his daughter so crudely, but he waited, knowing how upset Kyla had been when she'd come away from that tower. There was more.

She continued, her voice lowering as if she feared there were gremlins in the woods listening. "He's ordered her to be Simon de

La Porte's mistress."

Finlay let out the breath he'd been holding. That statement explained everything. Kyla had wished to stay and talk to Buchan more. She'd probably hoped to convince him his actions were wrong—an impossible task with a man like him. No one moved, everyone still absorbing the information she had just revealed. Jamie jerked his gaze from Kyla to Logan, apparently waiting for his uncle's reaction.

Logan Ramsay's voice came out in barely a whisper, "Well done, Kyla. You've done what no one else could do." His gaze traveled from face to face. "Now we know where the bastard is."

"You think he's on Buchan land now?" Jamie asked.

"I do. If not, he'll be there soon." Logan continued to stare at Kyla for a few moments before he turned to Finlay. "Explain why this upset Buchan."

"Uncle, I can tell you," Kyla said.

"Nay, I'll hear it from the one who told us to move out without hesitation." His hand motioned to Finlay to continue.

"Once outside the tower room, Glenn asked Kyla what he needed to do to gain Davina's acquiescence, and Kyla told him all Davina wished to do was take care of her daughter."

"There must have been more to it than that…"

"He wished for me to declare her daft," Kyla burst out, "and I said she was not."

Finlay nodded in agreement. "And he exploded, pulling his sword from its sheath and striking any place he could. He was too close to Kyla for my comfort, so I pulled out my own weapon to protect her. He didn't take to aught we did from then on. Just continued on about a daughter needing to do her sire's bidding. I did not understand him at the time, but now I do."

"What do you mean?" Connor asked.

"He wants Simon de La Porte to do his bidding, but my guess is the lout made Davina a condition of his agreement with Buchan. Davina is refusing. No Davina, no assistance."

"It makes sense," Logan said. "No doubt, he's also offered him plenty of coin, something Buchan seems to have in abundance."

"We have to help her, Uncle," Kyla pleaded.

Uncle Logan paced two more lengths of the clearing before he announced, "The rest of you see to your needs and mount up.

We'll not rest until we're closer to Grant land. Buchan is becoming unsettled and we must be careful. Kyla, I understand your concern, but we do not have the warriors to help her at this point. Molly and Tormod were unable to locate de La Porte in the castle, so he may not be there yet. I sent them to Edinburgh to speak with our king."

"And I know my sire's view on the matter," Jamie said. "We'll not attack until we know for certes that de La Porte is there and we have our king's permission to move forward. Hopefully, Molly and Tormod have found him and obtained that permission."

"Sorry, Kyla, but he's correct. We wait."

℆

Uncle Logan decided they'd camp for one night before returning to the Grant castle. Kyla sat on a boulder by the burn, her legs tucked close to her body so she could rest her chin on her knees, her hands underneath her chin. The sound of water tumbling down the stream and over the rocks calmed her insides, something she desperately needed. Her stomach had churned ever since Davina had mentioned Simon de La Porte. The war she had hoped to allay was beginning to seem inevitable.

"Kyla? May I join you?" Finlay's bootfalls crackled in the twigs and grass behind her.

She glanced up at him and nodded, setting her legs down so they fell over the edge of the boulder, a position she was sure her mother would prefer she adopted around a man. She patted a spot and Finlay hopped down next to her.

"Aught wrong?"

"Nay." She stared at the babbling water, mesmerized by the rhythmic sound and movement. She couldn't take her mind off the woman who'd been given to different men by her own father.

The look he gave her seemed to radiate warmth. "You did the best you could. I have naught but admiration for the way you stood up for your beliefs, not giving in to your fear of the Buchan."

Finlay's eyes were a cross between brown and red, she realized, almost like his hair. Predominately brown, they had auburn flecks in them that she loved.

"Are you sure there's naught wrong?" he asked, quirking his brow at her. Then a huge grin spread across his face. "Aye, 'tis true.

I am the most handsome of all. I'm sure 'tis why you stare at me so."

She giggled and reached for his hand, though her mother would for certes not approve of *that*. "My thanks for protecting me against the fool." She knew he was speaking in jest, but she could almost agree with him. He was one of the most handsome warriors in all of Clan Grant.

A fleeting memory crossed her mind: Sorcha telling her about how her perception of Cailean had suddenly changed—he'd gone from being one of the Ramsay warriors to *her* Ramsay warrior. Was this how it happened? Something so simple and ordinary?

He intertwined his fingers with hers and settled her hand on his lap, rubbing the back of it with the thumb of his other hand. "I was only doing my job."

Finlay was a bit of mystery to her. His humor confused her at times—it was hard to tell when he was serious and when he wasn't. But the heat of his gaze told her he was serious at the moment.

"I know, I know, you're my protector." She rolled her eyes, giving the last word a special emphasis.

He laughed, pulling her hand up to his lips and kissing the tender skin there, a move she hadn't expected at all. When she glanced up at him in surprise, his eyes darkened and he said, "I know you wish to return to save her, but your brother and uncle are correct. This is not the right time. Your protector would not allow it."

"When is the right time? When will we be able to go back and get her?"

"I don't think you need to worry about Davina. After all Buchan has lost, I doubt he'll hurt her. He's lost two sons already."

"Mayhap you are correct. But what if Simon de La Porte forces himself on her? What if *he* hurts her? Or worse, what if either of them hurt that sweet bairn? I cannot get Davina and the babe out of my mind." She stared at their interlocked hands, amazed at how strong his felt, how warm, how pleasing, enough so that she didn't wish to remove hers.

"Whatever happens, 'tis not your fault. Davina is a strong woman. She had to be in order to survive all the Buchans have been through. I would wager she is more than capable of caring for herself."

"Mayhap 'tis all true, but the Buchan is such a monster. Who would do such a thing to his own daughter? I cannot get past it. Thank the Lord above for my sire and my mama."

She reached to the ground and picked up a few sticks, twirling them in her hand, breaking them into pieces before she tossed them into the burn, listening to them hit the water. She could feel Finlay's gaze on her, but it made her feel...strange, and she didn't know what to do about that either. This mission was supposed to give her power. Instead, she felt more powerless than ever.

"I have to go back. Mayhap not now...I *do* understand the wisdom of waiting until I have guards with me. After seeing the fury in his eyes when he pulled on his sword, I knew I needed to exercise more caution than I do at home, but..." She tossed another stick into the water.

"But?"

Suddenly, she couldn't take it anymore. She needed to do, to act, to let out some of this turbulent emotion boiling up inside her. Kyla shot off the rock, moving toward the water, and grabbed at the stones at the water's edge. Then she flung them into the rolling stream as hard as she could, so hard that she lost her footing, tipping toward the stream, and would have landed in the middle of it but for a pair of warm hands that wrapped around her waist and turned her away from the stream.

She fell against Finlay, and he wrapped his arms around her to keep her from falling. She couldn't help but grab his waist to anchor herself, and her head fell against his chest.

They both froze in that position, both because she couldn't believe how she'd latched on to him so easily and because she had no desire to let go. The night was a wee bit cool and he warmed her from her chest down to her very core, sending a strange and alluring tingling through her.

She pushed away from him and sought his gaze, wanting to see how their embrace had affected him. Her posture had stiffened, and so had his. "My thanks for catching me." She cleared her throat, not knowing what else to say at the moment.

"You're angry," he said.

"Aye. I'm angry that someone would treat their own kin the way the Buchan treats Davina. He has no concern for his daughter at all." She wiped her hands down the wool of the tunic that she'd worn over breeches for this trip.

Finlay's expression was most serious. He set her away from him and dropped his hands, but his eyes never left her. Finally, he said, "Kyla, if I can find a way to protect you, I'll take you back."

"You will?" She was astonished at what he'd volunteered to do for her.

He blushed and said, "Aye, but only if I'm sure I can keep you safe."

She stood on the tips of her toes and threw her arms around his neck. "Thank you, Finlay."

Her breasts flattened against his chest, and they swelled in response to his nearness. When she pulled back, his gaze had darkened and he made a strange, husky sound. Without thinking, she moistened her lips with her tongue, and his lips settled on hers before she could even think about pulling back. He teased her with his tongue until she opened to him, parting her lips. Suddenly, her instinct to pull away shifted to desire. He angled his mouth over hers and deepened the kiss, and she leaned in, wanting more.

She'd kissed a few guards before, but never before had a kiss left her with such a craving for more. The sensation of his tongue against hers rocked her to her core, unlike anything she'd ever experienced. Finlay growled, a low sound from deep inside that made her feel both seductive and cherished as he sucked on her tongue. He pulled away so suddenly she almost fell against him, but he caught her and righted her, taking the opportunity to nibble on her lower lip before he let her go.

Then, for some strange, unknown reason, he dropped his hands and scowled before he spun on his heel and hurried off, leaving her panting in the middle of the forest. Her fingers came up to feel her swollen lips as if she wished to be certain she hadn't imagined their short encounter. The taste of him, the scent of him, the warmth and strength of his embrace were now seared in her mind forever.

Why had he run off?

Everything about her relationship with Finlay MacNicol had just changed dramatically.

CHAPTER FIVE

⨎

FINLAY'S MIND WAS JUMPING IN so many directions, he had trouble holding a steady thought for more than a moment. Memories of how Kyla Grant had felt in his arms kept bombarding him. They were headed home and on Grant land, so he should be wondering how his mother fared, and he did take the time to say a quick prayer.

But as soon as he finished, blue eyes and a pair of sultry lips popped into his head. He hadn't intended to kiss Kyla, but her rosy red lips had begged to be tasted, and he'd been powerless to stop himself. Their kiss had been so much more than he'd expected, and she'd responded to him in a way that had instantly made him wish to take it further.

Was there a chance for them? Probably not. She was the laird's eldest daughter, and she deserved her own castle, a husband of noble blood, and a bevy of servants to see to her every need.

Except *he* wanted to see to her every need. He chastised himself for thinking about Kyla when he should be thinking about his mother, his clan, or their conflict with the Buchan, and vowed to clear his head of his carnal desires.

They were almost to the gates of the Grant Castle when a small black bird flew directly into Finlay's line of vision. His gut clenched in reaction, praying it was not a sign of what he was about to discover.

Was his mother still alive? The closer they came, the more restless he felt, so he finally mumbled, "My pardon," to Jamie before he spurred his horse over to the cottages outside the curtain wall.

People were everywhere—talking, hugging, praying.

The worst had happened. He could tell by the number of clan-mates wandering about—not working, consoling each other. His mother must have passed while he was gone.

A bellow built inside him until he could no longer keep contained, and he let the wail out as he approached the castle. Silence greeted him as everyone watched his approach. He jumped off his horse and raced to his cottage inside the bailey, shoving the door open and running into the inside chamber, only to find it empty.

There were footsteps behind him, and then he heard his sire's voice. "Finlay, your mama's gone."

Finlay fell to his knees next to his mother's empty bed. He whispered, "When?"

"Last eve. 'Twas peaceful. Lady Brenna gave her herbs to keep her comfortable."

His brother entered the cottage behind his father. "I told you that you should have stayed."

His father barked, "Fergus. Enough! Finlay did what he felt he needed to do."

"Aye," Fergus replied. "But he could be shamed by the clan like Uncle Geordie was years ago. He's never returned."

His sire said, "Geordie had many problems. He does not belong here." He heard the anger in his sire's voice. Geordie was his sire's brother, though he'd been gone for so long Finlay barely remembered him.

Finlay couldn't stop himself. He took his fist and pounded it on the bed, his voice coming out in a roar. He cared not who heard him. His dear mother was dead, and he hadn't been here. He'd selfishly left on a mission.

He distantly heard his sire say, "Answer the door and leave me with your brother. I'll have a talk with him."

Fergus cast a furtive look at him—Finlay couldn't blame him for that—and then left, closing the door behind him.

A few moments later, Finlay managed to get off his knees and settled on a nearby stool. "Forgive me, Papa. I should not have gone." He hung his head, still struggling with the realization that he would never see his mother again in this life. He fought tears, unable to look his sire in his eyes because of the pain and judgment he knew would be there.

Nicol sat on the bed facing him. "Finlay, your mama told me

she'd instructed you to go."

"She did?" He lifted his gaze to his father's, surprised to see compassion there instead of judgment.

"Aye, she was mighty proud of both of our lads, as am I. After you left, she told me that she'd told you to go, made it her last wish. She fell asleep the morning after you left and never awakened. Do not feel guilty for leaving when she asked you to honor her request."

Finlay settled his elbows on his knees. "What about the others? Is Fergus right? Will I be shamed as Uncle Geordie was? He left his wife's side and the entire clan shamed him because she died alone. Will they do the same with me?"

"The situations are entirely different. Uncle Geordie was in the arms of another woman when his wife passed. That part of the story has been left out over the years."

"Where is Mama?"

"Celestina brought your mama to the keep. She is leading a group of women to ready her body for burial. If you'd like to see her, you may, but I do not believe you would benefit from it. Remember your mother when she was happy, not when she was ill." Celestina was the wife of Brodie Grant, his sire's closest friend.

There were voices in the other chamber, so Finlay forced himself to stand. His father embraced him, then said, "Shall we greet our visitors?"

Finlay clasped his sire's shoulder and followed him into their main chamber. Jamie, Kyla, and Logan Ramsay stood there, all looking quite uncomfortable. More than anything, he had the sudden urge to go to Kyla's side, wrap his arms around her, rest his head on her shoulder—to take comfort from her, and to give it, too. She'd tagged along behind Jamie and Finlay when they were young, so she'd known his mother for years.

More than anything, he wished he'd had the chance tell his mother about his feelings for Kyla, but it was much too late.

Logan spoke first. "Nicol, my deepest sympathies for your loss. She was a strong woman."

Kyla gave Finlay's sire a hug first, then Fergus, and then—finally—him. He wished for her to never let go, but he was pleased that she stayed by his side. "May I share one of my favorite memories of your mother, Finlay?" she asked softly.

Nicol turned to her and said, "Please, I'd like to hear it as well."

Kyla's voice trembled with her emotion, but her smile was sincere. "Do you remember how much she loved coming out to see the forts we built in the snow during the worst of winter? Jake, Jamie, Fergus, and Finlay would build their own castle in the snow and build guards in front of it. Your mother came out one day when the snow was as deep as I'd ever seen it. She helped you build a slide from the peak of your castle tower all the way to the moat."

Jamie laughed. "I remember. We fought over who was to go down first. Jake won, if I recall."

Finlay chuckled. "I fought Jake pretty hard for that right, but Mama said whoever could jump the highest could go first. Jake won."

"But Jake wasn't the one who went down first. A wee lassie came along and tugged on your mama's arm," Jamie added.

Kyla blushed and grinned. "Aye, she gave me the first slide. I sat on her lap and we giggled all the way down."

Memories washed over him. His mother wrapping her arms tightly around a wee raven-haired lassie as she yelled, "Catch us, Finlay! Make sure Kyla lands safely, Fergus!" He and his brother had taken off toward the bottom of the small hill, running alongside the castle of packed snow as their mother's gleeful laughter filled the valley. She and Kyla had ridden down the slide on a piece of curved metal the armorer had given to the lads.

Everyone joined in with their own stories, recalling the hours and hours they'd spent in that castle and the slide. Kyla had given him a gift he'd never forget.

Thanks to Kyla, his mother's laughter echoed in his mind as though she were standing next to him, encouraging him to take his own turn on the slide, telling him to believe in himself. It suddenly struck him that his mother would tell him to fight for Kyla, that he was a good lad and deserving of happiness. She would tell him that someone with noble blood couldn't love her or take care of Kyla the way he could.

His parents had always taught him to fight for what he wanted and for what he believed in.

He wanted Kyla Grant. Badly.

C

Kyla awakened early and found her way to the kitchens. "Dearest Cook, is there something I could carry to Nicol's family this morn? I'd like to make a quick visit."

Cook motioned to one of her helpers. "Make a basket for the men, will you not, Fiona? Some oat bread and fruit for the poor laddies. Kyla, you're a dear to take a basket to them, you have a heart just like your mother's. You're so sweet that I'm including a tart just for you."

Kyla made her way over to squeeze the woman's shoulders and kiss her cheek. "You're the best, Nonie. You know I still love your fruit tarts. Have you seen Mama yet?"

"Aye, she came to fetch your papa's porridge. He's moving slow this morn, so he's not coming to the hall."

Fiona handed her the basket of food.

"If you see Mama, please tell her I'll be back later."

She made her way out the back door of the kitchens and through the gardens. She loved this time of year, when the leaves were just starting to change colors and the nights turned cool. Her parents were busy, so her chastisement for sneaking away wouldn't come until later today. A deep sigh escaped her followed by a big smile. The first because she'd have to answer for her trip to Buchan land, the second because she'd found herself thinking, again, about Finlay's lips on hers and how lovely it had felt to be held in his embrace.

Nothing was better than knowing she'd caught Finlay's eye.

She shoved that thought to the back of her mind, focusing instead on his family's loss and how she could best show her support for them. When she approached their cottage, she slowed her steps, surprised to see Finlay sitting outside on a boulder. He was staring off into the distance, a mournful look on his face.

"Finlay?"

He jerked his head and rose to his feet as soon as he noticed her. "Good morn to you, Kyla."

"I brought some food from Cook for you."

"Many thanks." He accepted the basket with a smile and set it down.

"May I?" She pointed to the boulder, indicating she'd like to join him. He had to be going through a most difficult time.

Finlay nodded. "Aye, but wait a moment." He ran into the house and emerged a moment later with an extra plaid, which he arranged on the rock for her. "'Tis a wee bit cold for your tender sensibilities." He waggled his brow at her.

Controlling the urge to giggle, she murmured, "My thanks. Do I have tender sensibilities?" She sat down and peered up at him just as he plunked down next to her.

He stared straight ahead and whispered, "I'm quite sure I felt something tender on you by the stream."

She couldn't contain her giggle this time. "Tender, Finlay?"

"Shall I try again to find something tender? Mayhap I was wrong." His gaze caught hers and the butterflies started tormenting her all over again. His teasing grin warmed her. After all he'd gone through, he could still smile.

She thought of ten different responses, but she chose the less than proper one. "I hope you will try again another day." Halfway through, she felt her cheeks heat, but she managed to get the words out. She stared down at her hands for a moment before lifting her gaze to meet his. His smile had disappeared, and the look on his face could best be described as yearning.

She wasn't sure, but she thought he mumbled, "I promise."

He turned away, the moment gone.

"How have you been? How is your sire?" she asked.

"Better." He stared off into the distance again, leaning back on his palms. "She passed without any pain. I didn't dare say this to Papa, but a part of me is pleased we'll not have to watch her suffer anymore."

She covered his hand with hers, and he sat up so he could intertwine their fingers. "Do you believe in heaven?" she asked.

He thought for a moment, then said, "I do. Mama did."

"I do, also. Then the day will come when you will see her again."

He nodded. "Mama said the same. I like that idea. Thank you."

Kyla noticed her aunt and uncle coming their way, so she pulled her hand back. Finlay stood to greet her aunt Celestina and Uncle Brodie and she gave them each a hug. Others were coming down the path toward the cottage, so she whispered, "I'll visit another time."

He picked up the basket and said, "Again, my thanks." He held the door for the others and his gaze caught hers, staying on her until it felt like she'd melt into a puddle at his feet.

Oh, how she wished she could embrace him, touch him, and cuddle him whenever the urge struck her.

☾

Kyla's reckoning finally came that evening. Her mother had sent word that she was to meet her parents in the solar in ten minutes. After delaying as long as she dared, she trudged down the staircase and knocked on the door.

"Enter," her sire's voice boomed.

She peeked around the door, pleased to see only her parents inside, her father seated at his desk and her mother in a chair off to his side. Much better to face them alone than with a board of witnesses. "Greetings, Papa. You sound so much better. Is he better, Mama?"

Her sire narrowed his gaze at her. "Sit. You'll not distract us from our purpose, daughter."

She sat down in the chair in front of the desk, fussing with the folds of her skirt. "Mama, forgive me for my transgression. I…"

"How could you?" Tears fell down her mother's face, exactly what she did *not* want to see. "After everything your sire and I have been through, how could you put us through this worry?"

Her father clasped her mother's hand and said, "I'd like to hear Kyla's reasons, Maddie. Let's allow her to explain herself. She has rarely been defiant, so she must believe she had a good reason."

Her mother took out her linen square, dabbed at her tears, and folded her hands in her lap. "Aye, I wish to hear your reasons, Kyla."

She took a deep breath and began, hoping she could convince her parents she'd done the right thing. "After listening to Jamie and Uncle Logan talk about the mercenaries and their ill intent toward us, I could not just sit by idly and watch. We've been through too much, and so much of it is because of our quarrel with the Buchan and MacNiven. I could not watch my family be torn apart again.

"Papa, it was so hard when you fell in battle. We did not know whether you would see the next day." Tears began to fall down her cheeks, but she managed to control them for the most part. She would explain her intentions and gain their support. "After our celebrations for Jamie and Gracie and Sorcha and Cailean, we got back some semblance of what we'd been before. You were home, and we were happy again. Our clan was functioning again. I was proud of how we all pulled together, of the fine job Jake and Jamie were doing as lairds, and I…I was willing to do aught I could to keep it that way.

"We must persevere." Her tone changed and the anger she had about what her loved ones had been forced to endure seeped out. "Mama, I could not allow it. And why can I never go along on any missions? Connor is always left behind as well. 'Tis not fair to him."

Her father said, "We're discussing your situation, not Connor's. Your brothers have all been training for years in the lists to be able to protect themselves. You know how talented the Ramsay women are as archers, but you've never been interested in learning to fight. How did you plan to protect yourself?"

"There were plenty of guards with us. Finlay was assigned as my protector. I had a plan," she insisted, looking back and forth between her parents. "I wanted to speak to Davina. I believed that we could come to an agreement, woman to woman. My hope was that she would divulge what her sire was planning, and that I could convince her to help establish peace between our clans."

"And were you successful?" her sire asked.

"In a way, aye. Davina told me something no one else from our group uncovered. And we have to help her, Papa. Please tell me you'll help her."

"What did she tell you?"

She gave her attention to her mother, who had been grossly abused before Alex had rescued her from her stepbrother's keep. Her mama would want to help Davina; she was sure of it. "Mama, her sire gives her to whatever man he wants. She has no say in the matter. He wishes to give her to Simon de La Porte who will be arriving soon."

Her mother gasped, just as she'd expected.

"And she has a bairn now, MacNiven's daughter, and she only wishes to raise the wee lassie in peace. Her sire wanted me to convince her to do his bidding, I believe, but I would not do it. How could her own father treat her so poorly?"

"Is that the reason you were ordered off their land?" her sire asked.

"Aye, he was angry because I did not agree with him. He swung his sword over his head and struck a stone bench. Finlay pulled out his sword and protected me."

"So instead of helping, you hindered the attempt to make peace." Her father's voice had turned into that quiet tone they all dreaded, that tone of judgment that could make her cry at just the sound.

"But Papa." She sat on the edge of her chair, gripping the arms tight. "We must help her. Can you not see that? We must send an army back to get her away, take her and her bairn to a safe place. I promised her we would help her."

"Did you see de La Porte?"

"Nay, but I would not know him if I saw him. Uncle Logan never saw him. We must save her before he is forced on her. Even if she has a babe, 'tis still rape, is it not? Mama?" She had to make them understand.

Her sire got up from his chair behind the desk and moved around to the front. He sat on the edge and tugged her out of the chair, wrapping his arms around her and setting his chin on the top of her head.

The tears came and she could not stop them.

"Papa, am I not hurting you?" She sobbed into his chest, taking in her father's familiar scent and the warmth of his embrace as she melted into her favorite place in the entire world.

"Nay, you're not hurting me. The only way you can hurt me is if something happens to you."

"Don't you see I was afraid you'd never be able to hug me again?" She sobbed harder, her breath hitching as she swallowed her tears. "I must do something to prevent that from happening again. I just got you back, Papa. I cannot bear to lose you."

"You are too soft-hearted." He gave a large sigh as he rubbed her back. "Just like your mother."

CHAPTER SIX

$\swarrow$

THE DAY OF FINLAY'S MOTHER'S burial arrived. Finlay walked next to his brother as they headed up the hill to the keep where the women had prepared her body. His sire and Brodie Grant walked ahead of them. When they reached the keep, the women would release the body to the men, and the closest family would carry the body to the gravesite, finally putting Inga to rest.

His mind was numb.

As they moved along the path, others stepped out of their cottages to follow behind Inga's family, offering their support by their presence. Others stood outside their homes with their heads bowed as they passed, their hands clasped in prayer.

He passed by a group of lads and heard, "Should have been home."

Another whispered, "Shamed your family."

Another: "Shame on Finlay. What kind of son leaves his mama when she's so near to dying?"

The taunts continued as they moved along, but Finlay ignored them as best he could. He'd done what his mother had asked and his papa understood. The others' opinions did not matter.

Or so he tried to tell himself.

"Go home."

"Shameful."

Fergus whispered furiously, "They're right. You should have been here."

The words hurt more coming from his brother, but he reassured himself that he did not need to explain his behavior to anyone.

"Just like his uncle."

A few more comments about shaming were thrown his way before Brodie Grant spun around. He ushered the mourning family off to the side and then unsheathed his sword. "I've heard enough. Finlay has not shamed his family. Your taunting ends here, or you'll meet me on the lists after the procession. Who is interested?" He turned from group to group, walking back down the path a ways to confront Finlay's accusers, but no one spoke.

"I did not think so. Finlay's behavior is acceptable to his father, to me, and to his lairds. So it is acceptable to all of you. The shaming ends here and now." He sheathed his sword and returned to Nicol's side, continuing along the path as if nothing had happened. The comments instantly stopped.

Finlay whispered, "My thanks, Uncle Brodie." The laird's brother had told him and Fergus to call him uncle long ago, which they had done gladly. They had almost made it to the keep when three others joined them, Brodie's sons, Loki, Braden, and his grandson Kenzie. They fell in behind Finlay and Fergus.

Finlay couldn't have been more pleased with this demonstration of solidarity.

He moved through the rest of the funeral as if he observed it from a distance, unable to believe that his mother was gone. He saw many faces, but they all melded together in his mind.

The only thing he could focus on was the endless chant in his mind. "Shameful, shameful, shameful…"

Even though Brodie Grant had put an end to the others' taunting, it had moved into his own head. No matter what his mama had told him, he should have been there.

That thought stayed with him throughout the rest of the burial.

The men walked in silence to the Grant burial site, the women only following to the edge of the graveyard, where his mother's body would be laid to rest in the clan graveyard. Father McKenny said beautiful prayers, and before Finlay knew it, they'd settled her body into the ground. When he glanced over his shoulder at one point, wanting the comfort of seeing Kyla, her gaze was on him. It looked like there were tears in her eyes, but she was too far away for him to know for sure. How he wished she was by his side, the way his parents had always stood together through life's challenges…

He turned back to the proceedings and a lump caught in his

throat.

His mother was gone for good.

C

The feast after the funeral had been good for Finlay, or so she thought. The foolish comments about shaming had ended.

She'd not heard any sly remarks about shaming, though she'd been told about how horrid their walk to the keep had been. The thought of forcing more distress onto a grieving family bothered her in so many ways that she would have been forced to address the situation. She was proud of Uncle Brodie for taking a stand against those bent on the foolish shaming, something mostly done by the elders.

The only thing that worried her was that the two brothers did not converse at all. While she'd wished to stand by Finlay's side whenever possible, she'd decided it best to keep her distance. This was a time of respect for his dear mother, and there were many people who wished to show their support for him and his remaining family.

In truth, she also didn't know how to approach him. Was he interested in her, or had he formed an attraction to her simply because he'd been forced to act as her protector? She didn't know, though she hoped his feelings were true. The best practice for her was to tend to her own business and leave the next step to him. He was going through a most difficult time, and perhaps he needed to be alone for a while.

The following morn, Kyla caught up with Sorcha in the great hall. "Will you teach me to protect myself?" Her inability to defend herself was something that had weighed on her ever since the Buchan's near attack…and she sensed the conflict with his clan was far from over.

Her cousin gave her a knowing look. "How soon do you need to be able to protect yourself?"

"Soon," she whispered. "And I have another question for you." She glanced around to make sure no one was eavesdropping. "When did you know Cailean was the one?"

Sorcha quirked her brow at her cousin, a small smile on her face. "Finlay, aye?"

Kyla put her hand over Sorcha's mouth. "Hush. I'm not sure yet.

But there's something there."

Sorcha giggled. "You've kissed him, aye? 'Tis one way you'll know for sure. If his kisses are better than any other lad's. How are they?"

She blushed. "Pretty nice. But there must have been more to it. How did you know how he felt about you?"

"That part was easy. It's the way he looks at you. When he acts like no one is around but you, and you don't *care* if anyone else is around, then you know 'tis right."

She considered her cousin's advice, then said, "Nay, not yet."

Sorcha tipped her head, a knowing look on her face. "Must be you're on your way to falling—"

"I have more important things to discuss," Kyla said, cutting her off. "Back to protection."

"So who do you need to protect yourself against?"

"I'm not sure. I just felt so vulnerable at Buchan Castle. I would have felt so much better if I hadn't needed to depend on a man for protection once we were inside."

"Then a bow and arrow is not what you need and 'tis the only skill I can teach you. Maggie is the one you want." Sorcha beckoned to her sister in the crowded hall.

Maggie came over and plopped down on the bench across from them. "What is it?" Her gaze shifted expectantly between the two of them.

Sorcha whispered, "Kyla wants to learn how to protect herself."

Maggie smirked. "You've come to the right person."

"I have?" Kyla quirked her brows at her cousins. She'd never heard of Maggie doing harm to anyone.

Sorcha giggled, covering her mouth. "My sister has a dead eye with a dagger, but no one knows except for Bethia and me."

"Who taught you?"

Maggie said, "Well, my mama taught me long ago, but she doesn't know how skilled I've become."

"Can you teach me? Can I learn to hit a man a distance away in a short time?"

Maggie tipped her head and thought for a moment. "I may not be able to teach you to kill with one dagger, but you'll be able to injure a man enough to stop him in his tracks so you can get away or hurt him more."

Kyla dropped her voice. "And will you teach me how to hurt him more?"

"I will." Maggie's gaze never faltered, her expression unreadable.

A chill ran down the back of her neck. Kyla stared at her cousin as though she'd never met her before. Where had this person come from? She knew Molly and Maggie had come from an abusive background, but how bad had her life been? From the expression in her gaze, Kyla guessed it had been quite bad indeed.

"Will you help me?" she finally asked.

"Find yourself a good dagger. You need your own, one you can tuck into the folds of your skirts. I sew pockets in every garment I own and have bands around my ankles. Sometimes I carry three daggers. Sorcha and I can help you with that."

Kyla jumped out of her seat, intent on her mission. "I know just where to get one. Meet me behind the stables in an hour."

"Where are you going?" Sorcha asked.

"To find Kenzie. He's often practicing with daggers." She smiled, spun on her heel, and ran out the door.

She found Kenzie in the stables, rubbing down his sire's horses. "Kenzie, I need your help."

He immediately hustled to her side. "What do you need?"

"I need a dagger."

"For what? Who do you wish to use it on?" Kenzie's eyes were the size of big gold coins.

"I just wish to become skilled in protecting myself. 'Tis all I want, Kenzie. Will you help me?"

He giggled. "I'll show you my special supply." Kenzie ran down the passageway in the stables to the ladder and then scrambled up to the loft. He stopped on the top step, turned and beckoned to her. "Come with me."

It was easier for someone Kenzie's size to navigate the loft, but Kyla managed to walk around the mounds of straw and follow the lad to a small cupboard built into the wall. He carefully removed a long box from inside. As soon as he removed the cover, his eyes lit up. "You see? I have many. You may choose any of them except this one, my favorite."

"Where did you get these? Why must you keep so many?" She stared at the multitude of blades—long, short, thick, thin.

"For protection. If someone leaves one behind, I claim it. Someday I may be like my sire and need one to use against the Norse." His eyes danced with excitement. "Choose your weapon."

She looked inside and fingered one with a red handle. "What about this one? May I have it?"

Kenzie held her hand up, placing the dagger next to her palm. "Looks about the right size. 'Tis my gift to you if you take me along with you to practice."

"All right. I'm meeting Maggie shortly behind the stables. Then we'll go into the gardens to practice. No one will see us there."

"I'm quite skilled, too, if you must know. I'm not just good with my slinger."

"Kenzie, you have more skills than most grown men. I've no doubt you're great with your dagger. Will you help me?"

His chest puffed out a bit. "Of course. I'd be pleased to help you. Just let me hide my stash." Kenzie replaced the cover and carefully returned it to the cupboard, hidden from prying eyes.

"Why do you not take that home with you?"

He laughed. "I have one at home, too. One never knows when you'll need a weapon."

She couldn't help but smile back at him. "Come, let's find Maggie."

A few minutes later, the three of them were headed to the trees behind the gardens, Kenzie peppering the two of them with questions along the way. He was a most talkative lad.

"Who taught you how to use a dagger?" he asked Maggie. "Do you think you are better than me? Can you teach Kyla? She's never thrown one before. I have, many times. We can see who's the best among the three of us when we're done. Will you teach me more, too, Maggie?"

As soon as they found the perfect spot, Maggie turned to Kenzie. "Now you must listen carefully to my instructions."

A few hours later, Kyla stood poised in front of a line of three daggers set on the tree stump next to her. Kenzie yelled, "There's one in the oak."

Kyla flung her dagger and it landed with a thwack in the middle of the tree's trunk.

"There's one in the pine tree."

She winged another one and hit the pine square.

"Look out. He's coming from the ash tree to your left."

Another shot caught the edge of the tree. "Oh, I almost missed that one."

Maggie smiled. "Kyla, you are an excellent student. I can't believe how well you've done in such a short time."

Kenzie bolted across the grass, retrieving her daggers for her. "You're not as good as me yet…is she, Maggie? But you're pretty good."

A moment later, a voice carried across the courtyard. "Kenzie! Where the hell are you?"

"Och, 'tis my sire." He handed the daggers over to Kyla and ran off. "Coming, Papa."

Loki appeared behind them, Kenzie in tow, and asked, "What are you two doing?"

"Naught. Just chatting. We were tired of being inside," Maggie replied, staring at a hangnail on her finger.

"Hmmph. Why do I not believe you? Never mind. Just make sure you stay inside the curtain wall." He left as quickly as he'd arrived.

Kyla hugged her cousin and said, "My thanks. I feel much more confident."

"Now, be honest," Maggie said. "Who inspired you to learn this new skill?"

"Promise not to tell?"

Maggie nodded.

"Simon de La Porte."

᭟

Finlay strode into his cottage after dark. Their clan had brought plenty of food for them, so he suspected his sire would be at home rather than at the keep. Fergus stood from the table as soon as he entered. His sire stayed seated.

"Where've you been?"

"Thinking." He made his way to the pot on the hearth and filled a bowl with mutton stew.

"About what? How much you've shamed us?"

"Fergus, do not start that again," their sire said, his voice weary.

"Why, Papa? 'Tis the truth. Everyone is saying it except you and Uncle Brodie. The men in the lists are all saying he should have stayed home. I think I deserve an answer. Papa and I both told you to stay. You agreed you would, and then you left. Just like that."

"An answer to what?" Finlay strode over until his face was no more than a nose length away from his brother's. Finlay was the taller of the two, though he was a year younger than Fergus. He was also stronger. He could take his brother easily if he wanted to fight.

Finlay was ready for a fight. Part of him was desperate for one.

"Why you walked out on us. Do you not think we could have used you here when she passed? Do you not think it was tough on us when she did not awaken? 'Twas just Papa and me. Everyone else stayed away except the healers."

"I don't need to explain aught to you. I had my reasons."

"What could be more important than your own mother? Were you chasing after Kyla?"

The words sent a shock through his system. What did Fergus know about his interest in Kyla? "I didn't know she would be on the journey when I left. It had naught to do with her."

"You've been sniffing around her skirts lately. What makes you think you're good enough for the laird's daughter?"

Finlay grabbed his brother by the neck and threw him against the wall, pinning him there. "You'll not talk about her that way. Do you hear me? I'm allowed to talk to her as a Grant warrior and that's all there is to it."

Finlay had his arm against his brother's windpipe.

"She's the reason, is she not? You want her," he wheezed fiercely, unrelenting. "You forgot about Mama because of Kyla."

Their sire charged at the two of them, pulling them apart. "I've heard enough from both of you. If there's one thing your mama would want it would be for all of us to get along."

Fergus rubbed his throat. "Except Finlay is an embarrassment."

"Hellfire, I'm not. I did what I had to do."

His father stood back and said, "Finlay, tell your brother."

"Tell me what? I'll tell you what else I know. After you left, one of the last things that Mama said was 'Where's Finlay?' How do you think it felt for me to have to break her heart and tell her you'd left Grant land?"

"Papa, he can believe what he wishes," Finlay said. He didn't wish to defend himself to his own brother, someone he had believed would be on his side no matter what. He'd made a promise to his mother and he'd keep it.

"Fine. I'll tell him," his sire yelled, finally losing his temper. "Finlay left because your mama told him to go."

Finlay moved back to the table, grabbing his bowl of stew. Forcing himself to act like his brother's reaction didn't matter to him.

Fergus stared at their sire, a look of disbelief on his face. "She what?"

Their sire took a deep breath before answering. "She told Finlay to go. She made him promise."

"Why would she do that?" He glanced at Finlay. "If 'tis true, you have my apologies. I just cannot understand why she would have said that."

"She told me so herself," their father said. "Now, let there be an end to the tension between the two of you. There is to be no shaming in this household or anywhere."

"I'm sorry," Fergus said, trying to meet his gaze. "I'll be certain to tell the others."

Finlay finished his stew and cleaned his bowl before he brushed past his brother and said, "Don't bother. I can see it will trouble you too much. You prefer to think the worst of me." He strode out of the cottage and never looked back.

He had to get away.

He hadn't gone far when Brodie's son Braden caught up with him. He was with Braden's cousin Roddy. "Finlay, we have a proposal for you."

"Have I shamed you, too?" he snapped.

"What?" Braden asked. "Nay. Do not be foolish. I know you're grieving. Your brother is taking this hard, aye, but none of us fault you for leaving."

"What is it?" he asked wearily. "I need some time to myself."

"Molly and Tormod returned from Edinburgh. They couldn't locate our king, and Molly's headaches became so bad that Tormod made her come home. Uncle Logan is hoping she'll have one of her visions, but she hasn't had one yet. They didn't get much opportunity to search for the mercenaries. We've decided to make our own group of guards and travel to Edinburgh. See what we uncover about Buchan."

"On your own or does Logan know?"

"He's given us his support, and plans to meet us there as soon as he takes care of some business he would not explain. You know how he just leaves and scouts, never discussing his destination. We received a message from Uncle Micheil that he and his son are heading to Edinburgh and would like to see us. Going to see what they can learn. Uncle Logan made us promise to meet Uncle Micheil, 'tis his condition for allowing us to go. Gavin and Gregor wish to go with us." Gavin was Logan Ramsay's only son, and Gregor was his cousin and age mate.

He leveled a steady look at Braden. "So you, Roddy, Gavin, Gregor are all going? What about Connor?"

"Aye, so long as his sire approves. Jamie will stay back. We were hoping you would join us since you know more about Buchan castle than the rest of us."

Finlay rubbed his chin. He did need to get away from the weight of everything. From the dirty looks people were giving him. From the whispers behind his back, especially the ones spoken by his own brother. He'd have to find a way to see Kyla before he left, let her know why he was going.

On the other hand, perhaps if they uncovered something important, he'd gain some respect from Kyla's father. It was definitely worth a try. He'd be traveling with her cousins and brother.

"All right, if Jamie agrees, I'll go. When do you leave?"

"On the morrow, mid-morning. Meeting with Uncle Logan and Uncle Alex first."

"I'll be there."

Mayhap he'd travel with them and stay in Edinburgh. In fact, he wondered if that was where his shamed uncle lived now. Mayhap he'd pay the man a visit.

CHAPTER SEVEN

K YLA SAT IN THE GREAT hall early the next morn. The hall
door banged open and Uncle Logan flew through the hall
and into her parent's new chamber at the end of the hall. A lad she
guessed to be a messenger stood next to the main door.

Her heart thumping in her chest, she moved over to ask the lad
his intent.

"Message for Laird Alex Grant. Already given it to Logan Ramsay."

Kyla decided to play her mother's part and welcome him. "Please,
come in and I'll find you something to eat." She hustled into the
kitchen and came out with a huge trencher of stew from the previous night. "Here you go."

The lad was thin and his eyes darted everywhere, so much so
that she wondered if it was the result of some affliction. Once he
sat down, he said, "Do you know which one is Kyla Grant?" He
grabbed the utensil and began to shovel food into his mouth, his
gaze on Kyla.

"*I* am Kyla Grant. Why do you ask?"

He bolted out of his chair and reached inside his tunic for
another scroll, handing it to her. "A message for you from Davina
of Buchan." Having delivered both of his messages, he sat back in
the chair to finish his meal.

Kyla's hands shook as she fingered the parchment scroll. Had the
lass discovered what her sire had planned for Clan Grant?

Her gaze traveled across the hall, but none of her cousins were in
attendance yet. She glanced back at the messenger and said, "My
thanks," then rushed out of the hall.

Only when she was in the garden, where she could read her note in private, did she unwrap the scroll. She instantly gasped. Three words were written in large letters:

Help me, please.
Davina

Saints above, what was she to do? She tore back into the great hall to speak to the messenger, but he'd already left.

From the corner of her eye, she saw her mother striding out of the kitchens. "Mama." She chased after her.

"What is it, my dear?"

"Mama, I need your help. Do you recall what I said about Davina of Buchan? I'd like to bring her here to safety. As soon as possible."

"What, dear?" her mother said distractedly. She was glancing around the great hall as if searching for someone in particular. "You know I'll help you however I can."

"We must help Davina."

Her mother caught sight of Brenna entering the hall. Her eyes fixed on the healer, she placed her hand on Kyla's arm. "Excuse me, dear." She rushed across the hall to Brenna.

They were just close enough that Kyla could hear their conversation. "Alex is having some pain today, and I do not understand why," Maddie said. "Would you visit with him and see if he is hale? I worry about him doing too much."

Kyla crossed the hall to join them, walking up just as Aunt Brenna replied. "I thought I'd visit him today. I'll go right now." She patted Maddie's shoulder, smiled at Kyla, and headed toward the laird's chamber.

Maddie started to follow her, but Kyla stopped her. "Mama, please. I think Davina is in trouble."

Her mother turned back around to face her. "Why would you think that?"

"Because she sent me a message saying she needs help."

"Oh, Kyla. I'll not make any decisions about that. I do feel terrible about all the poor lass has suffered, but how can you help her? You must speak with your sire. He's in great pain, so please do not overtire him."

Kyla sighed, knowing she probably would not get anywhere

with her sire, but she had to try. She followed her mother into the bed chamber, and when her gaze fell upon her sire, she lost the ability to speak.

Alex stood not far from her, bent over at the waist and clutching his middle where his injury had been. Aunt Brenna stood beside him, trying to guide him back toward the bed.

"Is this new pain, Alex, or has it ailed you before?"

He didn't answer, but he was panting as if he'd raced in the courtyard for an hour. His breaths continued to come in quick gasps with each step he took backward toward the bed. He gripped the poster on the headboard so hard his knuckles had turned white. When the back of his knees hit the bed, Aunt Brenna said, "Go ahead. Sit, Alex. 'Tis just behind you."

He grabbed her hands and fell back onto the bed.

"There, now take some deep breaths. I can give you something to ease your pain. Would you like something?"

"Nay," he whispered. "I need a sound mind. If it continues, mayhap I'll take something before I go to sleep." He took a few minutes to calm his breathing, then said, "Every once in a while, it comes back. I know not what I did. 'Tis better now, Brenna. Thank you."

Her mother glanced at her, as if to remind her not to tire her father. She could see how the fine lines in her mother's face had deepened over the last few weeks, how nearly all her hair had turned nearly a beautiful shade of white. She hated everything they'd been forced to endure.

All of it.

"What is it, Kyla?" her father asked once he was propped up in the bed.

"Papa, I shouldn't bother you…"

"You will tell me why you came in, please."

She showed her father the note and he patted the bed next to him, encouraging her to sit. How she hated to see him in this weakened state, so diminished from the strong, proud warrior he'd always been.

He read the note quickly, then grasped her hand in his. "I know you are concerned about Davina, but you cannot return the way you did before. You'd not be welcomed by Buchan. Our best hope is to attack, and as soon as we have our king's permission, we will.

Until then, we wait."

"Aye." She leaned over and kissed his cheek. "I love you, Papa."

"I'm not going anywhere, daughter. 'Twas just a twinge of pain."

She smiled, then stood and said, "Take care of him, Mama." She kissed her mother's cheek and left, vowing not to bother either of them again.

She'd have to find another way.

She left the keep through the kitchens, not wishing to talk with anyone.

The day was overcast, but the chill in the air was leaving as it oft did in summer. Cool nights and warm days had prevailed of late. She traveled the periphery of the curtain wall, needing to think before she did anything she would regret.

Her instinct was to jump on a horse and chase off toward Buchan land, but after their last trip, she knew she needed more protection than just her dagger. She was desperate to help Davina, but if she traveled to Buchan land without a plan and got captured, it wouldn't do the other lass any good.

Halfway out to the gates, she noticed someone sitting in the garden.

Quite sure it was Finlay, she headed his way, only to slow her progress when she distinctly heard someone crying.

Could it be Finlay? The poor man had just lost his mother, and he hadn't been here when she passed. Others talked about shaming, something she did not believe in, but many of the elders disagreed with her there. Her heart, already broken for Davina, broke a little more.

She knew how her brothers spoke of men crying—any Grant warrior would be embarrassed to be caught shedding a tear—so she made some noise to warn Finlay of her approach. If she could, she'd wrap her arms around him and hold him close, but she wasn't sure he would welcome her touch at such a time.

He stood from the bench and turned his back to her, wiping at the tears that must have been on his cheeks.

"Finlay?" she called out to him.

"Aye. What is it, Kyla? I've been sneezing and sneezing enough to make my eyes itch terribly."

Kyla did not look at his face, giving him the chance to recover. She wouldn't let on that she'd heard him crying. He was as proud as her brothers and would consider it a sign of weakness.

"I must share something with you. Please do not inform Uncle Logan what I'm about to reveal to you."

He nodded but said nothing, looking extremely uncomfortable.

"Davina sent me a note with only three words on it. 'Help me, please.' What do you make of that?" She handed Finlay the scroll.

"Help me?" He unrolled the parchment carefully so as not to disrupt the seal. "When did you receive this?"

"A messenger brought something for my sire, and then said he also had a message for me."

"Have you asked your sire?"

"I did, but he's having a bad day. He said he'd wait to see what the king said about attacking. Papa's not well today, so I didn't press the issue. Finlay, when we left the Buchan keep, you said you'd help me. Will you?"

Finlay's eyes widened. "What exactly would you have me do?"

"Get me to Davina. If we help her, I'm certain she'll give us information about her sire's plans. About Simon de La Porte. She already promised to find out aught she can and tell me all. Will you help me, please?" She glanced up at Finlay, but he rubbed his face before staring off over her head, apparently lost in thought. "If this weren't important," she said softly, "I wouldn't ask, but I realize this is a bad time for you. I can find another guard who's willing to go with me."

After witnessing his torment, she couldn't help but reach for his hand and intertwine their fingers. He glanced down at her, a soulful expression on his face, and she wished to kiss him and hold him, tell him everything would be all right. But that would be a lie.

She couldn't bring his mother back.

"I know I promised," he finally said, "and I think there is a way. What will you tell your parents?"

"Well...they don't approve, so I'd leave a message for them. I'll tell them my goal is to get information. We cannot put ourselves in another precarious position. I understand that now. I'll talk to Maggie and Sorcha before we go, explain everything to them. One of them will pass along the message."

"Here's what I know. A group of your cousins are leaving later today for another scouting mission, this time to Edinburgh. I've been invited along and you could find a way to join us. The lads are so determined to get off Grant land, they'll not send you back. They want to be involved in clan matters, and they've been left out more often than not."

"Much like Connor."

"Aye. He might join the group, too. Your uncle approves of the journey because they are meeting his brother Micheil in Edinburgh. Molly and Tormod were unable to arrange a meeting with the king, and Logan is anxious to track him down. He has some secret business to attend to, but he plans to meet with the lads as soon as he's able. Molly is too ill to return to Edinburgh."

"Her headaches are that bad? Poor Molly."

"Aye. I believe I can convince them to allow you to travel with us."

She clasped her hands together and whispered, "Perfect. Which cousins are going?"

"Braden, Roddy, Gavin, and Gregor. Micheil and his son will meet them in Edinburgh. They are going to see if they can find out aught about the English mercenaries. They are still trying to determine if de La Porte has arrived in Buchan land. If we go with them, we can use it as an opportunity to check on Davina."

"Will they help me?"

"They've been begging to patrol for days. Give them a good reason to go near Buchan land and they will. You've got plenty of strong swordsmen and archers in that group. Gavin and Gregor are expert archers, they can protect us while we scale the curtain wall. Once we see Davina, we'll find out the truth. We'll decide what to do then." Finlay sat back down on the bench. "Lass, there's something else you need to know."

"What?"

"I can't promise to bring you home because I'm not sure I'll be returning right away. I may visit my uncle in Edinburgh. Your cousins will take care of you."

Shock shook her to her core. "What? Finlay, you cannot mean it. Have you told your sire and your brother?"

"Nay, and I want your word that you'll not tell anyone."

"I'll keep your secret, but why? You're an important part of our *clann*." She rested her hand on his arm. The expression on his face was not to her liking. His usual humor was gone and he had the look of someone lost, someone haunted. "Please reconsider."

His gaze caught hers, and the memory of their kiss in the woods shot through her, setting her insides afire. Every time she saw him, he grew more and more handsome. She didn't wish to lose him, not now that she'd just begun to see him in this new way.

"I'm not sure why, but I think 'twill work," he said, ignoring her request. "I'll tell them I'll catch up to them off our land, I just won't tell them I'm bringing you.

Kyla snuggled next to Finlay and rested her head on his shoulder. "I don't want you to leave."

He reached for her hand. "Why not? Do you not think I've shamed my family as others do?"

"Nay, 'tis a piece of foolishness. My cousins do not believe it. Nor do my brothers. 'Tis not a reason to leave. Besides, I was hoping…"

"Aye?" He rubbed his thumb across the soft skin on the back of her hand. "What were you hoping?"

"That we could…you and I could…" she stumbled on the words, but she couldn't allow him to leave, even for a short time, until she knew the truth. Did this mean he had no feelings for her?

"Lass, naught would make me happier than to ask permission for your hand in marriage. I doubt your sire is expecting to wed his firstborn daughter to a lowly warrior." He caressed her cheek, and she covered his hand with her own.

"But I could speak with my sire. You don't understand. My grandmama wanted us all to choose our own husbands. Aunt Brenna speaks of it frequently."

"Does your sire feel I shamed the clan by leaving when my mother was so close to death?"

"Nay." She dropped her hand.

"Have you asked him?" His hand fell to his side.

"Nay, but I'm sure he wouldn't feel that way. Uncle Brodie doesn't."

"But you don't know for certes."

"Finlay, please don't go. I'd like to get to know you better. Visit with your uncle, but don't stay away for long. We need you here."

"'Tis funny," he said softly, "my only goal in life was to be a braw warrior for the Grants, the fighters known as the strongest in all the land, but now that I am, I feel as though I am missing something. I don't intend to stay away forever, Kyla, but mayhap a little time is what I need. I'll make it a short visit."

"I know what your trouble is, and you'll not find the solution in Edinburgh. You're missing your mother. 'Tis what I would feel. Give yourself time to adjust to the loss. She was a dear woman to all of us."

"You may be right. I'll not argue with you on that point." He leaned over and gave her a chaste kiss on the lips.

She reached up and pulled him closer, kissing him with an abandon she'd never felt before. He teased her lips with his tongue and she parted her lips, mating her tongue with his. He wrapped his hands around her waist, lifted her and settled her onto his lap, slanting his mouth over hers, tasting her, tantalizing her until she wished to scream with delight.

She was not about to let him go. His tongue stroked hers until she wanted to cry out, and she gave back everything she could. His hands gripped her arms and pulled her so close that every part of their bodies melded together, her breasts pressing against his chest in a rhythm that fueled her need. Where did they go from here? How she wished she knew.

He ended the kiss, cupped her cheeks, then kissed her nose before he pulled back, his breathing as ragged as her own. "Lass, you torture me, but we have to stop."

"Why?"

"We're in a place where anyone could discover us." His hand moved to the back of her neck, caressing her until her entire spine tingled.

Moving to get up, she pushed against him, but he pulled her closer. "Stay. I like you exactly where you are—here in my arms."

She nestled her head into the crook of his shoulder, feeling the joy of being close to him, feeling also his pain and all he'd been through. "I'm sorry about your mother. I hope my arrival did not interrupt your thoughts." One of his hands settled on her hip, making small circles that she found quite soothing.

"I appreciate your words. I didn't expect...rather...I...I never understood."

Confused, she decided to push him a bit. "Understood what?"

"After your sire's injury, you had the appearance of someone who was lost. 'Twas as though you'd become a different person. I had no idea losing someone could affect a person so profoundly. Now I do."

"I couldn't bear to lose either of my parents," Kyla said softly. "My heart breaks for you. My father came so close... When they still weren't sure he would make it, I couldn't sleep at night. I kept thinking about Papa. Every time he led his warriors out, I would watch from the parapets because 'tis his favorite spot. He used to bring me there when I was lassie. He'd lift me into his arms so I could see over all of Grant land. His pride became my pride. Losing him is inconceivable."

"Your father is larger than life itself. He is an inspiration to us all. The Grant clan will be devastated when he goes."

"He's my papa, and 'tis the way I prefer to think of him. You lost your mama, the one who loved you without question, the one who always supported you."

"I...I never thought it would be so difficult," he said, still stroking her hip. "She's been declining for almost two years. I thought I'd have enough time to accept it when she passed, yet it feels as painful as if it had been a complete surprise."

"Do you wish you'd been here when she passed?"

He paused before answering. "Nay," he finally said. "I'm glad I was not. I don't wish to have that image of her taking her last breaths. My brother was upset that I wasn't here, but I think 'twas best for me."

She sat up to gaze into his eyes. "I'm sure your mama would understand."

He tucked a stray lock of hair behind her ear and then rubbed her cheek with his thumb. "My mother told me to go with Jamie. Brenna and Jennie had told me that she could pass any day, and I planned to stay home, but my mother insisted. She would not have it any other way. I foolishly thought she would wait until I came home, that she had some control over when she died."

"Oh, Finlay." She kissed his lips, then his cheek.

"A black crow flew in front of me on the way home, and I knew...I just knew."

"Aunt Jennie believes the dying do have some control over when they go."

"Then I feel worse."

"Nay, I think 'tis better."

"Why?"

She stared up at the stars. "Aunt Jennie would tell you that your mother knows your heart because you are her son…and that she knew 'twould have been too difficult for you to watch her go. Does that make sense to you?"

He thought for a moment, squeezing her hand tightly. "Mayhap. I'm not sure."

"This will sound silly to you, but I would want to be with my mother when she goes, but I could not handle being with my father."

"Nay?"

"Nay." Her eyes misted at the thought. "The sight of my sire who's always been so strong brought so low…I would throw myself on him and scream and cry." Then she laughed at the thought of how her sire would react to such thing. He'd open one eye at her, and then… "And then he would tell me to stop it."

She scowled and whispered, "Nay, he would say, 'Stop it, lassie.' And then I would cry harder. I love it when he calls me his lassie."

The sound of guards yelling in the distance brought them out of their quiet interlude. Finlay set her on the ground in front of him, kissed her cheek, and said, "My thanks. You helped me more than you know. Do you still wish to leave on the morrow?"

"Aye." Kyla squared her shoulders and sighed. "I cannot sleep knowing something could have happened to Davina and that wee bairn. If we wait, they could both be killed and it would be on my conscience."

"For certes, you'll not go alone. I'll meet you on the path just past the loch when the sun is high. Bring your satchel. I'll have a horse for you."

What had she done?

CHAPTER EIGHT

ℒ

FINLAY FOUND JAMIE IN THE stables early in the morn, just as he'd hoped. He wished to discuss his impending journey with him, mostly to be certain he approved. While part of him also wished to tell Jamie about Kyla's intention to join the trip, he wasn't sure how his friend would react. Kyla would be devastated if her brother prevented her from going.

"Good morn to you, my laird." He clasped Jamie on the back, a sudden vision of his dark-haired sister filling his mind. Did he dare broach the subject of courting his sister?

"Finlay. You've settled on traveling with Connor and my cousins, aye?"

"Only with your approval. As your second, I should be by your side at all times." He scratched the hair on the back of his head, wondering how to best explain the disquiet he'd felt since returning from the Buchans. "But I need to clear my head."

Jamie stopped brushing his favorite horse to turn to him. "My sister has clouded your vision that much, aye?"

Finlay was flabbergasted. "What?"

"You did not think I would miss what passes between the two of you, did you?"

He stuttered a few times and his friend laughed. Finally, he collected himself enough to say, "I like Kyla. And if I'm being truthful, my feelings for her grow stronger each day. But I doubt your sire would approve of a warrior marrying his daughter. I hoped some time away might help clear my thinking. And the answer to your question is aye, she clouds my vision that much."

"Don't dismiss my sire that easily. Aline is not exactly the lass we expected Jake to marry, but she is one of the strongest women I know. If you feel that strongly about Kyla, I encourage you to approach him. I believe both my parents would prefer that Kyla marry within the clan than for her to be sent to live with a neighboring laird. My father does not believe in building alliances that way."

"She's his eldest daughter. I would have guessed he had a member of the nobility in mind for her at this point. Wouldn't our king arrange a marriage for her?" Finlay did his best to ignore how pleased he was by Jamie's declaration, but he didn't wish to get his hopes up for nothing.

Jamie snorted. "Nay. King Alexander could try, but my sire has the largest warrior group of all the Scots. Add in the Ramsays and the other smaller clans that support us, and our king knows what he's up against. At this point, everyone's aware that my grandmama made Alex promise to allow his sisters to choose their own husbands. I doubt Aunt Brenna or Aunt Jennie would allow Alex to treat Kyla any differently. My sire also prefers for his close family to stay in our quarters. 'Tis why our keep is now one of the largest. Loki could have stayed if he had wished."

It was a better response than he could have hoped for. Mayhap they did have a chance. "I'll definitely consider your words."

"I understand you've had a difficult week, so if this is what you must do to get past all that has happened, I wish you a good journey."

Sudden feelings of guilt washed over him. He couldn't hide what Kyla had asked him to do. He valued their friendship too much…and he also wished to share an idea he'd had about Davina's message.

"There's something else I must tell you."

Jamie stood back and crossed his arms. "What has she talked you into? My sire informed me of the note Kyla received, and I agree that we should wait until we have approval from the king before we attack."

"She wishes to see Davina. She's convinced the lass is in trouble, but she thinks Davina might have information for us, too. The lass promised Kyla she would contact her if she discovered her sire was planning to act against Clan Grant."

"She did? Are you certain?"

"Aye, I was a witness to that promise. Jamie, what if she does know something? What if a disguised message was the only way she could communicate that? At first, I thought it was a bad idea to take Kyla with us, but what if she can learn all of Buchan's plans through Davina? The lass is not happy with her sire. Wouldn't we be foolish not to try?"

Jamie rubbed his jaw in thought. "You may be correct. There could be any number of meanings behind that message. Her sire could be turning daft, or he could be ready to march and plans to leave her behind. We'll never know unless someone speaks with her."

"You know I'll protect Kyla with my life. If we journey there together, mayhap 'twill help us decide if we suit."

"Aye, but you better not learn too much about how well you suit, if you get my meaning. I'll kick your arse if you touch her."

"Understood. I have the utmost respect for your sister." Was he considering approving Kyla's journey with him?

"I'll turn my head for now, but I'll talk to my parents after you've gone. You have archers with you. Use them. If Kyla goes with you, I will expect you both back as soon as you complete your mission."

"My thanks, Jamie. I'll go talk to my father, let him know I'll be leaving."

☾

A few hours later, Finlay tightened his satchel to his saddle. He'd told his sire and his brother he was going on a mission with the younger group of warriors, and they'd accepted his decision. His sire had begged him not to seek out his uncle, and he'd promised that he wouldn't. The purpose of this journey had changed completely in his mind. Now he sought to prove his value as a suitor for Kyla's hand. He wasn't ready to share that with Kyla quite yet, but he would tell her that he definitely planned to return to Grant land. She deserved to know his feelings were genuine.

If they could uncover the Buchan's plans and prevent any battle from taking place, perhaps her sire would consider him. He'd protect her with his life.

There was a rustling sound, and he glanced up in time to see Kyla running toward him. She'd wisely grabbed lad's clothing to wear, though the dark tunic and breeches did nothing to hide her soft curves. Her hair was pulled back in a tight plait tucked inside her tunic, and she carried a small satchel.

She came to a quick stop in front of him, panting a bit, but a huge smile covered her face. Visions of the two of them rolling around in the soft grass behind the horses broke through his thoughts, but he forced them away.

"Are you ready, lass?" Finlay took her satchel and attached it to the back of the saddle of the horse he'd brought for her.

"Aye. I'm ready, and before you ask, I'm sure."

He laughed. "You guessed my next question."

Kyla glanced around the area, and there was no denying her obvious discomfort. "Are you sure we'll be fine until we catch up to them? Do you not think we should bring guards?" She stared up at him with a look of trust he wasn't sure he deserved.

"Do not worry about the reivers. I've spoken with many of the guards and they've not seen anyone on our land. It seems likely they've all been attracted to Buchan's promise of coin. I doubt we'll see anyone. I do want you to know that I informed Jamie of our plan."

"You did? But he'll make me stay here, will he not?" She spun around, apparently checking to see if Jamie was indeed pursuing them.

Finlay reached for her hand to stop her. "Jamie said he'd turn his head. I explained that Davina had promised to send you a message if she found out aught about her sire's plans."

"But why did that help convince him? That wasn't what the message was about."

"We discussed how she'd never be able to get a messenger to take a 'direct' message. They wouldn't dare deliver his plans to his enemies. She'd have to disguise her message. I convinced Jamie that it was worth a try to see if this was her intent. He doesn't wish to see your sire go to battle any more than you do. I also told him something else."

"What?"

"He sensed something between us, and I admitted to my feelings for you. I also told him I'd return home to Grant land with you." He stepped in front of her and took both her hands in his. "I asked him if he thought I'd have a chance with a laird's daughter."

Her eyes widened and the biggest smile he'd ever seen spread across her face. "You did? What did he say?"

"He said his sire might agree, but *he'd* never agree to me court-ing you. Said I was an arse." He dropped his hands and turned his back to her to hide his smile.

"What?" She peeked around his shoulder at his face, and as soon as she saw his smirk, she grabbed his hand and squeezed it. "Finlay, that was not funny."

He grinned. "Aye, I thought it was."

"Tell me exactly what he said. Everything. Tell me right now." She wiggled in her spot as if a squirrel had climbed up her breeches.

"I told him I was interested in you, but only if you didn't become too bossy."

She swung lightly at his arm. "Finlay, you're horrible."

He couldn't stop laughing, so he gave in to the moment of hap-piness and picked her up, spinning her about, and then kissing her soundly until she slid back down his body. Cupping her face in his hands, he said, "He thought your father would consider my suit. 'Struth is, naught could have pleased me more. We'll find out what that bastard has planned and then return here, and I promise to talk to your sire as soon as we do."

"Oh, Finlay." She tugged his lips down to hers and she kissed him.

He groaned as soon as he heard a soft sound in the back of her throat, but he forced himself to stop. "You tempt me too much. I'd love to continue this, but if we don't leave now, we may not be able to catch them."

"Did Connor come along?"

"Aye, he did. Five of them plus five guards. They'll travel quickly, but I told them I'd meet up with them on the road."

"You didn't tell them why, did you?" Kyla chewed on her lip.

"I told them that I needed to spend a little more time with my sire."

He grabbed her waist, kissed her quickly, and tossed her up onto her saddle, where she landed with an oof.

She cast a puzzled look his way.

"Because I wanted to, that's all. Or would you prefer this?" He got down on one knee in front of her and held his hands to his chest. "Your beauty slays me. I am unable to do aught but kiss your plump lips."

She burst into laughter. "Aye, I think I would like you to fall to your knees and attest to my beauty more often."

He stood up and rolled his eyes, adjusting his plaid. "Don't get too attached to that."

When she was able to keep her laughter in check, she said, "I cannot tell you what this means to me. I've been overcome with worry for poor Davina and her daughter."

"Don't fret. We'll convince Connor and the others to help us, especially after my discussion with Jamie." He mounted up and led the way down the path, setting the pace and giving her space to ride next to him.

"I wish my sire was still strong enough to attack the Buchan Castle and put an end to this chaos. The Buchan is not a rational man."

"No matter how strong he is, your sire would never do that without the king's approval. I'm guessing your uncle Micheil will broach that topic with our king while he's in Edinburgh."

"I have a bad feeling about all that is taking place around us. 'Tis why I feel I must do my part. I'm hoping Davina will be able to tell us more about her sire's plans."

"Aye, 'twould be to our advantage for certes." He spurred his horse into a gallop. "Come. We have to move along to catch up with them."

They rode in silence until dusk was upon them. They'd made it off Grant land, but Finlay didn't like the look of the clouds above. "Lass, I fear we have a storm coming."

"I hope not."

He could see the terror in her expression. "If my memory serves me correctly, your fear of thunderstorms is almost as grave as your brother Jamie's. True?"

As soon as he finished his sentence, a bolt of lightning lit up the sky. Kyla flinched, her arms jerking up to cover her face. "Aye, 'tis true. I hate lightning. The thunder only troubles me when it tells me a storm is coming."

Her fear probably had the same source as Jamie's—a former stablehand of the Grants had been killed by a strike of lightning.

"There's a cave about an hour ahead. If we ride fast, we may make it ahead of the storm. Can you keep up?"

"Aye. Just go."

He flicked the reins and they galloped across the meadow, watching the storm as it veered closer to their area. Darkness fell when they were almost to the cave.

"Hurry, Finlay. I can feel the raindrops starting. It could turn into a downpour in a matter of minutes."

"The cave is directly ahead. There's a nice overhang that will keep the horses dry as well. I'll leave some feed just inside to keep them near."

Once they were close, he dismounted and climbed up the small hill to the cave, struggling to lead the horses to a place they weren't interested in going. The animals calmed down as soon as they reached the flattened area in front of the deep cave. The overhang was even better than he had recalled. He reached for Kyla and set her down just as the rain started to pour over them. "Go. Get inside. I'll get your horse settled."

She ran ahead as two lightning bolts shot across the sky, illuminating the way. He heard her squeal, but she continued forward until she was well inside the protection of the cave. He'd just managed to get the horse feed out and the beasts under the protective overhang when the sky opened up, gushing rain like he hadn't seen in some time.

When he stepped inside the cave, he paused for a moment to allow his eyes to adjust to the dark. Then he saw her huddled in the back, shaking. He rushed to her side and wrapped his arms around her. "Kyla, I know we were in danger outside, but now you're safe. You're shivering terribly."

He noticed a large boulder off to the side and moved over to it, sitting down and tugging her onto his lap. "Open your eyes."

She'd had them squeezed shut since he'd first noticed her in the cave. "I do not wish to see what's happening."

"Never mind, please keep them closed. As long as your eyes are shut, naught can happen to us."

The teasing lilt of his voice made her chuckle. "Finlay, must you jest like that? I cannot change my fears."

"If it makes you laugh, I'll tease you more often, not less."

She stopped her giggling and opened her eyes to look at him. Her gaze settled on his lips.

"Ah, lass. If you keep that up, we're headed for trouble."

She lifted her gaze to his, but said nothing.

He leaned down and pressed his lips to hers, teasing her into parting her lips for him. Hell, but he loved the taste of her. He pulled back just for a moment. "Kyla, you taste so sweet. Only trouble could come of this, but kiss me again, lass."

She did, leaning toward him until he could feel her curves meld against him. He groaned, thrusting his tongue inside to taste every part of her delectable mouth, surprised to see that her passion seemed to match his own. She pushed him for more, and he wanted to lay her down on a spot of soft moss and make sweet love to her.

When his tongue met hers again, she moaned, a sound that traveled straight to his cock. He devoured her mouth, his hands suddenly out of control, roaming across her back to her front, circling around until he cupped her breasts through the tunic. It was too heavy for him to feel her like he wished to. Fumbling for the bottom of the tunic, he slid his hands under the fabric until he found the soft mounds of her breasts.

"Kyla, I swear you have the most beautiful breasts ever." He kissed her neck and she shoved at him. He moved back, doing his best to get his breathing under control when she did the one thing he never would have expected. She tugged at the bottom of the tunic and yanked it over her head, flinging it off to the side in one smooth movement. Her thin chemise followed.

He growled, his head dipping to her breast, and his tongue traced a path through her delicious cleavage, across the underside of one heavy mound and up the middle until he stroked her nipple.

"Oh, Finlay."

Her hands gripped his shoulders as she pulled him closer. He did as she asked, switching to her other breast and suckling it until she gasped, writhing beneath him. He scraped her taut peak with his teeth and she squealed.

His cock was now so hard that he feared he would lose control like a wee laddie, so he reminded himself who sat on his lap. She had as much passion as he did, and if he took her, he'd have her screaming his name louder than the thunder.

But he couldn't. He pulled away, forcing himself to do the right thing no matter how much it hurt. Innocent that she was, she seemed baffled by why he'd pulled away. She whispered his name, an act that almost put a knife through his heart. "Finlay, is something wrong?"

"Nay, lass. 'Tis as right as ever. Naught pleases me more than having you in my arms." He did his best to get his panting under control, something that had come out of nowhere and overtaken him. But he could not allow it to overtake his sense of honor.

"Then why did you stop? Kiss me again."

He cupped her cheeks and kissed her forehead. "Naught would please me more, but you tempt me beyond my control. I'd love to make you mine, here and now, but I force myself to remember who your sire is."

"What does that have to do with us?" She gripped his forearms, keeping him close.

"Your sire is formidable man, lass. I'll not take your maidenhead before I stand in front of him to ask for your hand in marriage. I just won't do it. Even I have a hard time not believing you deserve better, to be the mistress of your own castle, but…"

"But?"

"But." He kissed her lips, a tender kiss to let her know how much he did care. "But I like you too much to give up without trying. I can only hope he views me as worthy."

She lost her smile. "I'm glad you'll try, but I hate it when you say you aren't worthy. You're as worthy as any man."

"Still not taking your maidenhead, lass, no matter how much you beg me. Please stop begging me." He set her on her feet and got up to grab her clothing.

She giggled at his playful tone and allowed him to help her dress, but it didn't stop her from speaking. "Finlay, I've told you—my sire will allow me to choose my own husband. He'll not force anyone on me. Please don't push me away."

"I appreciate what you're saying, but you must understand where I'm coming from. If I think only of my own desires, I'll have you stripped down to naught but your skin, lying underneath me and carrying my bairn before the next round of thunder echoes through the land. Try as I might, I can't picture your sire staring at me and saying, 'Well done, lad.'"

Kyla laughed so hard she turned her head away from him and rested her forehead on her arm. "Finlay, you're so funny."

He sat back down and set her on the stone next to him. "Och, you think I'm jesting? I just planted that idea in my head, and now

I need to walk away before I am unable." He reached for her wrist and caressed the tender skin on the inside with his thumb, the spot where he could feel her life force beating inside her.

She shivered. "Why do you do that?"

"I had an idea. Whenever I touch you like this, you'll know I want you more than anything in the world. I can't always kiss you or hold you when I want, but this will tell you how much you mean to me." He chuckled. "Just in case your sire is nearby."

She stared at his thumb on her wrist in awe. "Oh, Finlay."

He kissed the spot before releasing her wrist. He strode over to the opening to the cave and looked out over the land. "Look, did you even notice it has stopped raining?"

She joined him at the mouth of the cave, her hands hugging her body against the dampness. "Then I guess we would have had plenty of time before the next round of thunder."

He hauled her up next to him, doing his best to warm her. "Stop begging me, lass."

She stared up at him and whispered, "Please?"

He shook his head. "Must I remind you that your sire is not the only one I should be worried about? Jamie warned me to keep my hands to myself before we left." He dropped his arms from around her. "I didn't listen well, did I?" He reached for her again. "Your uncle is also Logan Ramsay. You heard how he threatened Cailean MacAdam, aye?"

She laughed again. "Even I would be afraid of Uncle Logan. I don't blame Cailean for that."

"Good, because he scares the hell out of me."

"All right, Finlay. I understand. We shall hold off until we are back on Grant land, and we'll both talk to my sire. Will that suit you?"

"Aye, 'tis a most suitable arrangement. My thanks."

He glanced at the storm around them. "I don't think we'll catch them as quickly as I'd hoped. This storm is northeast. They may not have been slowed by it at all."

"What will we do?"

"I hate to travel at night, but 'tis the only way we'll make up the time. Take care of your needs. Then we must head out. I'll not travel to Buchan land alone."

"Aye, I'd like to have some guards along."

"Now, lass, there'll be no kissing me again, will there?"

She laughed and ran behind a bush, the lilt of her voice soothing to him. How he hoped all would go well.

He couldn't help but feel unworthy of Kyla Grant, no matter what she and Jamie had said. If he could just handle this situation right and help put an end to this trouble with Buchan, he'd stand a much better chance.

He'd convince Laird Alexander Grant he was a worthy suitor for his daughter or he'd die trying.

He had a bad feeling about that thought.

CHAPTER NINE

THEY'D ALMOST MADE IT TO Buchan land before they found the group. Finlay let out a bird call as soon as he caught sight of Connor near the rear of the group. Connor and Braden both heard him and called the others to a halt.

"What the hell?" Braden asked as they came riding toward them.

Connor chuckled, glancing at his sister. "Your plan worked again, dear sister, but this time with a different guard. She tricked you, aye, Finlay?" Connor motioned for them all to dismount in a clearing off to the side. "And what is your intention this time, Kyla?"

"Who's leader of your group," Finlay asked.

Four sets of hands pointed to Connor. "He's the eldest," Roddy said.

"Connor, we'd like to request your assistance, and I have Jamie's approval."

"Truly?" Connor quirked a brow at his sister. "Davina again?"

"Aye, she sent me a message asking for my help."

"And you trust 'tis a true message?" Braden asked. "What did it say?"

"It said, 'Help me, please.' True, it could be false, but I have to see her for myself. Will you not guard us? Finlay and I were in her tower room before. We know where to go."

Finlay said, "I spoke with Jamie about this. Davina promised to inform Kyla if she learned of her sire's plans. It's possible there's more to the message than there appears to be. It could be that Davina's discovered something useful. Jamie agreed the possibility is worth investigating if we think we can get in safely."

"I doubt Buchan will allow you in after our last visit. Or have you forgotten the way he kicked us out, Kyla?" Connor asked.

"Nay, I've not forgotten." She crossed her arms and gave her brother a menacing look. "Just remember, I'm older than you."

The look on her face forced Finlay to step in. "Look, Davina lives in the only chamber in the tower. I can get your sister over the back curtain wall. We can be in and out of there in less than an hour if need be, but not without some protection. If we need to get Davina and the baby out, we'll decide what to do once we've assessed the situation. Will you post two archers on the curtain wall?"

Connor sighed, but then glanced at Gavin and Gregor.

The two exchanged a look, followed by a nod. "We did the same for Jake. Why not Kyla?"

"Lead on," Connor said. "I'll leave the five guards at the periphery. Gavin and Gregor will take the wall. Braden will scale it and wait for your return. If they don't return within two hours, Braden, you're to go in and find out what happened. Roddy and I will make our way around the curtain wall to see what we can learn of the rest of their operation. I want this done before dawn."

"My thanks," Finlay said. "We'll leave Kyla's horse back here. She can ride with me."

Connor spoke to the head of the guards and they discussed their plan while Finlay tied Kyla's horse in a hidden area. He helped her mount in front of him, and as soon as they were ready, Connor gave the order for everyone to continue toward Buchan land.

They hadn't gone far when Finlay felt the fine tremors in Kyla's body. He whispered in her ear, "Why do you tremble, lass?"

"Nervous. I know not what will happen. I do not want aught to happen to my brother or my cousins. Think you all of us are safe?"

"Aye, who is better trained than the Grant and Ramsay lads? And we have two of the finest archers in the land. They will protect us." He rubbed her arm, hoping to calm her fears.

Truth was, he felt ill. A strange feeling pulled in his chest each time he thought of something happening to her. He'd be the only one guarding her once they stepped inside that tower. He wiped the sweat from his brow at just the thought of her in the hands of her sire's enemy.

He'd been so intent on getting away and pleased at the thought that she'd be with him that he had not properly thought this through. If anything happened to her, he'd never be able to live with himself. A vision of Glenn of Buchan swinging his word flashed through his mind.

"Kyla, promise that you'll listen to me. If anything is off, we're leaving. I'll not put your life at risk."

"I promise."

She gazed back at him with those beautiful blue eyes and her pouty lips that begged to mate with his. She leaned her head against his chest and he sunk his fingers into her plait at the back of her neck, rubbing his hand rhythmically against her skin. This closeness with her was veering his thoughts in the worst possible direction.

Damn, but he liked the feel of her in his arms. He'd do whatever she asked of him.

"All right," he whispered. "Please remember your promise, no matter what transpires."

She nodded and tugged his lips down to hers, kissing him, sucking on his bottom lip before she pulled away from him.

She'd just kissed him in front of her brother and cousins, and he was pleased—it was as good as a declaration of their intent to marry. The woman continued to wreak havoc on his senses, and he was glad of it. Hellfire, but he was in deep trouble. He prayed his dear mother was watching over them from above.

☾

Getting up the wall had been a challenge. Finlay had thrown a rope from his satchel into a tree branch until it caught just right so he could climb up onto the wall. Gavin, Gregor, and Braden had followed. Once they'd determined all was well, Finlay had climbed back down to help Kyla up the rope.

She'd ignored the drop beneath her, knowing Finlay was there to help her. The wall was much taller than she could handle, but the lads had all easily scaled it. When they finally reached the top, Finlay hoisted himself onto the lip and dropped down to the walkway before motioning for her to jump into his arms. He caught her, and her heart sighed at the nearness of him, but there was no time to savor the new pleasure of his touch. They crept over to the door of Davina's tower chamber, pointing out their destination to Braden. Once at the tower, she peered up at him, her heart racing, and said a quick prayer for safety. He opened the door and stepped into the darkened interior while she waited outside. A few moments later, he tugged her inside, putting his finger to her lips.

It took a moment for her eyes to adjust to the darkness. As soon as she could see movement, it was already too late. Something came crashing down on Finlay's skull just before her world went dark.

𝌆

Finlay's eyes opened to a harsh voice, followed by a slap to his face, first one cheek and then the other.

"What the hell?" He bolted upright and grabbed for his sword, only to find it wasn't there. He found himself staring into the eyes of a red-haired stranger. The man was missing two teeth, and he had a grin that told Finlay he needed to be careful and move with care.

The only thing he could think about was Kyla. He didn't move, just searched the room with his gaze as memories came floating back to him. He stood on one side of the dark chamber, his guard seated at the only furniture in the room, a table with two stools. The man was greedily sucking down an ale.

Finlay reached up and felt the dried blood on the back of his head where he'd been struck. "My companion," he managed to say. "Where is she?"

The man said, "She's dead to you. 'Twould be better for you to forget her. I see your sire has trained you well, just as I expected, just as I told the Buchan."

"Who are you?"

He snorted. "What? You do not recognize your favorite uncle, dear nephew? 'Course, it has been a long time since you've seen me, since I was sent out of Clan Grant. Foolish bastards. I knew someday I'd have the chance to get my revenge. My own brother never stood up for me. Banished…just banished."

"Uncle Geordie?" he asked in shock.

The man's eyes lit up. "Och, you do remember me, lad. Glad to hear my brother kept my memory alive."

"I do. Now, I need to find the lass I was with and take her home. This was all a mistake. Just let us go."

"Can't do that, Finlay. Have a seat and I'll explain how things have changed. Before you start searching, I'll tell you right away that I've removed all your weapons."

"Why? You're my uncle. I've done naught to you."

"Business, lad. I needed coin, and Buchan offered gold coins to anyone who joined him. Plus, he offered me extra. Simple as that."

"Offered you extra coins for what?" Finlay had a sickening feeling deep in his gut, one he didn't like at all.

"To help you accept your place here. 'Tis simple—they set you up. 'Twasn't my idea, but I have to admit 'twas a good one. I saw you the last time you were here, lad, and I could tell you'd be a mighty fine warrior. The Buchan's men have had little training. He needs someone like you to train his men for the upcoming battle...and he also needs a hostage. He had that note sent to your little lassie to lure both of you back here. Now you'll do as we tell you."

Finlay exploded. He reached across the table and grabbed his uncle by the throat and pinned him up against the wall. "You're right—'tis simple. You'll get me out of here, or I'll kill you."

The door flew open and three other guards came in, yanking Finlay away from his uncle and beating him until he couldn't move. He fought with every ounce of strength he had, but he was only one man. He couldn't fight three guards.

Once they had him contained, another man stepped into his line of sight. "Allow me to explain everything to you, fool," the man said. Something told him this was Simon de La Port. "I paid to have that note written and sent. I knew you'd come with her, and you did, solving two of my problems." He spat into the corner disdainfully. "Davina is fine, and now Kyla is mine to do with as I wish. When we're ready to attack, we'll bring her beaten body along for Alex Grant to see so he'll surrender his castle to us. 'Twill be his choice: his castle or his daughter. Since we have you to thank for bringing her along, we've decided to use you.

"Your uncle tells me anyone trained directly by Grant and his brothers is mighty with a sword, so you'll train some of our men since they're mostly useless."

Finlay spat the blood accumulating in his mouth off to the side. "The hell I will. I'll not do aught for you. Free Kyla and I'll take her home. Otherwise you'll have all five hundred Grant warriors along with three hundred Ramsay warriors here in two days. Alex Grant will call the Camerons, the Menzies, the Drummonds, and more. You have no chance."

"Do I not? If I place his daughter on a platform above my gate with an archer on either side of her, arrows aimed at her heart, do you truly think he'll bring eight hundred men down on me? Nay. He's not that foolish. He'll do his best to think of something, but it will take him time to plan, and time is something he does not have. We practice for two days, and then we move. All my mercenaries will be here by then.

"Now, you're going to train our guards in the lists, and if you don't, I'll beat Kyla in front of you. Or I'll let you watch me ruin her, unless…" A twisted grin broke out across his face. "Have you already taken her maidenhead, lad? Hmmm. Mayhap I'll have to find out." De La Porte's laugh was cruel and cold.

Finlay's mind spun in so many directions, he knew not what to do first. "Touch her and I'll kill you with my bare hands."

"Sure you will. My thanks for being foolish enough to come alone." He started to move toward the door. "She certainly is a beauty. I can see why she moved your cock. She's soon to be known as Simon de La Porte's woman."

Finlay did his best to focus on the errors in the bastard's statements. They hadn't come alone. There were five of the best Grant and Ramsay men in the area with more guards not far away, and if the lads didn't arrive in Edinburgh soon, mayhap Micheil and David Drummond would come looking for them… At least he knew the group had not been discovered.

"Leave her be! Do what you will to me, but leave her be, you slimy bastard." He fought against the holds on him, but to no avail.

His uncle left soon after de La Porte left. "Sorry, nephew. Each man for himself."

He couldn't take his mind off the horrifying thought of Kyla in the hands of Simon de La Porte. He would have to believe in her strength. She was Alex Grant's daughter, and while she couldn't wield a sword, she'd said something about daggers. If he ever got out of this, Alex Grant and Logan Ramsay would kill him and hang him in front of the whole clan. And what would Jamie think of him? The thought of how horribly he'd let Jamie down made him wish to heave. He'd hardly acted like the laird's second.

The three men yanked him to his feet and led him into the courtyard to jeers and guffaws of all those around him. The leader stood in front of him and said, "You are to defend yourself against one of our warriors, one-on-one. They'll learn from you, and if you have any foolish ideas, you heard what de La Porte intends to do."

"Just give me my sword." Finlay spat a stream of blood again, wiping his mouth on his tunic. He'd find his way out of this, but first he'd have to watch and plan. He did his best planning with a sword in his hands. And he'd kill every one of the fools who dared come close to him.

He'd kill them all just to get back to Kyla.

CHAPTER TEN

🙠

BY THE TIME KYLA AWOKE, it was the middle of the night. That was the first thing she realized, and the second thing she noted was the pain in her head. Everything came back to her as she sat up, scanning the area around her to determine her location.

Finlay was nowhere to be seen.

The sounds of a closing door jolted her, but the figure that rushed to her side was slender yet curvy. She sat up on the edge of the pallet and the woman, Davina, she realized, grabbed her hand. "Kyla, I'm so sorry. How do you feel?"

"Not well, but well enough to get out of here. Where's Finlay? And why did you send me that message? You look fine to me." Her hand moved up to check the bump on the back of her head.

"I didn't send you a message."

"What?" She stared at Davina, praying she'd heard her wrong. She'd be ill for sure if it turned out this was naught but trickery. "Aye, you did. It said, 'Help me.'" Upon closer inspection, Davina was a mess—her clothes dirty, her hair unkempt—but she didn't look like she'd been harmed.

"Nay. It did not come from me. I fear it has something to do with Simon de La Porte and his mercenaries. They arrived not long ago and de La Porte is ruthless. I will help you any way I can, but I have little power here."

"Why would they want me? I don't understand. And what have they done to Finlay?"

Davina crossed her arms. "Truly? You cannot think of a reason why they would want you? You are Alex Grant's daughter." There was no judgment in her voice. Just sympathy...and the plain-spokenness of someone who was accustomed to poor treatment.

Kyla dropped her head into her hands. "Nay, nay, please. My sire has been through so much already. Please, no more." The helplessness of her situation made her wish to sob until she had no more tears.

The door flew open and slammed shut. A beast of a man stood in front of her, his arms crossed and his legs spread wide. He turned his head to spit, but Davina yelled at him. "Do not dare spit in my chamber, Simon."

Kyla wished to scream loud enough to reach the top of the Highland mountains. The ill-reputed de La Porte stood in front of her.

He narrowed his gaze, but opened the door wide and spat back into the staircase. "Foolish chit."

Brown hair the color of mud fell in long strands to his shoulders. His eyes dark enough to appear black—a token of his black heart, she decided. He was not an ugly man, and he was much younger than she would have guessed. He had a strong jawline and his beard was in need of a trim. His body was fit, with broad shoulders and a trim waist, though Finlay was much more muscular. There was one thing that surprised her about him—Simon de La Porte was short for a man.

And yet there was something deeply wrong about him. The energy he gave off felt pure evil, as if he were the spawn of the devil.

When de la Porte's gaze turned to her, the only way she could describe the feeling of being under his scrutiny was to say that his eyes bore through her, in one side and out the other. She shuddered and pushed her back up to the wall.

"Greetings, my dear." He grinned, and Kyla had never seen a more deceitful expression than the one on Simon de La Porte's face. He spoke differently, his accent reminding her of how her mother spoke. Dear Alice had sounded that way too before she had passed on.

She turned her head away from him, not wanting to look into his eyes.

"If it isn't a snobbish Grant in front of me, just like her sire and her brothers. They look down their noses at everyone, believing they are better than all the other Scots in the land. Maybe they are, but they're not better than the English. All will know that the downfall of the great Alexander Grant was caused by Simon de La Porte and no other."

"Leave me be, and leave my sire alone. You've already done enough damage. Why can you not leave us be? And where is my guard?"

He chuckled. "I'd be happy to leave you be. As soon as your sire relinquishes his castle and all his lands to me, I promise to never bother you again. Until then, I'll haunt his every moment. I'll not stop until I get what I want."

"Why should he give you his castle?" she snapped. "He built it and protected it all these years, not you."

"Are you not a bit mouthy for a mere female? Keep your opinions to yourself and we'll get along just fine. Speak too much and I may have to take action."

Kyla didn't dare ask what kind of action he meant.

"That's better. Now, tell me everything I wish to know, or you'll be punished for it. Understood?"

Kyla refused to acknowledge him.

He moved closer and his fingers grabbed her by the chin, forcing her gaze up to his. "I asked you a question. Understood, Lady Grant?"

Kyla spat on him.

His fist immediately swung out and hit her cheekbone. Her world went dark again, but this time, she didn't mind.

*

Connor stood in the middle of the clearing, his hands on his hips, staring at the sky.

"I couldn't see any sign of either of them when I went inside," Braden said. "What do we do? Gavin and Gregor are still up there, and it has been almost several hours. The sun will be up soon. Finlay said he'd return in an hour. Something has happened."

Gregor came flying toward them, Gavin close behind him. "Connor!"

Connor held up his hand to silence Braden and motioned for Gregor to say what he needed to say. "Gregor?"

Gregor came to a halt directly in front of him. "We just heard a couple of men talking of taking prisoners. Two of them. Hit them both over the head. One was laughing about how hard they fell; the other was excited they had another female in the compound."

"It must be Finlay and Kyla. Did you hear aught else?"

"Just that Simon would decide what to do."

Connor shook his head. "De La Porte is here. Hellfire."

"Shall we go after them?"

Roddy and the guards had all gathered round, waiting for instructions.

Connor said, "I promised Uncle Logan we would not attack anyone with only ten men, so I cannot. Gavin and Gregor, take three guards and head to Edinburgh to find Uncle Micheil. Do whatever he suggests. The rest of us will return to Grant land immediately. If Simon de La Porte has Kyla, I'll let Papa decide what to do next, along with Uncle Logan and Uncle Quade. This is a troubling situation. I'll not be the one to make the final decision."

He rubbed his chin before he said, "Hurry. Everyone go. We cannot waste any time. Kyla and Finlay are depending on us. As soon as we have reinforcements, we'll take action. We've just given my sire a reason to attack."

☾

Finlay swung his sword over his head at his most recent opponent, but as soon as he knocked the fool's sword out of his hands, he fell to the ground. He could not go on any more.

He needed water, he needed sleep, but more than anything, he needed Kyla. He'd fought off so many guards, he'd lost count. None had been able to beat him. He stood in the middle of two lines of torches, a field set up inside the bailey for practice. Clearly, de La Porte planned to work the men around the clock to prepare them for battle.

He listened to their whispering amongst themselves. One man said he was a Grant warrior and it showed. Someone else commented on how he'd done this *after* being knocked out for an hour. He heard a voice behind him—de La Porte—but didn't turn to acknowledge it. "Tell Morgan and Horas to take him back to the dungeon. Bring him water and oatcakes. He's earned it today."

A younger voice said, "He knocked down more than twenty of our men."

"Aye, he's good with his sword. I need him to train more on the morrow. I'll let him rest for a short time."

"Aye, my lord."

He waited, gasping to catch his breath. When two men came along, he pushed himself to sitting. When one of the men attempted to kick him, he grabbed the lout's boot and flipped him onto his back. He heard the sound of a lad's laughter as he pushed himself up to standing. "Keep your hands to yourself," he said.

He stood and faced one of the men, waiting to see if he would retaliate, but this one was quite a bit smaller than him. The larger one, the one he'd flipped, said, "Horas, he's a wise arse. We'll teach 'em a thing or two after he's done what Simon wants."

Morgan, just now standing up, cursed and spat. "I'll take the first swing when it's time."

A deep voice from behind them said, "Well, it isn't time yet. Leave him be. I need him for two days. Lead him back to his cell. Gillie can get his food." De La Porte spun on his heel and left.

He guessed it to be around the midnight hour, give or take. Horas gave him a shove, so he moved along toward the back of the keep. He ignored them, instead paying attention to everything he saw, trying to determine where he was in relation to where he'd climbed over the wall.

Could it be possible that Gavin and Gregor were still watching? He knew he needed to bide his time, learn what he could, but until he discovered where they were keeping Kyla, he wouldn't give them any cause to beat him. He had to find her.

The cell they brought him to had a small window that looked onto the passageway. The torch opposite it cast enough light to illuminate the cell. A pallet sat against the far wall and two buckets were arranged along the opposite wall. He guessed one was for pishing and he hoped the other held water, though he doubted it would be fresh. The only other piece in the cell was one stool.

He'd only been here hours, yet it felt like days.

That meant Connor and his group wouldn't have gotten very far yet if they'd left. Would they have gone back to the Grants? Or on to Edinburgh? He had no idea which way they would choose or whether they would try to gain entrance on their own.

He hoped they'd get Alex Grant and the others to join them.

He had to stay strong. He scanned the room for any possible

weapon but saw nothing.

The same voice he'd heard out in the yard returned promptly and set two oatcakes on the ledge of the window along with a small urn filled with water. He thanked him. "Is this it for the night, lad?"

"Aye, what do you expect for a piece of shite?"

"How old are you? You always talk so crudely?"

He grabbed the oatcakes and the urn in case the lad changed his mind. He heard the lad do his best to spit like de La Porte did, but he had to smile because the lad didn't quite have it perfected yet. "If I were you, I'd be copying someone else, Gillie. He's not one who will be around long."

"How do you know my name?" His face appeared in the opening with the bars. The lad looked to be about ten and three.

"I heard someone send for Gillie to deliver my food. 'Tis you, aye?" He took a bite of the oatcake, brushing the crumbs from his chin.

"Aye, I'm Gillie. There's no one smarter than Simon, and soon I'll be living with him in the biggest and finest castle in all the land. He promised me I could train as one of his warriors."

"Ah, Grant Castle is what he tells you, aye?" He settled on the stool and took a long drink of water.

"Aye, 'tis the best there is in all the land." The lad's face just made it over the window. He had fair locks that stuck out in ten directions.

"Laddie, 'tis a true statement."

"How long were you there?" The excitement in his voice put Finlay in mind of wee Kenzie.

"All my life. 'Tis a wondrous place with all the mountains and the stags, but 'tis mighty cold in the winter."

"As long as I can sleep indoors, 'twill suit me." His reply spoke of his innocence. Of his desire for a better life. Once again, Finlay found himself thinking of Kenzie.

Wee Kenzie had been adopted by Clan Grant, just as his sire, Loki, had been adopted before him. Both had been urchins found in the street—Loki by Brodie Grant, and Kenzie by Loki. Their rough upbringings had made them strong, wily, and useful, and something told Finlay that Gillie could turn out to be his best tool.

"Where are you from, lad?"

"Edinburgh. I was in Edinburgh when the men came through looking for more mercenaries, so I joined them. I was tired of sleeping in the streets. Tell me more about Grant Castle."

"It has four towers and the biggest hall you'll ever see. The view from the parapets cannot be compared. Where are your parents? How old are you?"

"Ten and four, and my parents died three years ago. They caught the heaves and died."

The lad was a bit small for his age, which explained why he wasn't wielding a sword yet. "And you did not?"

"I did catch it, but I got better."

Finlay could hear the wistfulness in his voice. "I know what 'tis like to lose your mama, Gillie. I just lost mine. 'Tis not easy." He decided to test the lad a bit. "Do you know where they keep the lass?"

"Aye. I know all that goes on here. She's pretty."

"She is indeed a beauty. Is she awake?" He hoped she hadn't been hit as hard as he had been.

"Aye. She's with Davina. Is she yours?"

"If I'm lucky, some day she will be." He breathed a sigh of relief. At least she was with Davina instead of de La Porte—perhaps Davina could keep her safe.

Gillie startled at the sound of footsteps down the passageway. "Got to take my leave."

And then he was gone.

But the lad had given Finlay hope.

CHAPTER ELEVEN

K YLA GROANED AND OPENED HER eyes. Davina stared down at her. "Keep your eyes closed whenever anyone enters," she said urgently. "He said you're to stay here until you're awake. Then he'll move you."

"To where?" Her fingers came up to feel her face where she'd been punched. Her eye was swollen and sore.

Davina took her hand. "Do not touch it. You are a sorry sight already. You could make it worse. I know not where he'll take you, but my guess is to his chamber. You don't want that. We must avoid it for as long as possible."

Kyla closed her eyes again. "How long have I been asleep?"

"A few hours. 'Tis early morn. Go back to sleep until the morrow. You need your rest. Finlay lives and Simon has told the men they may not beat him yet, so have faith your clan will return for you."

She set her head back down on the soft pillow and mumbled, "My thanks, Davina."

The next time she awakened, it was past mid-day, and a beast stood in the chamber. He'd swung his foot out and connected with her leg, the sharp point of his boot catching her shin. "Wake up. You're a prisoner. You're not to be treated any other way. I did not hit you that hard."

She attempted to push herself up—then thought better of it and let herself fall back onto the pallet.

De La Porte reached down and grabbed her chin. "You'd be wise never to spit on me again. I care not if you're a lass, I'll still beat you senseless." He flung her away and turned around. "Find a tub and get her bathed, Davina. She'll be with me tonight."

As soon as Simon left the room, Kyla pushed herself up onto the edge of the bed. "Help me, Davina. You must get me out of here. Find Finlay and he can help me."

Davina opened the door and yelled for her guard. "Send Gillie with a tub." She closed the door and leaned against it, closing her eyes and taking a deep breath.

"Kyla, I understand you'd like me to help you, and if there was anything I could possibly do, I would not hesitate, but I live in this tower and see no one. I cannot do anything for you except follow instructions. Since I don't heed my sire's word, I am basically imprisoned here. It suits me fine."

Kyla felt for her dagger. "Where is it? My dagger? I must have it."

"That I can do for you. I took off your breeches and hid the dagger. I have one gown with a pocket sewn inside that should fit you. You can conceal the dagger there easily. But please be careful. Simon is not afraid to hurt women."

"I'm not afraid to hurt *him*."

A knock sounded at the door, so Davina peeked out. She opened the door, revealing a lad not quite a man yet. This had to be Gillie. Small though he was, he hefted the tub in by himself.

"Here I am," the lad said. "Simon said I was to do whatever you ask, but do not ask for stupid tasks. A tub is here and water is coming. Who is she?" He boldly stared at Kyla.

"This is Kyla Grant. Gillie, will you answer her questions and not repeat them?"

"I can be trusted," he replied with a scowl. "I'm not an idiot either. I'll not make de La Porte angry, but I'll do aught else. I know all that transpires here."

"Good," Davina said.

Kyla asked, "Where is my friend, Finlay?"

"You mean the Grant guard?"

"Aye, he's tall with dark red hair. Verra muscular."

Gillie grinned. "He's verra good in the lists, my lady. Glenn sent ten of his men to test his sword skills, one at a time, of course. He beat them all. Then Simon sent ten of his men against him, and he beat all of them, too. He's got a mighty fine sword."

"That's what he's doing? Fighting?"

"Nay, my lady. Do you know naught? You must be a dolt."

"Gillie!" Davina barked.

"Sorry, my lady. He's training our soldiers. Glenn wants to know how mighty the Grant warriors will be. Now he knows. He tells his men to imitate and practice everything the Grant man does."

"Is he out there now?"

"Aye. They keep him there all day. At night, he returns to his cell."

"Will you get a message to him for me? Tell him I'm fine. Tell him…" She glanced at Davina and her friend shook her head. "Just tell him you've seen me and I'm fine."

Another knock came at the door, and two men brought in buckets of steaming water and dumped them into the tub. On their way out, one said, "Gillie, come along. You've tarried too long."

Gillie winked at Kyla and ran off. "Aye, Morgan. Coming."

Davina's daughter started to cry, so she moved into the adjoining room to tend her. Kyla stripped down and climbed into the tub, wishing to wash every bit of this place from her skin. She fought back tears, forcing herself to be strong.

She'd been warned many times about going off on her own. As she sank into the hot water, she thought about her cousins, wondering where they were. How she hoped they'd gone quickly back to Grant land. Her sire would come for her, or he would send his army along. So would Uncle Logan. She just had to make sure she held on.

Knowing that Finlay was hale made her feel a wee bit better. They could have easily killed him, but instead he was fighting off dozens of soldiers to keep himself alive. No doubt he'd phrase it as a joke. Forcing her eyes shut as she soaked, she tried to imagine what he would say to her if they could speak. He'd tell her to be strong, she knew, and to have faith in her sire and all the Grants.

She opened her eyes again and took a deep breath. That was exactly what she would do. Davina needed to protect her daughter, so she could not ask her to sneak out of the tower. It was up to her and her alone to fight Simon de La Porte.

She'd make Finlay and her sire proud.

After all, she was the daughter of the great Alexander Grant.

*

Finlay's shoulders ached like he'd been thrown against the side of a mountain a hundred times. How many men did they expect him to fight? Apparently, his exhaustion was evident because in the middle of the afternoon, Glenn of Buchan arrived and said, "Morgan. Move him under the trees and guard him well. Give him water and food from the kitchens."

Morgan and Horas led him over to a large oak tree and pointed to the trunk. He collapsed and propped himself against the tree while Morgan left for the kitchen. He took it as an opportunity to study Buchan Castle. True, he'd been here before, but he needed to learn as much as possible if he wished to have any chance at freedom.

A burly warrior stopped to speak with him. "You know the Ramsays?"

Finlay nodded, not wanting to start up a conversation with any of Buchan's men.

The man continued. "What know you of the daughters of Logan and Quade?"

Finlay had no idea where the warrior was going with his line of questioning. He answered as vaguely as possible. "Naught."

"Are they still on Grant land?"

"Probably. What's your name?"

"Bearchun."

Finlay tried his best not to react too much to his name. "I've heard that name. Why?"

He gave him a smug smile and a slight nod. "Because I have a reputation." He spun on his heel and left.

If he ever gained his freedom again, he'd be sure to inform Logan Ramsay of their conversation.

Freedom. All morning, his mind had dwelled on one thing— how he'd failed. Hot shame filled him when he thought about how much he'd let his best friend down. Jamie had encouraged him to pursue Kyla, and he'd even allowed him to take her here, and now they were prisoners, the victims of terrible trickery. He wondered how Jamie could ever forgive him. He had always been proud of his position as his second, knowing that someday Jamie could be the clan's only laird, but surely that position would be taken away from him—*if* they survived this.

In his foolhardy quest to appear worthy of Kyla Grant, he'd put her in a life-threatening situation, and he had no idea how they were to get out of it.

True, he was not the only person who'd considered their plan solid…and yet, he could not deny his role in the way these events had unfolded.

He'd been too wrapped up in his own problems to see the situation clearly.

He'd never be allowed back on Grant land. If he found a way to save Kyla, he'd take her home and then leave. He did not think he could bear to face her father. How could his laird forgive him for what he'd done? The simple answer was that he couldn't. Alex Grant would run him through with his own sword.

His fate was sealed. There'd be no wedding, and he'd have to find a new home.

He no longer deserved to wear the Grant plaid.

☾

The man named Morgan led Kyla down the stairway and into the main keep, then up another staircase and down a passageway before stopping at a door. He knocked, and when they were bidden to enter, he grinned at her and said, "Have fun, my dear."

He retraced his steps and let out a chilling laugh as she turned the handle on the heavy wooden door.

The chamber was cold and stark. One chest had dirty clothing piled atop it, and a table covered with weapons sat in front of the hearth. Two chairs waited in front of it.

Simon de la Porte sat in one chair, his gaze perusing her. He beckoned her forward, but she didn't move.

"Come here." He pointed to the spot in front of him.

"I've done naught to you. Set my friend and me free." She stared back at him, refusing to be intimidated by the bastard.

"And here I believed you to be a fair head…instead you strike me as a featherhead." He grinned at her. "Do not be foolish. I enjoy breaking women, especially those who belong to my enemies."

"Let me go."

He stood and sauntered over to her. "Have you ever gotten on your knees to service your friend, my dear? Because if you have, it would make this much easier. I truly do hate to have to instruct a whore on how to take care of my needs." Once he was close, her ran his finger down her jawline.

She slapped his hand away. "Our king will love to know how you treated Alexander Grant's daughter and Logan Ramsay's niece."

He slapped her hard across her cheek, splitting the corner of her lip.

She refused to cry out, instead positioning her hand near her dagger, ready to use it if necessary.

"I don't care what your king thinks. Get down on your knees, bitch." His voice came out in a low tone, his jaw grinding while he waited for her to comply with his wishes.

She didn't move. His hands shifted to her shoulders and attempted to force her down. She locked her knees and gritted her teeth, vowing not to give in to him, no matter what the cost. There was no way in hell she would service this beast. She'd heard talk of this before, and she refused to bend to his will.

"Down on your knees," he ground out, still putting pressure on her shoulders in an effort to force her down.

"Rotten bastard," she cried. Try as she might, she could not hold her strength against the force that propelled her down. As soon as her knees buckled, she reached for her dagger and stabbed the flesh of his thigh as hard as she could. Blood stained his breeches as he grabbed her hand.

He jumped backward, cursing her, but she didn't stop there. She grabbed another dagger from the table and flung it across the room, catching him in his left shoulder. Maggie's lesson had served her well.

De La Porte's bellow brought men running down the passageway. Once he managed to remove both daggers, he came at her. As soon as the door opened and two of his men came inside, she slipped out past them and raced down the passageway.

"Stop her, you fools!"

Two more men came running toward her, and they grabbed her and spun her around just in time for her to see Simon de La Porte charging at her, his fist pulled back and flexed for a blow that landed directly on the side of her head. Her knees collapsed as pain shot through her head, and she dropped to the ground, wrapping her body into a ball to protect her head and face.

His boot swung out and kicked her over and over again as he called her every vile word in his vocabulary. Maggie had given her brief instructions on how to protect herself, but all those lessons had left her.

Now in a fetal position on the floor, her body screaming in pain, she thought of Finlay. How she wished she'd had the chance to love him. Instead she would die here at the hands of her sire's enemy.

A loud voice rent the air. "Stop! Stop, you stupid fool! Do not kill her, I care not what she's done."

"Foolish bitch took a blade to me twice," Simon turned toward the voice, heaving from anger.

"If you kill her, we have naught. Put it back in your pants and leave her with me. I told you this was one condition I would not bend on." She recognized the newcomer as Glenn of Buchan, now standing in front of her. His voice dropped. "You've done enough damage today. Go see my healer and get your wounds tended." He glanced at Morgan and said, "Bring her to my chamber, and if you touch her, I'll cut your bollocks off."

Morgan lifted her and she promptly fainted from the pain.

CHAPTER TWELVE

A LEX GRANT SAT IN HIS solar, mulling over all he'd just heard. His eldest sons and acting lairds were there, along with Quade and Logan Ramsay, and the group that had returned with the news—his youngest son, Connor, and Roddy and Braden.

Logan had just returned from a journey intended to uncover new information about the mercenaries and Buchan's plot—a mission that had proved unsuccessful. The man had started pacing the room the moment he'd entered it, and he now turned to the younger men and barked, "What the hell were you thinking, taking Kyla straight to the enemy? I could order lashings for all five of you. And Finlay? I'll kill him with my bare hands. You've given the enemy just what they wanted, something to use against us."

"Admonishments will get us nowhere at this point," Alex said. "They used the innocence and inexperience of our young people against us. Now, we must do what's necessary to right the situation. The bastard has my daughter, and we need to settle on a strategy to get her back. Jake, make a call to arms. Three hundred men will march with me on the morrow. Get them ready. Get their mounts ready. Jamie, find messengers and send them to Menzie land and Drummond land. I would ask for one hundred guards from each of them. Micheil has likely brought Gavin and Gregor back to Drummond land with him, but we can send another messenger to Edinburgh to be sure. And someone should be sent to Cameron land telling them we're coming and bringing our women for safety. Aedan's to keep his guards at home to protect his land and the abbey. Dusk outside Buchan land on the morrow."

"Send a messenger to Torrian," Quade added. "Tell him to ready two hundred."

Jake and Jamie left the room to carry out their instructions.

Logan continued to pace. He stopped for a moment and said, "Alex, are you sure you're ready to sit on a mount for that long? It will take nearly a day to get there."

"Aye, 'tis perfect. We'll attack at night while half of them are in their cups," Alex said.

Connor said, "I doubt they'll be in their cups. We saw no evidence of such."

Logan sat down and said, "Connor, Roddy, Braden. Tell us every detail of what you know."

The door opened and the Grant's brothers came in quietly and sat.

"De La Porte and his mercenaries had just arrived," Connor said. "We saw no more than two hundred men."

A knock sounded at the door. Brodie said, "I'll go."

Alex nodded. His brother opened the door to find Maddie standing there.

"A messenger," Maddie motioned to the door.

Brodie returned a few moments later, holding a scroll. "A messenger handed me this and hustled away." Maddie followed him in.

All conversation stopped as they waited to hear what Brodie had to say. Alex motioned for Maddie to come to him behind the desk.

Brodie read the message on the scroll. "This is from Glenn of Buchan," he said, looking up. "He has Kyla and promises no harm to her in exchange for..." he paused, reading it again as if to convince himself of what it said.

Alex pulled Maddie down onto his lap, afraid she would collapse onto the floor. He could feel her fine tremors. This was too much for his wee wife.

Robbie stared at him. Alex said, "Go ahead, Brodie."

"He'll return Kyla to us safely when we relinquish Grant Castle to him. We have two days to decide."

Maddie gasped and fell against Alex, but after a moment, she stood up and squared her shoulders.

She folded her hands in front of her and said, "Husband, you need to put a dagger in that man's black heart."

Finlay sat down on the pallet in his prison after accepting more oatcakes and ale from the lad. "My thanks, Gillie."

He fell flat onto his pallet after the lad left. His exhaustion was complete. Every muscle in his body hurt, and he knew he'd sleep as soon as he lay back—but probably not for long.

According to his calculations, if Connor had made haste back to Grant land, the earliest he could return with a sizeable force would be late tomorrow, but only if there were no obstacles. The one thing in his favor was that the Ramsays were still on Grant land because of their hesitation to travel in the current conditions. Aedan Cameron had returned home but left Jennie behind to visit with family.

There would be plenty of reinforcements from the clans they were linked to through family. Camerons. Menzies. Drummonds.

Help should be arriving on the morrow. All he and Kyla needed to do was survive one more day, and they'd have a fighting chance.

One more day. After he finished his meager food, he settled back on the pallet, his eyes drifting shut in an instant.

A voice wrenched him out of sleep.

"My lord, my lord!" The urgent whisper came from the small window in the door.

He bolted up off his pallet and reached the door, staring down at Gillie standing in the passageway. "What is it?"

Gillie glanced in both directions before he spoke. "He beat her bad."

"Kyla?" His fists clenched at the thought of anyone touching her.

"Aye. She's alive, but she's bad off, my lord. You must help her, please. She's in my laird's chamber, and he's gone to visit his daughter."

Raucous laughter rang out from the end of the passageway, so Gillie took off. "Sorry, my lord. They'd kill me."

Finlay understood, but he thanked the Lord the lad had come to him. He'd take care of it in his own way. He picked the stool up and pounded the door with it, making as much noise as he could. He let out a Grant war whoop in the hopes of bringing any fool his way.

Morgan appeared in less than a minute. "What the hell is your problem? You'll not be allowed out for any reason, prisoner."

"Get de La Porte. I need to see him now. Tell that weak bastard to come down here, take me on in hand-to-hand combat. I've been fighting all day, and I'll *still* kill the arsehole." Fury shot through his body, and he did nothing to slow it down. He needed that fury.

Simon de la Porte strolled down the passageway moments later, his cold laughter filling the space. "You have a problem, captive? Don't you understand the rules here? It doesn't matter to anyone what you want, but we would sleep better if you'd shut up."

De La Porte stood in front of the door, his arms crossed in front of his chest.

Finlay took one look at the raw knuckles on his hand and said, "Do you feel like a tough man when you beat a woman with your fists?"

De La Porte's gaze narrowed and the smile left his face. "And how would you know who I beat?"

"I don't. 'Tis an easy guess. You're a wee man, so you could only hope to best a lass. Does it make you hard to beat someone weaker than you?"

"Open the door."

Morgan grabbed the key and scrambled to fit it in the lock, but he dropped it and had to crouch to retrieve it.

Finlay continued to taunt de La Porte while Morgan fumbled about. "Where did you get that wound on your shoulder? From a lassie? I'll bet my Kyla gave you that, didn't she? Hah! A wee lass battered Simon de La Porte. I'll spread the word to everyone."

When Morgan finally had the door open, he stood back and pulled his sword from its scabbard, though it wasn't a weapon anything like the Grant swords.

De La Porte held a dagger in his right hand. There was murder in the dark gaze he cast at Finlay.

Moving to the back of the small cell, Finlay whispered a silent prayer that both of them would be drawn inside. They positioned themselves perfectly.

De La Porte opened his mouth and said, "You'll regret your words, fool."

Finlay kicked the sword out of Morgan's hands and then leaped at de La Porte, throwing him against the wall and twisting the dagger from his grip until it fell into his waiting hands. He spun the bastard around until he held the dagger at his throat. "Take me to Kyla."

"You want to see what I did to your woman after I put my dick in her mouth? I'd be glad to take you to her. She's a fighter, just like you. Alex Grant teaches you well, but as you said, I took her down. I'll be happy to show you how she fares."

Morgan, a stunned expression on his face, glanced from one face to the other, uncertain of what he should do next. He picked his sword back up and took a fighting stance.

"Morgan, you worthless arse. Stand down, or have you not noticed he has a knife at my throat? I'll relent just this once. Take us to Buchan's chamber so he can see his sweet lass."

They made their way down the passageway to another section of the castle, meeting a few others along the way.

"Stand down and do not follow us. Only Morgan goes with us."

Finlay wished to kill the bastard, but he needed to see Kyla first. Then he'd wrench de La Porte's neck; he'd take pleasure in snapping it with his bare hands.

Morgan opened the door, lit a torch, and hung it in a sconce. There was a large bed in the center and a small one off to the side. Kyla lay in a heap on the small bed, blood dripping from her face. She looked dead to him, and a fist punched him square in the gut, though not an actual blow by de La Porte.

"Kyla?"

She didn't move.

He wanted to go to her, but he couldn't let de La Porte go free. The bastard said, "Morgan, lift her head."

Morgan moved to her side, his eyes darting everywhere before he finally reached over and tugged her by the hair to do his master's bidding.

"Kyla!" he screamed. She had to be alive...she just had to be. "Wake up, Kyla. Please, I need you to wake up. I cannot help you if you do not."

Her eyelids fluttered, and she almost managed to focus on him before they closed again. Morgan dropped her head back on the bed.

She was alive. At least she was still alive. "One day, my sweet. One more day and your sire will come for you."

"Now," De La Porte said, "You have fifteen seconds to drop the dagger at my feet, or I'll have Morgan slit her throat. Your choice. If you've a mind to, you can watch her bleed out and gag on her own blood."

Finlay had no choice. He dropped his blade and Morgan picked it up. Two more men came in behind him, ready to do battle, but he paid them no mind. He punched de La Porte in his face and then wrenched the dagger from Morgan's hand and tossed him against the wall. Fury consumed him and he pounded every body part within his reach. He kicked one of the newcomers back out into the passageway, and snapped the arm of another, but as soon as he sent two out of the chamber, four more replaced them.

De La Porte kicked him in his bollocks so hard he nearly vomited. "Now, do you think six of you could hold one man?" the Englishman quipped. "Beat him senseless, but do not kill him. Throw him back into the cell when you're done."

Finlay drifted in and out of consciousness, giving as many punches as he could, taking down a couple more before he was done. When he fell to the ground, he fell face down. He opened his eyes and Kyla filled his vision. His beautiful Kyla had been beaten to near death, and he could do naught to help her. "Kyla?"

She didn't move, but all he could think was that he'd never have the chance to show her how much he loved her.

CHAPTER THIRTEEN

GLENN OF BUCHAN FLEW DOWN the passageway toward his chamber. "Out. All of you out of my chamber. What the hell are you doing in there?"

All of the men left except for Simon, who stood wiping blood from his mouth.

Glenn glanced at the floor. "What the hell? You beat our prisoner? He was the only chance we had to get our men trained, de La Porte."

Simon snickered. "You mean your wastrels? My men are well trained. I don't need this arse for anything."

"He appears to have beaten all your men, as well."

"Lucky. My men will do the job when necessary."

Anger rose up in Glenn, hot and fast, and he rushed over to grab de La Porte by the tunic. "You're out of control. You won't get another payment until Grant Castle is ours. You promised that I had final say about everything, including battle strategies. Did you consult me about beating our two prisoners? Look at them. They can't even lift their heads. How in hell can I place them on horses when the Grant arrives? You fool!"

De La Porte shoved at Buchan. "Take your hands away from me. I don't like to be touched."

"What leverage do we have against the Grant if his daughter and her guard are both dead? You're a fool. You are driven by emotion instead of sound battle strategies." If his sons had survived, he wouldn't have needed to take up with this mad man. Hellfire, MacNiven had possessed more sense than this hothead.

"We don't need leverage. My men will take care of Grant's men."

Their voices had grown loud and heated, and there was a line of men listening in the passageway.

"Grant could be here tomorrow. If he finds out his daughter is all but dead, the king will have us both in chains, or have you not considered that?"

"I don't give a shite about the King of the Scots. I answer to the King of England and he'll do nothing to me. He is afraid of me and my men."

"I'm in charge, and you'll do naught to stop my orders now. After all your talk, you only brought a hundred men, and you think they can take the two hundred men I have? You're a bigger fool than I thought, de La Porte. Some of my men need training, but you're well outnumbered. Get the prisoner back in his cell. Gillie?" he called out. "Where the hell are you, Gillie?" At least the lad they'd found had made himself useful.

The lad hurried into the chamber. "Aye, my laird?"

"Get the healer. Bring her here first to tend the lass, then take her to the prisoner."

Gillie took off and Glenn stepped into the passageway. "No one is to touch these prisoners again, or I'll have your head on a pike outside my gates. Understood?" He called to his own second. "Stu, you are in charge tonight. Keep these men outside. The only ones allowed inside are the healer and Gillie to assist the healer. Stu, have ten of your men guard the entrance to my keep. Now go. All of you. You better get your rest this night because the battle could begin any time after high sun on the morrow."

❦

Finlay groaned. It must have finally happened. He'd crossed Logan Ramsay and the beast had beaten him as though he were a hedgehog on a stick. A hand pushed on his shoulder and he turned his head, doing his best to see who had touched him.

An old woman sat on a stool next to a pallet. "Lad, you took a terrible beating, but I think you'll live."

"Kyla?"

She smiled, revealing only a few teeth in the front of her mouth. The green in her eyes attested that she was a compassionate soul. "She took a worse beating, but I think she'll also live. At least the lassie gave him a couple of wounds to remember her by. She's a feisty one. A beauty, too, beneath those bruises."

"No sleeping potions. I need to be able to protect myself."

"Aye. I'll just put a poultice on your cuts, try to prevent the fever, though your conditions down here are not the best. Here, drink this ale. You need something."

She had a soothing touch as she applied the poultice to a cut on his hand and a slice in his side. "Lad," she said, "I'm a seer. Mayhap this sounds strange, but I must ask you a question."

Finlay scowled. While he'd heard of Molly and her special skills, he was far from sure he believed in seers. He certainly didn't believe this stranger was one. "Go ahead."

"You've lost someone dear to you recently, have you not? A woman much older than you?"

Hell, but his skin bristled at the thought that she might be speaking of his mother. Could it be? "Aye, I have."

"Family member? Someone close?" She rubbed more poultice into his skin.

"Aye." He hesitated, but what did he have to lose? "My mother died not long ago."

"Och, must be her. A sweet woman who's beside herself trying to get a message to you. Brown hair peppered with gray, kind brown eyes, and she rambles incessantly, so much so that I'm struggling to understand her. She's searching for a way to get a message to her son before she moves on. I'm thinking 'tis you."

Finlay smiled. "Mama rambles whenever she's upset. Papa always had to go to her and grab her shoulders to calm her."

"If you think 'tis your mama, she sends you a message."

"What's the message?" His whole body tensed, wondering if his mama would judge him for his actions. Was she ashamed of him? Was she ready to chastise him for his decision to bring Kyla to Davina?

"She says three things. You have shamed no one. Fight for your clan. And listen to your uncle."

He closed his eyes, savoring the first messages. She had not judged him or told him to leave the clan. Instead, she'd told him to fight. He wished he could reach into the heavens and hug her right now.

The seer patted his arm. "She wishes the same."

He snatched his arm away as if she'd burned him.

"Aye, while she's with me here, she can sense your thoughts."

I miss you, Mama. The seer patted his arm again as if she'd read his mind. Then the third comment suddenly struck him. "The first two make sense. But listen to my uncle? Are you sure you heard her correctly? He's their ally. You must be wrong."

Frowning, she closed her eyes, grasped both of his hands, and hummed for a few moments. The heat that radiated from her hands was so intense he tried to pull away, afraid his skin would burn.

She tugged on his hands. "Not yet. Do not break the bond. You'll not burn."

She had not lied. His hands continued to heat, but he never burned. When the warmth left him, she opened her eyes and said, "Your uncle will return. Listen to him."

He wanted to disagree with this last statement, but he wouldn't argue with the old woman.

She stood and returned her jars and bandages to her satchel. "I'll be back on the morrow to check on both of you. Rest, my son. You'll be needing all the strength you can muster."

Hell, but he hoped that wasn't another of her premonitions.

☾

Alex Grant sat in his solar, staring at the wall of weapons. They were symbols of his ancestry, of the clan that he held so dear, of his pride in his land, and he was suddenly acutely aware he was at risk of losing all of it.

But nothing frightened him as much as the possibility of losing his eldest daughter. Kyla, with eyes the color of Maddie's and a heart as big as they came, was in the hands of brutal men, and he was almost close to vomiting over it. He knew what bad men did to women, had spent half his life fighting against it.

This was his daughter. His enemies could bring him to his knees.

What unsettled him most was how powerless he was. Aye, there had been many threats over the years, but he'd always had a strong sword arm and worked hard to maintain that strength. His recent injury had changed all. His wife would remind him that he'd spent years training their sons and nephews to be equally mighty.

Would it be enough?

A knock sounded at the door and he heard his wife's voice.

"Come in, Maddie."

Maddie stepped inside, a small smile lighting her face and her blue eyes sparkling. "Alex, I have something to tell you."

"Wonderful, Maddie. Come sit with me." He patted his lap.

"Oh, Alex. I'm quite sure I shall cause you pain. I can sit in my own chair."

He shook his head and tugged her to him, plopping her down on his lap before he kissed her.

She pulled back and placed both hands on his chest. "Alex, I have good news."

"Go ahead. I could use some about now." He settled his hands on her hips.

"Before Kyla left, Maggie taught her how to use a dagger. She said our daughter was the quickest learner she'd ever seen."

"Aye, that is good news."

Maddie hung her head, absently rubbing a circle on his chest with one hand.

"What is it, wife?"

"I am troubled that Kyla did this after the previous trip, but I know how upset she was about Davina. She came to us about her, and we both turned her down. She made this decision because of two reasons. First because she was worried about us. Jamie said she truly believed she could convince Davina to talk to her sire and stop the battle. The second reason is she could not believe what Davina's sire had forced on her in the past, and what he planned to do. She is so innocent, she couldn't comprehend such cruelty."

"Aye, I think you're right. The problem with our eldest daughter is that she has a big heart. Her concern for others outweighs her sense of danger, and I cannot fault her for that. She believed Davina needed help to get her out of a terrible situation. I also believe she didn't wish to cause us any concern. She was here the day my pain returned."

"Aye, it makes sense."

"'Tis not defiance but consideration that guides her. I recall a young lass who wished to stop my pursuit of two monsters because she didn't want anyone hurt on account of her." He trailed his finger down the line of her jaw and over her chin. "Do you not recall something similar?"

She latched on to his hand. "Aye, I remember. Do you think she is so headstrong about Davina because the lass has been abused as I was?"

Tears misted his wife's eyes, and he set his finger under her chin to lift her gaze to his. "Do not ever think that you have done aught but raise a beautiful soul who is generous of heart."

"I'm sorry, Alex, if she's gone on this venture because of me or my past."

The tears in her eyes grew as big as his thumb, and he brushed them away as fast as they fell. "Know this. I do not fault Kyla for going after a cruel bastard, nor do I fault Finlay for assisting her when she became headstrong. They were both raised with the honor of our ancestors and I am proud of them. Mayhap this will be good for all in the end."

She rested her head on his shoulder and sobbed. "I miss her, Alex. Go get her…and get Davina, too. Find Finlay and bring him home. The poor lad just lost his mother."

"Our clan is strong and has many allies. We will bring Kyla and Finlay home. If Davina wishes to come here, we will welcome her with open arms." How he needed to believe his own words and make good on his promise to his wife.

A knock sounded at the door. "Enter." His wife sat up and wiped the tears from her eyes.

His brother Brodie came inside with Nicol and Fergus. Alex had been expecting they would pay a visit. "Nicol would like to speak with you, Alex," Brodie said.

"You are free to speak."

Nicol struggled for words but then said, "My laird and mistress, please forgive my son for his part in this travesty. He has a good heart and he is a hard-working lad and warrior…"

Alex held his hand up to stop him. "There is no need to apologize, Nicol. I know my daughter. If she decided to do something, she would see it through to completion. I am pleased Finlay went along with her. Think you I would feel better if she was in the Buchan compound alone? Nay, I will thank Finlay when I see him again, and we will see him again soon."

Another knock sounded at the door. "Enter," Alex called out.

Logan Ramsay joined them in the room, followed by Alex's twin sons. "We're ready to report to you when you're ready, laird."

Brodie leaned over to give Maddie a hug and clasped his brother's shoulder. "My thanks. I'd also like to apologize for the hand Braden had in this."

"And if we had not sent those five lads, we probably would not know where Finlay and Kyla are at the moment. It happened for a reason. Tell Braden to have his sword arm ready. I believe we have a major battle coming. Nicol, you and Fergus may take your leave. Brodie, please stay."

The two left and Logan closed the door as soon as Quade entered. Those who'd stayed in the solar took their seats. "All the messengers have been sent, as discussed. I plan to take my leave within the hour, and I'll take my family with me, all but Brigid, whom we'll leave in your care, Maddie.

"Molly and Tormod will travel back to Edinburgh to make another attempt to meet with the king, although there's a good chance he's not there. I think they will return to Buchan land to meet us. If Molly fares well enough, we could use her skills with the bow. We've plenty of talented archers to go over the rear curtain wall. Gwynie and I will make the plan for them. Gavin and Gregor already know the area, and I doubt Buchan will have anyone at the back of the wall. 'Tis not a place we could attack on horseback, so I doubt he'll waste having any men there."

"Where will your archers position themselves?"

"We'll come around the wall and find raised locations, trees if we must—places that give us a good vantage point of the curtain wall. I want these bastards, Alex. I'm taking Cailean, stubborn bull that he is, and he and Tormod will protect my archers. Once the archers are all in their places, I'll take some of our Ramsay men for face-to-face combat. We train many that way, and I know you train more for horseback."

Quade asked with a smirk on his face, "Are you sure you want Cailean along with you? He is one of our best, and we all know how you feel about him…"

"Have your jests, but there's no one who will protect my daughter as well as that beast. He stays with me."

Alex said, "It's a sound plan. Now I only need you to help me strategize for the final face-to-face encounter…"

Logan said, "I'm glad this has happened. Now we can finally attack as we see fit. You know how I am. I'm not interested in waiting until Buchan can assemble and train his forces before he comes after us. This gives us a sound reason to launch a full-scale attack on the bastards. Our king cannot question our motives now."

He paced a bit more before he stood next to Alex. Logan set his hand on Alex's shoulder. "We will finally put an end to this man's reign of terror."

CHAPTER FOURTEEN

⌇

FINLAY WOKE UP THE NEXT morning and could barely open on eye. His face was so swollen that it pained him to lie on his side. He remembered all that had transpired the previous night: Kyla's beating, Gillie's warning, his beating, and the healer's advice. Something about listening to his uncle. The sound of the key in the lock brought him to a sitting position. He needed to force himself awake to re-evaluate his situation and what he should do next.

The door opened and he lifted his gaze to his uncle.

Hellfire. There were many strange things transpiring. It was beyond his understanding.

"Uncle Geordie?"

"Aye. I brought you something to break your fast, along with an ale to ease your pain a bit." He sat on the stool and handed him a trencher and a goblet. He tipped his head toward the corner. "Broke a stool, I see. I had to search to find another."

He watched his uncle warily, uncertain how to take his visit. Did he have something to tell him?

"My thanks for the food."

"I saw you battle to protect the lass. While I've known the Buchan for some time, I've only just met Simon de La Porte. I do not like what I see." He sighed, one that seemed to go on forever as he ran his hand through his thinning hair. "I was ashamed of what I've done. I remember you as a wee lad. I always loved you and Fergus. I wished you were my own sons. I've watched you fight with such honor these past days, and it has brought me back to a different time in my life, one that I miss. You made be proud to be your uncle...but ashamed of how I've treated you.

"I've been up since last night trying to decide what is best for you. I've done some things I shouldn't have in my life, but now I believe 'tis time to do something right. I'd like to help you. You can defend yourself, but that poor lass... I remember how Alex Grant would carry her around in a plaid strapped to his chest when she was just a bairn. He was such a proud papa, and she always had a smile on her wee face." He stared at his hands. "De La Porte is wrong. He's gone too far. I expected this to be a battle between men, not brutality to women. That, I cannot tolerate."

Finlay wished more than anything to ask his uncle for suggestions on what to do, but if his mother had truly given him the advice, he knew it would be forthcoming from his uncle.

"You must get free. I could let you out of here, but you're in such bad shape that another beating could kill you. I know you'll not leave without the lass. Hear me out before you dismiss me." He swallowed hard and ran his hand across the back of his neck before he continued.

"I think you should join forces with the Buchan."

Finlay's eyes widened and he opened his mouth to deny his uncle, but then he remembered his mother's message.

"I know you will balk, but 'tis the only way you'll be able to pass through the keep without being beaten. The Buchan does not plan to attack the Grants. He sent a message demanding that Grant give up his castle and all his lands in return for Kyla's life. I'm sure there will be a contingency here from your clan, but what you need to do is to steal Kyla away before there's a confrontation. You'll not be able to do it locked in this cell. Convince Buchan you'd like to switch sides and he'll give you some freedom. He's bent on revenge, but he's not cruel like de La Porte, and he believes he needs your skills. If you can convince him you're on his side, he'll treat you well and keep Simon away from you. The way things are, I fear de La Porte might kill both you and Kyla outright."

He said nothing, giving Finlay time to process his thoughts.

Finlay wanted to refute everything he said, but his idea held merit. He would do what his mother had suggested and consider his uncle's idea.

"Well?"

"Mayhap you're right. 'Struth is I'm not sure I'll be allowed back on Grant land anyway. Coming here with Kyla was a mistake. Mayhap I'll travel to Edinburgh when this is done. I might need to run that far to escape the Grant's wrath."

"Nay, lad. You belong with the Grants. If I know Alex Grant well, as long as his daughter comes back hale and hearty, he'll forgive you. And there's no one with a bigger heart than Maddie."

"Do you know where Kyla is?"

"Aye, Buchan is keeping her in his chamber." He held his hand up. "He knows her value as a hostage, so he's keeping her away from de La Porte. He slept elsewhere and the healer stayed with her last night. She gave her a sleeping potion, which is likely why the lass has not awakened."

"If I agree to your plan, then I'll have to convince him soon. The first contingency of warriors could arrive *today*."

"Agreed. I could bring you to the Buchan at the midday meal. He's meeting with de La Porte. You'll have to be strong."

"Aye. If you or Gillie could find me a horse, you could leave it somewhere near the back curtain wall. With your help and Gillie's, I could get Kyla out and hide her until either our clan or the allies come along. I'd just have to find a well hidden spot."

"True, because once they discover you two are missing, they'll have men everywhere." Geordie reached over and patted his leg. "Think on it and I shall return in a couple of hours. If you agree, I'll take you to the Buchan then."

"Thanks, Uncle Geordie. If I make it out, I'll tell Papa you helped me."

"I'm doing my best to right one of my wrongs."

As his uncle was on his way out, Finlay said, "Send Gillie to me."

Barely any time at all passed before Gillie's voice came from down the passageway. "I'm here, my lord."

Gillie appeared in front of the wee window. "Why do you need me?"

"First, I'm Finlay, not 'my lord.' I may need your help. What must I do in exchange for your assistance in something?"

"Promise to take me away." Gillie bounced up and down on his toes, his eagerness at the possibility of leaving Buchan castle apparent in his face. "'Tis not as I thought 'twould be. De La Porte is too quick with his fists. 'Tis not honorable to beat a lady. I'm not of noble blood, and I know that."

"Where do you wish to go?" He could bring the lad, but he'd need another horse if there were three of them.

"With you. Can I not join Clan Grant? I'm ten and four. I could start training to be a warrior. I saw you fight in the lists—you could teach me to use a sword!"

"Have you ever fashioned a slinger?"

"Nay, but I'd like to. Can you not show me?" His eyes looked wide and hopeful in the small opening in the door. Finlay couldn't dash the lad's dreams away.

"Agreed, but you'll have to find two horses since there'll be three of us. Can you do that?"

The lad nodded vigorously.

"Good. And when this is finished, I know the perfect person to show you how to use a slinger. He's a few years younger than you, but he's talented."

"He is? Is he as good as Loki Grant was at the Battle of Largs? I heard about his slinger and he was only eight summers."

"Aye, the lad I'll introduce you to is Loki's son. You'll get to meet Loki, too. But first you must promise to be Kyla's protector for the rest of my time here and tell me aught you hear about her. The horses are important, too. If you don't find two, I won't be able to take you along."

Gillie nodded again, his hands gripping the edge of the small window. "Aye, I'll do it. You can count on me, my...um, Finlay."

"Come back after the midday meal, and I'll tell you my plans." One more thing occurred to him. "And find Kyla and tell her to have faith in me."

How he hoped she wouldn't think him a traitor.

☾

Kyla opened her eyes, surprised to see Davina seated on a stool next to her. "What's wrong?"

"How do you feel?"

She tried to sit up but fell back on the bed. "Awful. My ankle is swollen. I don't know if I can walk." Turning it from side to side, she couldn't help but grimace at the pain. "Where is Finlay? How is he? I have a vague memory of seeing him in this chamber, but he looked terrible. Did I dream it?"

"Nay, 'twas real. Finlay forced de La Porte up here at knifepoint.

There was a big brawl, and Finlay punched Simon and caused serious injuries to three of his men. They overpowered him in the end. 'Struth is I know not if Simon would have stopped until he killed both of you. My sire intervened, and now he won't allow Simon to touch either one of you. Papa has finally realized Simon's a bit daft. You know, he was always terrible about forcing me to give… my favors to men, but he never allowed any of them to hit me."

"What is happening now?" She rubbed her temple, hoping to ease the ache in her head, but to no avail.

"Word reached my sire that the Grant warriors are on the move. He expects them here before midday on the morrow. They've sent word there's to be an exchange. He's hoping it means they've decided to relinquish the castle in exchange for your life."

Kyla did not wish to consider such a travesty. She couldn't imagine her mother or her family living anywhere else but Grant castle. And she would have to live with the crushing guilt and shame for the rest of her days.

"Kyla, if the opportunity arises, I'm leaving," Davina said. "I will head to Lochluin Abbey or find my way to Edinburgh if I can free myself from here. If you wish, you may join me."

"Nay, Davina. I'll not leave Finlay. I love him and I trust him. Come to Grant Castle with me. You'll be happy there, I promise."

"You may not be going to Grant Castle if my father has a say. You may have to live in this horrid place, and I have no desire to stay here. I wish to get away and start a new life."

"But I can help you." She clasped her friend's hand, trying to think of a way to convince Davina that a better life awaited her. "Traveling with an infant will not be easy."

"I know. And yet living the life of a nun with my daughter sounds rather appealing. No man will bother me there."

"But you could have more bairns if you found someone to love."

"One is enough for me. I just thought I'd take the chance to say farewell to you. I appreciate how you've tried to help me."

A knock sounded at the door, and Kyla glanced over Davina's shoulder, pleased to see it was Gillie. "Come in, lad."

"Hush," he whispered. "I have a message for you." He glanced over his shoulder.

"What is it?" Kyla asked.

"Finlay said to tell you to have faith in him."

"What does he mean by that?" She hoped he was making a plan to get them both to freedom, but perhaps she was making a wrong assumption.

"I'm not sure, but he said I'm your new protector. He assigned me." Glancing at the door again. "Now I must go and see to something, but 'tis secret business."

Gillie disappeared as fast as he had appeared.

"What do you suppose that means?" Kyla asked.

"I don't know, but my guess is that much will happen in the next day. Stay alert if you can. Your sire will come for you, and Finlay will fight for you. Two days from now this will be over, and you may be on the way home. I just hope I can get away to the abbey."

Davina gave her a light hug and left.

CHAPTER FIFTEEN

🖎

AFTER MUCH TURMOIL AND PONDERING, Finlay decided to follow his uncle's advice. It would be the only way he'd be allowed to move about the compound. His only hesitation was over Uncle Geordie. Was he being honest or using trickery? The seer's words from his mother finally balanced the scales for him.

As if on cue, his uncle arrived. "What have you decided, lad?"

"I'll go along with you." He stepped over to the door. "You'll not give me away?"

Uncle Geordie sighed. "I don't expect you to trust me. I'll bring you to Buchan and do my best to convince him. He's anxious for any inside information on the Grant, something he's peppered me for time and again, but I always tell him my information is old. 'Tis your best way to get him to believe you. Give him aught you can think of about Alex, his sons, his strategies."

Finlay quirked his brow at his uncle.

"Och, mayhap not his true strategies."

"Take me to him."

Geordie found the key and opened the door to the cell, motioning for Finlay to follow him to the great hall. Once they stepped inside, all conversations stopped. Finlay took a deep breath, knowing he had to be convincing or they could kill him. He glanced around the hall, deciding they must be at the end of the meal since there were only a few warriors present. Glenn sat at the dais, and Simon was two seats away from him. All eyes were on him as he crossed the hall behind his uncle.

His uncle stopped in front of the dais. "My nephew wishes to speak to you. Please listen to him. If you think on it, he can be of some assistance to you."

Simon guffawed, stopping long enough to say, "Do not believe the lout, Buchan. He takes you for a fool."

Glenn glared at Simon, then said, "Go ahead. You have three minutes."

Finlay swallowed and began, "I've decided I'd like to go to Edinburgh after all is done. I'll not be welcomed back into Clan Grant after all that has transpired. I'll be blamed for the lot of it, and I care not to be tied to a whipping post by Alexander Grant." That comment caused both Glenn and Simon to snicker, though a whipping post wasn't one of Finlay's fears. It wasn't the Grant's style. "I'm willing to fight for you, tell you what I know, if you'll consider setting me free when this is done, and I also ask you not to beat Kyla Grant anymore."

De La Porte snorted. "Of course, you would attach a request like that. I don't believe him, Buchan."

Glenn held his hand up to silence de La Porte. "I'd like to hear what type of information you have. What could you possibly tell us that would be helpful to our cause?"

Finlay cleared his throat, doing all he could to reign in his need to jump over the table and choke de La Porte. It sickened him to offer the man any kind of loyalty, even if it was a lie. "I have acted as Jamie Grant's second for several years now, and he and his brother Jake are now acting lairds of the clan."

"What?" Glenn of Buchan came out of his chair but then sat back down.

This was the kind of response he'd hoped for. "As you know, Alex Grant was almost taken out in the last battle on Grant land. He was near death, thus the *dearbh fine* voted for the laird's twin sons to act as co-lairds until Alex is fit to return to his duties."

"And is he fit?" Glenn was so entranced by the news that he almost drooled, his hand reaching up to wipe the spittle from the corner of his mouth.

"Do we have an agreement, Buchan?"

Buchan screeched for a serving girl, who appeared in front of him in a matter of moments. "Aye, my lord?"

"Bring this lad a big trencher of mutton stew." Then he pointed to the trestle table in front of him. "Take a seat. We have an agreement. You'll help prepare our men, give us the information we need, and we'll set you free when this is ended."

"And I'll not be locked up again?"

"No cell," Buchan agreed. "But you're not free to leave until we have Grant Castle."

"Leave the lass alone until her sire arrives."

To his surprise, Buchan stared at the table and sighed. "Aye, she's had enough."

Simon sat forward, his eyes narrowed and squinting, his mouth twisted into a wicked grin. "I don't agree to that. In fact, I'd like to test your loyalty, lad."

"What in hell are you talking about, de La Porte?" Buchan fired at him.

"I'd like to ensure he's loyal to us now. Get the lass," de La Porte said, turning to Buchan's second. "Bring her here."

Finlay felt ready to heave. He didn't like the smug expression on de La Porte's face as the bastard paced the room. If he touched Kyla, he'd lose it and go after him again.

Had that gotten him anywhere last night when he'd launched himself at the fool?

"I want her alive," Glenn ground out.

"Aye, and I'll make sure she's alive. I just wish to see if this man is being honest with us."

This was exactly what he'd feared—this man intended to use Kyla against him. Again. It was for this reason alone that he'd sent Gillie to Kyla with his message. He'd have to remain indifferent to her or they'd see through his ruse.

Could he do it?

Sweat broke out across his brow, but fortunately the maid returned with his trencher, saving him from the need to speak or react for the time being. He'd have to ignore anything they did with Kyla.

For now. The bastard would pay later.

The guard returned with Kyla. She was limping badly, and her face bore the bruises that had been left on her soft skin, but at least she was able to walk on her own. Simon grabbed her and set her down on his lap. Finlay did his best to act ambivalent, but he couldn't help but glance at her out of the corner of his eye. *Mama told me this was the way.*

He almost choked on the bite of stew he'd taken when he heard her soft voice call his name.

Kyla pushed away from Simon. "Do not touch me. You disgust me."

He slammed her back onto his lap and said, "Do as I say unless you want your throat cut." His hands reached up to fondle her breasts, and that was all Finlay had to see to completely lose control.

"Take your hands off her!" he snarled. He bolted out of his chair and went after de La Porte, grabbing Kyla first and moving her behind his back.

That man would not touch his Kyla.

He'd kill anyone who attempted to touch her again. He'd so needed to see her again, to touch her himself, to see that she was awake and alive.

Two guards came after him while de La Porte backed away, but he flipped one onto his back, then picked the second one up and tossed him against the wall. "Buchan, you agreed that she was not to be touched."

Two more guards came after him, but Buchan stood up. "Stop, all of you."

They did, and Finlay took the opportunity to reach for Kyla and hold her against him. De La Porte laughed and stalked the hall, chanting, "You're a fool, Buchan," but Finlay's attention was focused on the laird.

"Buchan, do we have an agreement? I'll not deal with this fool pacing like a wild boar in a small pen."

Kyla clung to him, her face buried against his chest. He couldn't control his breathing no matter how hard he tried—the fire in his belly wouldn't relent. Grateful that his love was in his arms again, if only for a few moments, he kissed the top of her head and glared at Glenn of Buchan.

"We do," the man finally said. "Take her back, Morgan."

She gripped Finlay's hand and gave him a look that shot straight to his heart. He couldn't handle disappointing her, but he had to believe his uncle's advice would work. Buchan was guaranteeing her safety at least until the Grants arrived. He'd be worse than foolish not to take advantage of that.

Before he released her hand, he rubbed the inside of her wrist with his thumb, hoping she'd remember their conversation in the cave. The gaze in her eyes told him she did.

Buchan said, "Do not touch her again, Simon." Turning to Morgan, he said, "Return her to my chamber, and have the healer tend her again."

The man picked her up, no gentleness to his touch at all, and Kyla moaned in pain, sending another arrow straight through Finlay's heart.

He watched her until she was out of the hall, then returned to the table and finished his trencher. He'd need it for strength. He took a long gulp of ale, saying a quick prayer to the Lord to take care of Kyla until he could get to her.

Glenn moved off the dais to sit across from him. "Now, lad. Prove your worth. Tell me something about Alex Grant and how he fights. Who guards him the closest?"

"His son Jamie and his brothers, Robbie and Brodie."

"And where does he fight from?" Glenn leaned forward while de La Porte paced.

"He fights from the right side."

De La Porte stopped in his tracks. "That's a lie. He uses his sword in his right hand. Like all others, he would fight from the left side of the field." The two turned their faces to Finlay, awaiting his response.

He shrugged his shoulders, giving them the chance to ponder his response. "Alex Grant has only been taken down in one battle. Why do you think that is? He likes to keep his enemies guessing. 'Tis what makes him great."

Glenn bounded off his stool, full of excited energy, and started to pace the dais. "Simon, you train the men to make a path for me. I'll come from the back…"

"You're a fool to give your strategies away to this lad," de La Porte shouted.

Glenn dropped his voice, but Finlay could still hear him. "I'll come from the back right, catch him off guard. I want him, de La Porte."

One more day. Clan Grant and Clan Ramsay would be here today or on the morrow at the very latest. Kyla only had to hang on for one more day.

One of the Buchan's guards threw the door open and hurried

across the hall to stand in front of de La Porte. "What is it?"

"Our scouts have seen clans gathering."

"How far away?"

"Four to six hours."

"Get our men ready. Finlay, out to the lists with you."

☾

Kyla fell into the pallet with a groan once Morgan returned her. Her skin still crawled from de La Porte's touch.

But she had also felt Finlay's light caress on the inside of her wrist, the place he had told her about in the cave. What had he said? That it would let her know that he wanted her more than anything in the world. Whatever he'd been discussing with Buchan, whatever had transpired between them, that simple touch had told her everything she needed to know. She trusted him.

Once the guard left, she sat up, allowing the tears to fall while she did her best to bear her weight, but she failed. She'd almost fallen from the dais when de La Porte had stood up abruptly to avoid Finlay's attack. Her ankle had been weakened before, but it was of no use to her now.

She kneaded her foot, hoping it would ease the pain, but the swelling just continued to grow.

The door flew open and Davina rushed over to her side. "Is it true?"

"What?" She did not even look at her friend.

"Finlay turned traitor against the Grant. He's going to fight with my sire."

"What? I don't believe you."

"Aye, 'tis what I heard. And…I also heard your clan is on its way here."

Kyla sobbed with relief and rubbed her eyes. "I hope so. I cannot handle much more pain. I don't know what to make of Finlay and his discussion with your sire, but I cannot believe he'd truly turn traitor."

Davina's gaze narrowed as she paused for a moment. "Did you not hear something odd from Gillie recently? You were hit on the head, so mayhap your memory is not serving you proper."

"What do you mean, odd?"

"What did Gillie say to you when he was here last? Did he not bring you a message from Finlay?"

"Aye," she whispered, doing her best to remember his exact words. "He said I needed to trust Finlay."

"Do you suppose Finlay's plan is a ruse for my sire?"

Kyla laid her head back on the pillow Davina had given her, closing her eyes. Could she be correct? Had he feigned loyalty to Buchan in order to help them find a way out?

She remembered again that soft stroke on the underside of her wrist.

Kyla believed in Finlay MacNicol. She believed in the man who held her heart.

CHAPTER SIXTEEN

A LEX GRANT STOOD OUTSIDE THE Cameron stables, waiting for his horse to be readied for him. Loki and his men had joined them along the way, and Kenzie provided an entertaining distraction as he raced from place to place across the grass, using his slinger at this or that—all energy.

Logan Ramsay came flying across the moor, headed straight for him.

"What is it?" Alex's stomach lurched, fearing he would hear bad news. He reached for his wife, tugging her close in case they found out the worst.

"Naught to worry yourself over. Thought I would lead you to the group gathering outside Menzie land, not far from Buchan."

Quade limped over to them, coming to a stop behind Alex. "Did you find our lads, Logan?"

"Aye, they were with Micheil. Molly and Tormod came back from Edinburgh. The king is not in residence. Not feeling well is what they heard. Still in mourning is my guess. He's not been the same since he lost his family.

"We carry on. We have a sound plan for the archers, and Gavin and Gregor were able to give us a good idea of the layout of the trees around Buchan castle. We will await your war whoop, Alex."

"Our warriors?" Quade pressed.

"Will be there within the hour—Torrian and Kyle are both leading them. We'll get the bastards."

The stable lads brought out Quade's horse, then Alex's, the offspring of his dear Midnight. Maddie moved over to the tall stallion and offered him an apple. Alex couldn't help but smile as he listened to his wee wife whisper soft words to Black Lightning, appropriately named by Kyla. Maddie had always promised his horse sweet treats upon his safe return. While others thought it foolish, Alex did not question her methods. Mayhap there was something to it.

"We'll be ready, Alex." Jennie gave him a long hug, and Brenna did the same before she helped Quade mount. His sisters would stay behind with his wife. "Just remember, Kyla's as strong as her parents."

Everyone moved away except for Maddie, who returned to his side and took his hand. "I have three requests, Alex."

"Go ahead." His thumb caressed her cheek, his way of telling her how beautiful she remained after all these years. "I'll honor what I can."

Her blue eyes stared into his and she whispered, "Bring our daughter back. Be careful."

She stared at the ground. He knew it to be her way of controlling her tears. He lifted her chin with his finger, this woman whom he cherished beyond belief, who had given him five of the most beautiful children in the world. He would do whatever she asked. "And the third thing, wife?" He bent down and kissed her.

When he ended the kiss, her blue eyes blazed.

"Kill those bastards."

☾

Chaos erupted around the courtyard. "The Menzies and Drummonds are headed our way."

Simon de La Porte strode over to Finlay, who'd been practicing his sword skills with the Buchan men. "I'll take that sword. You're to stay inside the great hall. If we want you, we'll send someone for you. No weapons."

Finlay nodded and then handed the hilt of the sword to one of the guards and headed toward the keep. He slowed his steps to listen for as long as he could.

Finally, someone said something useful. "Buchan, take your men and head out," de La Porte shouted. "Find your location so you can attack the Grant the way we planned. I'll take care of everything from here."

Another guard rushed up to them. "Ramsays are on their way.

Two hundred warriors, at least."

Glenn raced to his horse, and Simon barked orders at his men, sending them in different directions. He arranged the archers where he wanted them along the front wall.

Having heard all he needed to, Finlay hurried into the keep. As soon as he stepped inside the door, he met Gillie. "Is everything set?"

"Aye. Behind the grove of ash trees."

"I'll get Kyla. Follow me when you can."

"Aye, my lord."

Taking two steps at a time, he raced up the stairs and down the passageway to Buchan's chamber. He burst inside, found Kyla asleep on the bed, and scooped her up into his arms. She pushed against him until she realized who held her, then wrapped her arms tight around his neck. "Finlay, 'tis you."

Finlay covered her mouth with his hand and said, "Shush, I'm taking you away from here."

The pain in her eyes nearly destroyed him. He vowed he'd fight anyone who dared to come near her again.

"Finlay, why did you say you would help them?"

"I had no choice, but know that I love you. I'm taking you away." He kissed her lips, a soft kiss to tell her he meant every word. "Did you not feel me caress your wrist? Have you forgotten my words so quickly?" He rolled his eyes at her. "If so, I'll hesitate to ever give you soft promises again."

She giggled. "I did. Naught could mean more to me than your caresses. 'Twas just that Davina heard you'd turned against my sire. I didn't believe it, but I couldn't rest until I heard the truth from you."

"I would never forsake your sire. Forgive me, I'll explain more later. We must go now. I vow I'll not let you down again."

He rushed back out the door, down to the end of the passageway, and then into Davina's tower. "I'll not leave you alone," he said as he stumbled along. "I love you." But his promise fell on sleeping ears. She'd lost consciousness. Soon, they were standing in front of the door they'd come through what felt like years ago.

"You can trust me, lass. Rest all you need." He paused in front of the door, bending down to pick up a sword left there by Gillie and sheathed it.

He crept out the door. Just as he'd expected, there was no one behind the keep. He found a rope Gillie had left for him and lifted Kyla up over his shoulder so he could climb. Gillie met up with him and said, "Hurry, my lord."

"Hold the rope still for me, Gillie."

When he reached the top, he said, "Come along." Gillie scrambled up the rope and jumped down the other side. Once at the bottom, he said, "I can catch her."

"Nay, I've got her. Go fetch the horses."

The lad took off and Finlay slid down the rope, his arm wrapped tightly around Kyla. "I know you cannot hear me, but I'm never letting you go again."

Gillie arrived with the horses and they headed out, galloping as fast as the horses would carry them as soon as they emerged from the dense forest. Two hours later, Gillie led them off the path, pointing toward a burn. "This way, my lord."

Gillie led him through the forest until they came upon a waterfall. Once they dismounted, Finlay sent him off again. "Please look for any warriors, then report back. According to the Buchan guards, the Ramsay and Grant warriors are close. The Menzies and Drummonds are also on their way, but likely further out. Red plaids, blue plaids, anything."

"Will there be enough to overtake the Buchan, Finlay?"

"Aye, do not worry, lad. When you see the Grants and Ramsays fight, there'll be no doubt in your mind."

"Do they fight as good as you?"

He chuckled, "Some better. Now off with you."

Gillie spurred his horse back in the direction they came.

Finlay glanced at Kyla, but she still hadn't moved. He carried her behind the waterfall and found a boulder to settle on. He cradled her and let his tears fall. "Kyla, wake up." His hand cupped her cheek. "Please, love. I'm so sorry I had to do what I did, but 'twas my mother's words. I knew it was the only way we could be free. I promise to find your sire. Wake up. For me, please?"

Her eyes fluttered opened, but then immediately closed again.

"That's my love. Open your eyes for me. You're so much stronger than they are. I'll return you to your mama and papa, I promise." He ran his finger down her jawline and across the lips he loved to taste.

"Finlay?" She grasped his arm. "Where are we?" Her gaze caught his. "Are those tears? What's wrong?"

He buried his face in her hair. "I feared I lost you. Tell me you'll fight. I love you, lass." He did his best to smile for her, his hands cupping her face as much as her dared.

"I love you, Finlay." Tears misted her eyes. "I thought we'd never be free. Are we far enough away?"

"Aye, do not worry. Gillie has gone off to fetch your sire or one of your uncles."

"What happened at the castle? I know 'twas a ruse, but why did you do it?"

"The only way," he choked out again. "I knew not how else to get out of the cell they had locked me in. The healer…she's a seer, too. She told me Mama was sending me a message to listen to my uncle's plan. He suggested that if I went along with Buchan, they'd free me from my cell."

"Oh, Finlay." She kissed his tears away. "Your mama knew. I'll heal. Do not worry."

"I made them promise not to hurt you again," he could feel the tears still burning his eyes, but forced them back. "But when de La Porte touched you, I lost all control. I want you to be mine forever." He breathed in her scent, kissing her cheek, her neck, and her nose. He finally took her lips with his, being as gentle as he could. He pulled back. "Am I hurting you?"

She shook her head and tugged him back for another kiss. "Thank you for protecting me. 'Twas horrid to be so close to him."

"Shhh…He'll not touch you ever again. He'll pay. I promise."

The sound of hoofbeats vibrated across the ground, slowing as they grew louder. He prayed it was Gillie or any Grant. "My lord, my lord," Gillie cried out. "They're here! I saw the line of warriors. 'Tis more than I could ever count. The red, the blue. Plaids everywhere and horses riding and some men marching. I saw the Grant at the front with the banners."

Finlay set his hand on the lad's shoulder. "Slow down, lad. Here's what I need you to do. You're to go straight to Alexander Grant and tell him we're here, and that Inga and Uncle Geordie helped me."

Kyla reached inside her gown and pulled something out. "Give him this. He'll know 'tis mine."

"Then what shall I do?" The lad stepped back and hopped from one foot to the other.

"Bring Alex Grant here."

"*Here?*"

"Aye, Kyla is his daughter. He'll want to see her, lad."

Kyla's eyes fluttered shut.

Gillie nodded and mounted his horse, but Finlay called him back. "If you locate her sire, tell him she's..." He pointed to her bruises and cuts. "Not the same."

Gillie nodded. "Understood."

After Gillie departed, Kyla opened her eyes for a moment, then settled her head back against Finlay's chest. "I don't feel well. I must sleep now."

She fell asleep a moment later, and her breathing slowed.

He prayed she only needed rest.

☾

Alex Grant rode with a heavy heart. Not at his peak, he worried he'd fail his daughter and his wife, yet he pushed himself onward. His side ached after being on horseback for so long, but it was nothing he couldn't handle. But how long could he swing his sword? He'd been practicing privately so as not to worry Maddie, but his strength had been slow to return. He was no longer the best swordsman in the Highlands, and mayhap that title would never be his again. Still, Alex had chosen his usual war garb, his leine and his red and black Grant plaid. While some warriors fought in muted plaids, he wished for his enemy to remember him well.

Despite his lingering ailments, he was confident in their plan. Logan had his archers all ready, and he knew his old friend would do his job well. Numbers were in their favor as well. Aedan had offered to send men with them, but Alex had advised him to keep all his warriors at home to protect Lochluin Abbey and his land. It comforted him to know that Maddie and his sisters were safe.

Then something miraculous happened. Alex led his warriors over the last hill on their way off Cameron land, only to see a sea of warriors waiting below him—there were blue Ramsay plaids, Menzie plaids, and he was quite sure he could see a slew of Drummond plaids, too. There were horses everywhere and banners waving in the wind. This stood for everything his clan had built over the years, all the friendships they had nurtured. He glanced at his brothers to his right, both clearly feeling the same pride that swelled in his chest.

Together, they would get Kyla back and end Clan Buchan's reign of terror.

Once in the valley, he held his hand up to halt his guards behind him so he could move forward to speak with the group of leaders who awaited him—Torrian, whose sire had already joined his side; Micheil; and Drew Menzie. "Any news of Kyla or Finlay?"

Micheil shook his head. "We'll get them back, Alex. 'Tis time for us to put an end to this treachery."

Alex was about to speak when a noise interrupted him. He turned his head to see two of his warriors, one of them Finlay's brother, escorting a young lad he didn't recognize toward him. Though he looked small on his horse, he held his head high.

Fergus held onto the reins of the lad's horse. "My laird, our pardon, but the lad says he can take you to Kyla."

"Fergus, 'tis probably a trap," Alex rumbled. "Let him go." He'd had enough of Simon de La Porte's games.

"Your pardon, my laird," Fergus said. "I think you should hear what the lad has to say."

Alex glanced to his brothers and his sons. He knew Fergus was upset about Finlay's situation. Could he really be objective? Connor, Loki, and Brodie all nodded at him, so he decided to listen. Besides, there was something about the boy that called to him. "Speak up, lad. Your name first."

"My name is Gillie, and Finlay sent me here because I was assigned as Kyla's protector."

His words came out in a rush so fast that Alex could hardly understand him.

"My real name is Gilleasp, but everyone calls me Gillie, Finlay promised me that if I helped him he would bring me to Grant land to live because I don't want to live with the Buchan anymore but I helped Finlay with the horses and we got Kyla out and he has her behind the waterfall and I'm to bring you to them and then he offered to take me with him to Grant land." He let his breath out and stared up at Alex. "Are you truly Alexander Grant, the one who fought at the Battle of Largs?"

"I am, lad. Now tell me why I should believe you. How do I

know Buchan did not send you to lead me into a trap?"

Gillie whispered, "Och, I almost forgot. Finlay said to tell you Inga and Uncle Geordie both helped him," the lad paused. "And he said to give you this. Kyla said you would know them."

Fergus took something out of the lad's hand and handed it over to him. Alex opened his palm and stared at the necklace of pearls, the same ones he'd placed around his wife's neck before they married. Maddie had told him she had given them to Kyla.

CHAPTER SEVENTEEN

᭶

"ARE THOSE PEARLS NOT THE ones you gave Maddie?" Brodie asked.

Alex nodded.

"You're certain?"

"Aye." He held the clasp up for Brodie to see. "I had the jeweler engrave it with FMG for Father MacGregor, who gave me the idea. Maddie adored him."

He placed the pearls in his sporran and said, "Brodie, Jamie, you'll come with me. Jamie, choose ten other guards to join us." He saw Nicol out of the corner of his eye—the man had ridden up to speak with his son. "You, too, Nicol." He then turned to the lad and said, "Gillie, take me to my daughter."

Gillie took the reins of his horse and was about to turn around when he stopped. "Oh, Finlay said I'm to warn you that Kyla was beaten bad. She does not look too good…my laird. That is, I hope you'll be my laird."

Alex motioned for him to continue, and they headed into the forest, leaving the lines of warriors behind. She was alive. That was all that mattered at present. He needed to see her for himself.

"She's a strong lass like her mother and sire, Alex," Brodie said. "Remember that."

He nodded, unable to speak due to the huge lump that had found its way into his throat. They hit a meadow and Alex waved to Gillie to speed his horse into a gallop.

It felt like they rode for an eternity, though it had to be less than an hour, before Gillie led them to a burn. They followed it as it widened, and a short time later he heard the musical sounds of the waterfall nearby. Alex said a quick prayer that this was indeed Kyla and Finley and not a trap. If his daughter was indeed safe, Gillie would be joining Clan Grant soon.

Gillie tipped his head back and whistled a bird call. Within seconds, Finlay stepped out from behind the waterfall, carrying Kyla in his arms. He could see the tears rolling down the lad's face and his gut clenched. Had they come too late? Was she gone? Her eyes were closed, but her color, what he could see past the bruises and swelling, was not the worst he'd ever seen.

Dismounting, he pulled on his inner strength not to fall to his knees, instead moving over to stand in front of Finlay, who'd stepped into the grass, still clutching Kyla to his chest.

"Is she alive, Finlay?"

Finlay nodded. "Aye, she still breathes."

"Are you alone?"

"We have not been followed."

Alex reached for his daughter, but Finlay stepped away from him. "I would like to, my laird, but movement pains her terribly."

Alex stood back and nodded, his eyes traveling across his daughter's beautiful face. It was covered with purple and blue marks, one eye was badly swollen, and her lips were cut and scabbed. As his gaze traveled the length of her body, fury built inside him like a raging fire.

He'd experienced a fury like this once before, when he'd watched a depraved bastard take a lash to his wife's back, but this was different. Now, he was older and more capable of controlling his fury, channeling it into vengeance. This was fury that would turn him into a predator, a cat that would pace around his enemy until he had the bastard just where he wanted him.

They had done this to his daughter, the one who had been strapped to his chest as a bairn, her giggles and blue eyes ensuring she had a special place in his heart all her own.

This. Was. His. *Baby.*

He leaned down and kissed her forehead, letting the tears fall onto his cheeks unabashedly. He wished to cuddle her as he had when she was a bairn, keep everyone away from her.

Finlay nodded to Alex and the others. His sire, Nicol, took a step toward him. The warrior finally spoke, "I have something I'd like to say."

Alex nodded. "Go ahead. You have a few moments before I send her to Cameron land. My sisters can help her heal."

Finlay kissed Kyla's cheek and said, "My apologies to all of you for my hand in this travesty. My laird, I need you to know that I love your daughter. Naught would please me more than to ask for her hand in marriage, but I understand that first I must prove my worth. I foolishly thought I should leave Clan Grant after my mother's passing, but now I realize that there is no place I'd rather be than by this woman's side. I set out to prove my worthiness to you as a suitor for your daughter, but I bungled everything terribly. I will accept your decision, whatever 'tis, but I do love her with all my heart."

He waited, his gaze on him. Alex had been struck speechless. It was the last thing he'd expected Finlay to say at this moment. "Lad, I think 'tis something I need to think on…"

Kyla opened her eyes and did her best to smile. "Papa? 'Tis you truly? And Finlay…would you mind repeating what you just said?"

Gillie hurried up to her and shouted, "He says he loves you and wishes to marry you."

Finlay chuckled and kissed her gently. "Aye, I do love you. But I know I must prove myself."

"Finlay, set her down please," Alex said.

"Nay, it pains her to stand, my laird. Either her ankle is twisted or her foot broken, so with all due respect, I cannot set her down in good conscience."

"Is there a boulder I could sit on behind that waterfall?" Alex pointed in that direction.

Gillie said, "Aye, there are two large ones."

"I'd like a few moments alone with my daughter. Please hand her to me." Alex reached for his daughter and scooped her into his arms as carefully as he could.

She winced but was able to grab his shoulders, and he carried her behind the cascading water, feeling a few cool splashes on his face. It helped ground him in the moment as he settled on the boulder with Kyla on his lap. "You are comfortable enough to talk?"

"Aye, Papa. I'm so sorry for all the trouble I've caused. Finlay only came along because I swore I'd go alone without him. The message was a ruse, but I believed it. I was terrified for Davina."

He rested his chin on his daughter's head as she continued to babble, explaining her actions, but all he could do was take in the familiar scent and softness of his wee daughter. Kyla had become such a strong woman, just as her mother was. How could he fault her for doing what was right and fighting against the abuse of women? Nay, he was proud of her, and Maddie would be, too. "Daughter, I do not fault you for your good heart, nor do I fault Finlay for protecting you. The fault lies at Buchan's feet. Forgive me, but I must ask. Were you raped?"

Kyla pulled her head back and cupped her sire's cheek. "Nay, Papa. Finlay and Davina and Gillie protected me. I may not walk for a while, but I'll survive. Oh, Davina is fine and so is her daughter." She brushed away the wetness she found on his cheeks. "Papa, I'm sorry. What will happen now?"

"Do you love Finlay?"

"Aye, I do love him. After watching my brothers and my cousins find such happiness in marriage, I was afraid I'd never find the same, but my love has been in front of me all along. And the best part is that he's part of our clan. I'll not be leaving you and Mama. I couldn't bear it."

"You've been through much, so we'll not decide now. Uncle Brodie and Finlay's sire will escort you to Cameron land. Your mother is there with your aunts, who will to tend to your wounds. I need to finish this so the Buchans and de La Porte will not disrupt my clan again." He stood, lifting her with him, then stooped to kiss her cheek. "I love you, lassie. My heart was nearly broken from worrying about you, but I am proud of you."

He stepped out from behind the waterfall and said, "Brodie, Nicol, please deliver Kyla to her mother on Cameron land. Take seven guards with you."

After Brodie mounted, Alex carefully lifted Kyla up to him. "Papa, be careful," Kyla said. "I love you and Finlay."

"What about me?" Gillie asked. "Where do I go?"

Alex beckoned to the lad and gestured for him to stand in front of him. When Gillie did as instructed and lifted his gaze to him, Alex set his hand on the lad's shoulder and asked, "Are you not my daughter's protector?"

He grinned and said "Aye, my laird." His eyes grew wide, waiting to see what would come next.

"Welcome to Clan Grant. You may ride with Nicol. Take care of my daughter until Finlay and I return for her."

"Aye, my laird." He raced to Nicol's horse and jumped so high he almost flew over the back of the horse, but Nicol caught him. It was good to see the man grinning—the loss of his wife had weighed on him.

After taking a final look at his daughter, ensuring himself she was okay, Alex moved over to speak with Nicol. "Your son made me proud today. I do not fault him for what transpired. He brought my daughter back to me safely."

After the group bound for the Camerons left, Alex motioned for Jamie and the other two guards to patrol the area. "Jamie, I'll speak to Finlay alone, then we shall head back. Give us a few minutes."

Alex strode up to stand in front of Finlay. Hell, but when had the lad grown so large? He remembered him as a little sprite of a laddie, just as he remembered all of these young ones. He could see the lad bore his own share of bruises, telling him how hard he'd fought to free Kyla from her imprisonment.

"Finlay, my thanks for returning my daughter to me and for joining her in her endeavor to ensure she did not go off alone. I know how headstrong she can be, so I do not need the particular details. I lay all the blame on Buchan and de La Porte. You are still a valued member of our clan, should you choose to stay."

"I do, my laird."

"That pleases me." He glanced up at the sky, pausing before he dropped his gaze back to Finlay's. "Then I only have one other question for you. Which one would you like—Glenn of Buchan or Simon de La Porte? I'll give you first choice."

Finlay smiled. "I choose de La Porte. I've dreamed of killing that bastard."

"He's all yours. I will gladly take on Glenn of Buchan." He moved over to his stallion and mounted.

"Time to end this."

☾

While they rode back to the main group of warriors, Finlay brought his horse abreast of Jamie's. "My apologies if I let you down as your second, my laird."

Jamie glanced at his sire, then said, "You protected my sister, exactly what I would hope for my second to do. My thanks for that. You know I'd welcome you as a brother." The last part he said with a grin. "Now, did you learn anything inside that will help us?"

"I did."

"Save it until my sire can listen."

As soon as they stopped, Finlay's gaze carried across the sea of warriors gathered on horseback. They covered the knolls and valleys around him practically as far as his eyes could see. No wonder Gillie had been so taken with the vision of all the plaids together.

Jamie called his father over. "Finlay has some information about the Buchan to share."

Alex motioned for him to proceed.

He swallowed and forged ahead. "I had to pretend to turn traitor. 'Twas the only way I could get out of my cell so I could reach Kyla. I heard Buchan discussing strategy with de La Porte, so I told him you prefer to fight from the right. I believe he plans to stay hidden until you are there. Then he intends to come upon you from the rear as an act of surprise. But he should come on the right side of the field instead of the left where you usually fight."

"Well done. Jamie, choose two men to watch for this maneuver. Now, I don't know about you, but I'm anxious to end this. Let's not tarry any longer."

Finlay breathed a sigh of relief now that all was out in the open. The leaders of the various groups of warriors met together, discussing the final plans for the attack. Alex was in charge, though Jake and Jamie were acting lairds. Their sire had far more battle experience than they, so they valued his wisdom. Logan had returned with his archers and reported they were ready to take their places whenever the Grant wished to move.

Torrian asked, "Now that Kyla and Finlay are free, do you suggest a straight attack instead of feigning that we are bartering for Kyla's life?"

"Finlay, did anyone see you leave?" Quade asked.

"Nay. They may not know yet. Their scouts had just arrived, updating them on the number and location of the warriors. I'd been sent into the keep without a weapon. When I climbed over the back curtain wall, no one was around."

Logan added, "Aye, 'tis what we saw. No good staging area for a fight in the back, so they ignored it. 'Tis where our archers will gain entrance to the wall and some of the trees. Buchan and his men are in chaos, arguing about their best mode of attack, though the foolish laird clings to the hope you'll give your land up easily."

Alex was quiet for a long moment, no doubt mulling over all of the information he'd been given, then said, "I will approach as if I fear for Kyla's life. This will allow us to get close, which will give us added knowledge of our enemy—we can see where they are, who is leading them, and what weapons they carry. I will suggest that we will give up our castle as soon as we see Kyla. Then, when I judge the time to be right, I will signal with our war whoop to attack. We will attack when they least expect it." His gaze shifted to encompass all of the leaders who'd joined them. "We attack with all seven hundred warriors. I want this ended quickly to avoid loss of our men."

All agreed while he gave each leader his individual orders for the approach. "Let it be known that Simon de La Porte is Finlay's. I've promised him that right, and Glenn of Buchan is mine. I suspect he'll try to use some trickery in his approach, even beyond what Finlay has said, but trust that I will take care of the Buchan. I want this finished. I'll not allow Glenn to walk away and plan another attack."

"What about our king?" Robbie asked.

"Our people went to Edinburgh to seek him, but he was not available, so I must make my own judgments. I say this needs to be ended, and the only way that will happen is if Glenn of Buchan is dead or behind bars." His glance shifted to his sons. "While I have been practicing, I wish you to know I'm still not as strong as I once was. I ask your assistance, lads."

The leaders waited to see if Alex had any other comments to make. He nodded, acknowledging the show of respect, and said, "The Lord has been generous this day and returned my dearest daughter to me. Now he will go with us as we end the torture that has become acceptable to the Buchans."

He nodded to each of his leaders. "Carry on and Godspeed."

He led the march out, Jake on one side and Jamie on the other, Finlay directly behind Jamie.

Simon de La Porte was about to get his due.

CHAPTER EIGHTEEN

W HEN THEY ARRIVED ON CAMERON land, it was near
dark, but Kyla knew she would not be able to sleep.
"Uncle Brodie, I hope Mama is still up."

He gave her a sideways glance. "Lass, I doubt your mother will
get a wink of sleep until your sire, your brothers, and you are all at
home. She has Elizabeth and Maeve with her, but this is the first
time she's been without so many of you."

Uncle Brodie took his horse directly to the steps of the Cameron great hall. Nicol had left his horse at the stable, and he and
Gillie and a stableboy followed them on foot to the keep. The stableboy would take the horse back once they dismounted.

"Where are we, my lord?" Gillie peered up at the towers around
the Cameron wall with such an obvious sense of wonder, Kyla
herself felt as if she were seeing it for the first time. "And what was
the big building we passed? It looked like a kirk."

"That was Lochluin Abbey, and this is Aedan Cameron's land,"
Nicol said. "He married Kyla's Aunt Jennie. Get the door for me
and see who's in the hall. Hopefully, we'll find Kyla's mother. She's
been riddled with worry ever since Kyla was taken captive."

Nicol helped Kyla down from the horse while Gillie scurried up
the steps. Her uncle dismounted and supported her other side. She
set her foot down carefully to test it, but the pain was excruciating.
"I cannot walk on it, Uncle Brodie."

Then her mother appeared in the doorway, hand-in-hand with
wee Maeve, and everything else fell away. "Kyla?" Maddie said on
a gasp. "Is it truly you?" Then she let go of Maeve's hand to rush to
her side. "Oh, Kyla. Thank the Lord above you are here."

Maddie hugged her, and Kyla could feel the fine tremors in her mother's shoulders and the wetness of her cheeks.

"Forgive me, Mama."

Since it was dark, Kyla guessed her mother hadn't noticed her condition. Uncle Brodie stood behind her so she wouldn't fall, and she clung to her mother's shoulders as much to keep herself from falling as for comfort.

Her mother took a step back, her hands still on Kyla's shoulders, and asked, "You are hale?" Then she paused, brushing the hair back from her face, and Kyla knew why. "Oh, Kyla." Her mother had noticed her face—the swollen eye and the horrible bruises on her cheek. Maddie's hand reached up to touch her, but she didn't. "I know exactly how you feel, lass. I'm so sorry." She could see the tears falling in rivers down her mother's cheeks.

"Mama, I'll heal. Do not worry." She kissed her mother's cheek and rubbed her arm, hoping her dear mama wouldn't collapse in front of her.

"I was so hoping your father would get to you before anything happened."

Aunt Brenna, who had followed Maddie out the door, motioned to Brodie. "Bring her inside so Jennie and I can check her over. I want to look at her foot." Aunt Jennie had come outside with her and she nodded her agreement.

Her uncle carried her up the steps, Gillie trailing behind him. Once they made it to the hearth, the lad peppered her mother with his questions. "Are you Kyla's mother? Finlay and I saved her." He took Maddie's hand and tugged on it. "We got her out while Simon and the Buchan were arguing."

Her mother turned around, brushed her tears away, and asked, "Who is this?"

"I'm Gillie. I helped Finlay. He said if I helped him I could go to Grant land. And I met Alexander Grant and he said I could come along and be Kyla's protector and then I could go to Grant land. I can be in your clan." The hopeful expression in his gaze was sure to affect her mother.

Her mother stopped and patted his shoulder. "My thanks, lad, for protecting my daughter. I think you must have built up a big appetite working so hard. Would you like something to eat, mayhap a meat pie?"

"Do you have an extra one? I've not had a meat pie since Mama and Papa passed. My mama used to make the best mutton pies. What kind do you have? But I love them all, so any will do."

Kyla glanced at her mother and saw the new tears gathering in her eyes just at the thought that a lad had lost both of his parents. Her mother had such a soft heart, and she was sure to watch over Gillie for some time.

Uncle Aedan entered the keep just then, and he must have overheard Gillie because he said, "Here, come along with me. I'll show you the warrior's meal we have just for you."

Kyla said, "And something sweet, Uncle Aedan."

Aedan nodded, and the two went off together. Brodie set her down in a tufted chair in front of the hearth, squarely in front of the warm fire there.

"The heat feels good." She shuddered at the memory of Davina's cold tower.

Aunt Brenna took over. "Kyla, I want you to tell me all the places you hurt, and how you gained each of your injuries."

Once she sat in the chair, she said, "I'm verra tired, Auntie."

Uncle Brodie said, "She slept most of the way here."

"Her body needs to heal," Aunt Jennie said. "We should check her foot before she sleeps, Brenna. If 'tis broken, we'll need to straighten it."

Her mother said, "Brodie, why don't you and Nicol go with Aedan? You can find something to eat and get some ale for the guards outside."

Once they were alone, her mother whispered, "How badly, Kyla? Did they steal your maidenhead?"

"Nay, Mama. The thing that hurts the most is my foot. My hip is also sore, but not too bad. I have a headache from the fist I took, but 'tis tolerable. I just cannot stand."

Aunt Brenna removed her boot and assessed her foot, turning it and prodding it as gingerly as she could. She then checked her head and her eye, her aunt's quiet mannerism soothing her in a way she could not explain.

Kyla decided this was as good a time as any to tell her mama about Finlay. "Mama, I know I shouldn't have gone. 'Twas foolish on my part, but I was truly worried about Davina. The note was a trick to get us there. I was verra naïve and I apologize. Finlay helped only because I insisted, so do not fault him. I love him, Mama."

Her mother's gaze lifted to hers, a small smile spreading across her face. "You do?"

"Aye. Spending so much time with him made me see him in a new way. He's kind and he makes me laugh. If it hadn't been for Finlay, I would still be under the control of those awful men. He and Gillie watched over me. He did his best to protect me, and they beat him for it. He asked Papa for my hand before Uncle Brodie brought me home."

"He did?"

She'd never seen such a surprised expression on her mother's face, but it was one of happiness. "Can you believe it, Mama? I've finally found someone wonderful to love."

"And what did your papa say?"

"He said he would think on it. Finlay said he wishes to prove he's worthy of being a Grant. He thinks 'twas all his fault, but I convinced him to go. I would have found another to take me if he did not."

Aunt Jennie sent some lads off to set up a tub in one of the chambers. "And what did you have to say about this proposed marriage?"

"Papa asked me if I loved him and I said I did. I hope he'll ask me again when this is over."

"Kyla, I'm so pleased." Her mother gave her a light hug. "Come, we'll get you cleaned up."

Aunt Brenna said, "Aunt Jennie and I are happy for you, too. Another wedding so soon? I think 'tis wonderful. But first, a bath. You'll be surprised how much better you'll feel after scrubbing all that grunge off your skin. We need to see if you have any other wounds you haven't noticed yet. We must dress them all so you don't get the fever."

"Then I'll sleep for just a bit because I want to be awake when they return. We can watch from the parapets, aye, Aunt Jennie?"

"We'll all be there with you in a few hours. There won't be much sleeping tonight."

⁂

Finlay was so proud of his clan. He'd never seen seven hundred warriors together, and he kept staring back at them in awe. He also kept an eye to the periphery to see if any of de La Porte's mercenaries were preparing to mount a secret attack.

Jamie rode up to him with instructions. "I've already discussed this with Jake and our sire, but our scouts have not seen Buchan outside the castle walls. In fact, no one has been found anywhere. We're guessing they have discovered Kyla and you missing, so they are searching or planning, one or the other.

"We're sending you in the back way. Look for Logan and his group. Five warriors will go with you, and Cailean and Tormod will also be stationed back there."

"And who will act as your second? That has been my privilege all these years."

"I understand your hesitance, but Connor can act as my second. My sire has an inkling that Buchan and de La Porte are either inside the keep or planning to head out the back. If this battle turns sour, they'll be on the run. They would have had a chance with Kyla as a hostage. Without her, they haven't a chance. They'll change their tactics, especially once they discover the number of warriors we've brought. They'd be foolish to think they can take on a group of seven hundred warriors with the force they have. It would be a blood bath. We have enough that I'm sending many out to the periphery to make sure few of their men escape. Many of our warriors will probably never see battle. But we have to find Buchan and de La Porte, both slippery as snakes. I do not want them escaping.

"Hopefully, you'll run into both of them. You know the layout of the keep, so you can take Simon out, and detain Buchan. Take Cailean with you once the archers are in position. He is mighty with his sword and he won't sit idle easily. The other guards can stand watch."

"Aye, my laird. Consider it done. I'll search for the archers."

"Finlay, 'struth is I know my sire is not strong enough to battle long. As soon as we determine Buchan is not at the front of his warriors, I'll bring Papa inside and leave Jake to handle the situation outside. Glenn is no longer powerful either. He'll be hiding. Loki is formidable with his sword, and I'm assigning him as my sire's second. With you, Cailean, and Loki there, I'll feel better. Connor and I will follow as soon as we're able."

Jamie started to ride off, then stopped and turned back to him. "And Finlay? I never question my father's instincts. He's usually right. I doubt we'll see either one of those men. They'll be inside and we'll follow. We'll have to hope there's no tunnel. Be aware."

Finlay nodded, accepting his instructions without question. He just hoped Jamie was right and the two bastards would be there for the taking. He couldn't wait to see Simon de La Porte at the end of his sword.

It didn't take long for him to locate Logan Ramsay.

"Why are you here?" Logan asked, direct as ever. "It's so dense behind the curtain wall, there's no place for fighting. I told Jamie to send a few warriors to stand way out, but there won't be any of Buchan's men here unless they're on the run."

"Jamie sent me to cover the back. He requested that I take Cailean with me once you've got your archers settled."

"Alex had another one of his premonitions, didn't he?"

"Aye. He thinks they've discovered Kyla's missing and changed their tactics. They've lost their leverage, and he imagines they'll run now that they've seen our numbers. He thinks they'll be holing up inside or sneaking out the back. Jamie's going to try to get Alex inside quickly."

"Hmmph. Alex is never wrong, son. Expect to see them both inside, and I hope Jamie's sending Connor or Loki with his father. Those two have the mightiest swords right now. Though Cailean is good to take with you."

Finlay replied, "Loki is acting as Alex's second. Connor is Jamie's."

"Good. All my archers will be either on the wall or in the trees outside. I'll not move any inside until I know 'tis safe. They can hit targets inside the bailey from the trees." He strode over to Cailean, conferred with him, and then returned to Finlay's side. "Once he has Sorcha set, he'll join you here. Godspeed to both of you. Protect your lairds and take care of the bastards, would you? My archers will get many of the warriors in the front of the keep. I'll have two keep an eye on the back, just in case."

Finlay took a deep breath and nodded. He found the spot where they had hidden their rope and waited for Cailean. He instructed two guards to stay on the wall and three to guard the property behind the keep. Bending down, he checked that both of his hidden daggers were easily accessible, then placed his hand on the hilt of his sword.

A few minutes later, Cailean appeared at his side. "Anything I need to know?"

"Nay, only that Simon de La Porte is mine and Buchan is Alex Grant's. I'll lead the way. We wait for the war whoop. Once we hear the signal, we're off. I'll climb up and see if anyone is in the back."

He scaled the wall and searched the area, though he couldn't see beyond the kitchens in the far corner. Logan Ramsay hurried over and called up to him once he gave the all-clear sign. "Word from Gwynie is Buchan and de La Porte just headed inside the keep, arguing. Expect your signal soon."

☾

Alex Grant nodded to Jake and Jamie to give their final instructions to their men. He needed a quiet moment of clarity, something he often found helpful before battle.

He rode Black Lightning down the lines of horses covering the landscape. He found a small knoll and led his horse up to the top so he could look over the leagues of men here to fight for his *clann*.

Dusk was descending fast and he closed his eyes to feel the light breeze coming in from the mountains, the sweet Scottish air feeding his soul, exhilarating him like nothing else could. His nephews, David, Roddy, Braden, and his youngest son, Connor, all wore expressions of anticipation. They were eager to be involved in the action for the first time.

His eldest sons, Jake and Jamie, carried the hardness of experience across their cheekbones, their gazes discerning, always searching for something unusual, anything to help in their preparation for battle. He and Maddie had done a fine job raising their bairns.

Hellfire, he was a proud man. Proud of his wife and all she'd endured over the years, of his sons and daughters, of how deeply they'd connected with the Ramsay clan, of how both clans dared to bring women warriors along with them. He thought of his sire and mother and how proud they would be of all they had become.

The breeze lifted the Grant banner and the Ramsay banner not far away, the snapping and billowing of the flags the only other sound to be heard outside his sons' voices and the occasional shifting of horses' hooves. His sons finished giving the instructions necessary to guarantee they would fight strong and dominate the battle.

Good must triumph over evil today.

The last thing he did was to bow his head in prayer that the Lord would see them all through this battle and that he would fare better than he had in the last one, the one that had nearly cost him his life. All was quiet as his men followed him, honoring his moment of silence.

Black Lightning was so in tune with his rider that when Alex finished his prayer, the great beast lifted his front legs and stood on his hind legs, his dark head raised up as he whinnied, giving the warriors the signal that his master was ready for battle.

The Grant war whoop, uttered by hundreds, rang out over the valley.

The battle was on.

CHAPTER NINETEEN

֍

A LEXANDER GRANT'S WAR WHOOP CARRIED all the way to the back of the procession of warriors, followed by the rest of his warriors, with echoes of Menzie, Drummond, and Ramsay whoops easily overpowering the answering Buchan yells. Finlay motioned to Cailean and dropped to the ground, pleased to see the surrounding area was still empty. He made his way to the tower door, opening it a touch while Cailean caught up to him. There was no sound in the tower, so they moved carefully toward the door to the inside passageway that led to the great hall.

Once in the passageway, he held his hand up to Cailean, indicating that he should slow down and fall in behind him. Sure enough, Buchan and someone else were arguing in the great hall. They stayed to the side and listened because Finlay was sure he heard a woman's voice.

It had to be Davina.

Cailean whispered, "Is it Buchan and de La Porte?"

Finlay shook his head because he wasn't sure. The sound of a gob of spit hurled across the hall reached them and he said, "Aye, that's de La Porte."

Cailean started to jump to action, but Finlay pulled him back. "Not until we know why they argue. Davina's there with them."

They moved to the door that opened to the great hall, opening it just a fraction, enough to hear everything clearly. Besides Buchan and de La Porte, he saw no other men inside. Glenn of Buchan held his struggling daughter around the waist, refusing to release her.

"You're completely daft, old man. Step aside and let me pass. If you have not noticed, we're under attack by at least four hundred Highlanders, each one eager to spear the two of us. I'm doing as we planned and going out the back, but not until you pay me the coin you promised me."

"I promised you coin when Grant Castle was mine."

"And when my mercenaries were here fighting. They're fighting now. I want my coin so I can get the hell out of here. I'll go to the abbey to get the rest of what I'm due. I hear they have big coffers."

"You also promised another hundred mercenaries. Where the hell are they?"

The man would never make it anywhere near the abbey, not if Finlay, Alexander Grant, and the seven hundred warriors outside had anything to do with it.

Davina made another tug against her sire's arms. "Leave me be, Papa. Please!"

"Neither of you have done what I asked," Buchan bellowed. "I promised you coin for two things, de La Porte—bringing two hundred trained men to fight and getting my daughter with child."

Finlay almost choked, spinning his head around to stare at Cailean. Had he heard what he thought he'd heard?

"Nay, Papa. Nay!" Her screams had become sobs as she struggled against her sire.

"Your daughter wasn't interested, so let it rest."

"Fine, I'll give up all my hopes for a strong grandson, but you still have to kill the Grant and Logan Ramsay to earn your payment. You mishandled my prisoners and now all is nearly lost."

The door burst open and five warriors came in. "De La Porte, they're heading this way. We're here to protect you. Extra coin, remember."

"Extra coin!" Buchan hollered. "You'll not be paid until Grant Castle is mine. I'm taking my daughter and hiding in the tower. See this done and I'll pay you well. You know what to do. I'm too old to fight."

"Simon, they're coming closer to the keep."

"Are you ready?" Finlay asked, turning toward Cailean. "I'll not listen to the bastard any longer."

He grinned and nodded. "Seven to two. Just the odds I like."

Finlay burst through the door and ran across the great hall toward the group in the middle, stopping not far from them. "Let her go, Buchan."

Four men came at Finlay and Cailean, and Davina took off in a dead run.

"Kill them," de La Porte yelled. He grabbed his own sword, but rather than join the attack, he crept around them toward the door to the tower.

Finlay thought of Kyla and all she'd had to go through in this keep. He needed to go after de La Porte, needed to stop him, but two warriors came at him at once. He swung his sword from the side, slicing the first one open, causing him to fling his sword toward the second, who was forced to duck to save himself from injury. From his peripheral vision, Finlay noticed Cailean had already finished off one of *his* attackers.

The other warrior recovered and came at Finlay with his arms raised over his head, preparing to slice him in two. Finlay easily sidestepped the blow and thrust his weapon into the man's belly when he turned around. He yanked his sword out, kicking the fool to the ground as the last of the five came toward him.

Out of the corner of his eye, he saw de La Porte leaving through the tower door. Cailean, who'd already knocked his second attacker down, shouted, "I've got this. Go after him."

Finlay didn't need to be told twice. He followed the bastard out the door and searched the area at the back of the keep. De La Porte was heading for the wall behind the kitchens, so Finlay pursued him without hesitation. The bastard was almost at the wall when Finlay shouted, "You'll never get up there without my sword in your back. Fight me like a true warrior, or are you all talk? I never did see you use your sword in the lists."

Simon spun around with his sword in his hands and lunged at Finlay, first from the left, then from the right. They parried for a short time while de La Porte did his best to taunt him. "That lass of yours sure had nice breasts. Did she tell you I tasted her every-where while she was my captive? She offered me her maidenhead, too." His grin hatched from the devil itself.

Finlay blocked out his comments, fighting for all he was worth. Off to the side, he noticed two of Buchan's men about to join in the melee, but one was taken out with an arrow to his chest and the second took a dagger right between his eyes.

Logan shouted, "Say the word and I'll have one of my archers take him out, MacNicol."

"Stay out. He's mine." Finlay growled, then brought his sword against de La Porte's so hard that sparks flew overhead. Their dual continued, Finlay doing his best to drive his sword home. He needed to finish this for Kyla and for himself.

"You have no skills, wee laddie. You'll never beat me. I'm going to steal Kyla again as soon as I get out of here. All the Grants are here, so my path will be obstacle free. My guess is you took her to Cameron land, right near the wealthy coffers of Lochluin Abbey, which is exactly where I'm headed."

Finlay swung again, but was blocked. "See? You savages think being a Highlander makes you stronger than other warriors? See the truth in front of you. You're nothing. You don't deserve the lass. I'll take her with me. She'll gladly trade you for a true man."

That comment sunk in, so he tried a move he'd only done a few times. He brought his sword across without completing his swing, faking his opponent into blocking his blow. At the last moment, he changed the path of his weapon and brought it down on de La Porte's arm as hard as he could.

He connected with flesh, rendering the man's sword arm useless. Simon de La Porte stared at him in shock as blood poured out of his body.

"How are my skills now?" Finlay drawled.

Simon hadn't moved so Finlay brought his sword down again, severing the fiend's arm from his body. His blood shot out in a pulsating fountain, his other arm reaching for a way to staunch the bleeding. Moments later, he collapsed to the ground.

Shouts of support came from the archers above, but he couldn't take time to appreciate them. He wiped his sword across the now lifeless body of de La Porte and rushed back to the keep, hoping the others had taken care of Glenn of Buchan.

When he stepped into the great hall, he saw about a dozen of the enemy fighting five Grants. Jamie, Connor, Loki, Cailean, and Alex Grant stood near the back with Glenn of Buchan huddling in the opposite corner. There was no sign of Davina.

Connor, Jamie, Loki, and Cailean fought like beasts, downing every man who dared to swing a sword their way, but Alex was losing strength. He fought hard, taking a couple out, but he didn't have the power of the other three.

Then the worst thing possible happened. Glenn of Buchan came running from the opposite side of the hall, his sword arm raised and heading directly toward Alex Grant's back.

CHAPTER TWENTY

⚘

"**M**Y LAIRD, YOUR BACK!" FINLAY bellowed. He buried a sword in the back of the man Alex had been parrying with in front of him, freeing the Grant to face his foe.

Alex Grant spun around, and in a beautifully choreographed move, knocked the sword out of Buchan's hands and plunged his sword into the swine's heart. Buchan fell to the floor, cursing the Grants and the Ramsays as he clutched his chest.

Connor and Jamie finished the last two and they all paused, staring around at the carnage, gasping for breath. "Anyone injured?" Jamie asked. "Papa?"

"I'm fine." He glanced at Finlay. "Good timing, lad. I never saw him coming."

"My laird, you finished him. 'Tis what counts and what all the Scots need to know," Finlay said as he cleaned his sword and sheathed it.

"De La Porte?" Jamie asked.

Logan came in through the back, chuckling. "MacNicol made sure he'll never be taking a sword to anyone again." Then he frowned for a moment. "And damn if somebody isn't deadly with a dagger. I still don't know who threw the one that hit that bastard between the eyes before Molly could send off another arrow."

Finlay had a vague recollection of that happening out in back. At the time, his mind had been fixed on de La Porte.

Connor took his sire by the elbow and led him to one of the few upright chairs. "Papa, sit. You did what you set out to do—you ended this man's tyranny. But your color isn't good. Mama will have my hide if I don't watch over you."

Alex sat, heaving to catch his breath. "Jamie, Finlay," he gasped. "Check the progress outside." Connor hurried off to find him something to drink.

Finlay peered over Jamie's shoulder as he opened the door, but they both broke into huge smiles when they saw nothing but red plaids and blue plaids filling the courtyard, either standing or on horseback.

"'Tis done, brother?" Jake yelled out. "Father is hale?"

Jamie nodded. "Aye, 'tis done. Alex Grant took Glenn of Buchan out, and Finlay MacNicol finished Simon de La Porte."

Jamie and Jake nodded to each other. Then they lifted their swords in celebration as they led a chant of Grant and Ramsay war whoops that spread like fire down the valley and across the surrounding moors.

A few moments later, Alex came out the front door, Loki directly behind him, and raised his sword to cheers from his comrades, but his arm fell to his side quickly. His color had improved, but his face was drawn. He'd apparently seen enough battle. Finlay caught the looks exchanged between the acting lairds and knew they'd be taking the former laird home soon.

Torrian raced across the courtyard and up the steps.

"What is it?" Jamie asked.

"I need to see for myself."

The fierce expression on the Ramsay laird's face left Finlay with no doubt that the Grants would let him in.

Everyone in the Highlands had heard the story of the beginning of the Buchan's tyranny. Glenn had tried to force Torrian Ramsay to marry Davina. Together with Ranulf MacNiven, he had conspired to use trickery to convince their king that Torrian had taken the lass's maidenhead. The Ramsays had been able to prove the truth with the assistance of Torrian's wee sister, Jennet. But the Buchan's plan had almost worked. Moreover, the Buchan's sons had tormented both Torrian's wife and his sister.

Jamie led Torrian into the great hall, and Finlay and the others followed them inside. While Alex took to a chair again, Torrian strode to the back to see Glenn of Buchan.

Logan, still in the hall, moved over and placed his hand on the Ramsay laird's shoulder as a show of support.

"Stand back, Uncle Logan." Torrian whispered. "I need a

moment."

Logan did as his nephew asked, glancing at Finlay, Loki, and Cailean.

Torrian stared at the man, spat on him, then pulled his sword out, before going down on one knee before Alex Grant and bowing his head. "My thanks to you, Uncle Alex."

Alex grasped his shoulder and said, "My stroke was for Kyla, Finlay, and all the Ramsays." He nodded to Finlay. "There were many hands guiding my arm. His evil spirit did great harm, but it's done."

Torrian stood and turned to Jamie. "Any instructions, laird?"

Jamie nodded to his sire, giving him that honor.

"We're heading home," Alex announced. "We shall take one hundred guards with us. Have the rest bury the dead. Ten guards should stay to take Buchan and de La Porte to Edinburgh for the king to see."

Torrian said, "Kyle Maule and I respectfully request that duty."

Alex nodded to him. "See it done. Then we hope the two of you will join our celebrations on Cameron land."

"With pleasure." Torrian nodded and left.

"The others can be sent back to Grant land with the instructions to hold a celebration for all on the morrow. Logan, bring your archers back to Cameron land for our festivities there." He turned away but then stopped. "Finlay, see if you can locate Davina. Kyla will want to know."

"Aye, my laird. I'll check her tower."

Logan grasped Alex's shoulder. "I'll find Micheil and Drew. I'll stop at the abbey on the way to Cameron land, leave some guards. I heard de La Porte say he planned to travel there after leaving the keep. I doubt any of his mercenaries survived, but I'll advise them, just in case. Then we'll be along."

Finlay left to do as instructed, and he was surprised to see that Davina had already left. There was no sign of her or the babe in the tower except for a few dirty raggies left behind, even the small cradle was gone. He searched the rest of the keep before he returned to the group in front of the castle.

"No sign of Davina or anyone else, my laird."

Jamie nodded, "Then mount up. 'Tis time for us to leave this forsaken place."

After all of the final orders had been given, their group began the journey to Cameron land. Jamie rode on one side of Alex, Jake on the other, and Connor and Finlay fell in behind them.

They had made it quite a distance before the full implications of the day's events finally dawned on Finlay. A smile spread across his face as he listened to the various bellows and whoops of their group.

He was free.

He and Kyla were both free, and he was free to pursue her as his future wife. How desperately he loved her… He'd never guessed it possible that he could feel this way about another person. He wished to tell everyone how he felt, and most of all, he wished to tell her—again and again.

Hope blossomed inside of him, almost bringing tears to his eyes, when he compared where he'd been a day ago with where he was now. He thought of the seer, the message from his mother, and how his uncle had helped him…but most of all, he thought of Kyla.

The woman he loved had been treated horribly in that hole from hell, but she was strong. She would recover, and he'd do aught he could to help her. He'd stand by her side every day for the rest of his life if he had his choice.

Exhausted yet exhilarated, he galloped along behind his *clann*, the very group he'd briefly thought of leaving. What a foolish plan that had been. He glanced at the men around him, reveling in their smiles, their pride, their friendship. This was where he belonged.

True, he'd lost his mother and he would miss her terribly, but after what he'd just been through, he was confident she'd always be a part of him, watching from afar.

Before he knew it, they were almost at the Cameron Castle. Jamie turned to him and yelled, "I see my sister waiting for you. Here, the flag is yours."

He couldn't stop the smile from bursting across his face as he leaned over to grab the flag before he searched the area for her.

There she was, the most beautiful sight he'd ever seen, sitting atop a horse with a smile on her face.

⟨₆

Kyla sat on her stool on the parapets next to her mother and

Elizabeth. Aunt Brenna and Aunt Jennie paced back and forth on the torched walkway. Darkness had fallen, but a full moon lit up the landscape. She had no idea how many hours had passed.

Kyla squeezed her mother's hand. "Mama, I've made up my mind and please do not try to change it. If Finlay and Papa and all my brothers come home safely, I want to marry Finlay right away."

"Right away?" Her mother stared at her in surprise, but she could tell the suggestion pleased her. Her aunts both joined them, waiting to hear more.

"Aye. I do not need anything fancy. After all that has transpired, I'd like to get married in Lochluin Abbey. 'Tis the right place." She glanced over at Aunt Jennie, whose face had broken out in the biggest smile.

Aunt Brenna said, "Maddie, it makes sense. We're all here. Quade will want to head home in less than a sennight. We've been away too long."

"You'll never have us all together again," Aunt Jennie added. "There'll be even more of us in one place than there were for Sorcha's wedding. Micheil and Diana will be here. Avelina and Drew. Even though they aren't your relatives, they love you truly."

"Of course, we have to speak to your sire." Her mother glanced from one person to the next. "What do you think, Elizabeth?"

"Aye. I love weddings, and the abbey is a lovely place for one. Kyla, you'll be the most beautiful bride ever." She ran over and hugged her sister. "I was so afraid for you. I'm so glad you're back."

"I'm sorry I worried you," she said, stroking her sister's hair. Looking up at her mother and her aunts, she added, "All of you."

"Do not be sorry, lass," Aunt Jennie said. "'Twas not your fault. And if this puts an end to those nasty men, we'll all be thanking you. Buchan's clan has been a blight on the Highlands for years."

"Especially on the Ramsays and the Grants," Aunt Brenna added.

"I hope Finlay hasn't changed his mind." Kyla stared at her hands in her lap, then lifted her head to check the horizon. "I think I see a torch coming." Staring off in the direction of the first flicker, she hopped off her stool and hung onto the parapets for balance.

"I cannot see that far," Aunt Brenna said, squinting. "Nor can your mother or Jennie."

Jennie frowned. "I can see fine. I'm much younger than you two."

"Can you see them?" Maddie asked.

Jennie shook her head.

"I do," Elizabeth shouted. "Over to the right. I saw two flickers."

Kyla gripped the stone wall as she fought to keep herself upright on one leg. "The Buchan healer gave me a potion to help me sleep, and it has not fully worn off yet."

"Probably a good thing, based on your injuries," her mother said.

"I know, but I cannot seem to balance verra well." Aunt Jennie had fashioned a crutch for her, but she hadn't learned how to use it. When she tried to walk with it, she spent more time sprawled on the ground than upright. "They're coming. The flickers are growing. I'm going to mount up."

"Kyla." Maddie caught her before she moved. "You will not leave the courtyard until we determine they are our warriors. I know it is unlikely, but it is possible they could be Buchan's men sent to take you or another one of us captive."

"I'm staying here with you, Mama." Elizabeth hugged her mother. At ten and six, she should be more independent, but she'd been her parents' wee bairn until Maeve had been welcomed into the family.

"I'll be careful, Mama," Kyla said. "I am not interested in being held captive ever again, but I need to see Finlay."

"We shall stay up here until I see your father. Then we'll move down below."

Aunt Jennie said, "Here, allow me to help you down the steps, Kyla." She glanced at Maddie, a guilty expression on her face. "I'll check on the lassies after I help her down." She'd sent Riley and Tara to bed with Bethia, Jennet, Brigid, and Maeve. Brin was with his sire, and Gillie had joined them.

Aunt Brenna's eyes widened. "I'm coming. I need to see Quade and Gregor for myself. 'Tis Gregor's first time in a big battle."

Kyla made it down the stairs with her aunt's help, though it was not difficult. Uncle Aedan was already down in the courtyard, and when they joined him, he turned and said, "I believe it's them."

"Do you have food and ale ready?" Aunt Jennie asked.

"Aye. I'm ahead of you women. I've set up two different spots for celebrating—one inside the courtyard and one near the loch."

"Near the loch?" Jennie asked.

"Aye, fresh from battle the best thing is to wash the dirt and blood off. 'Tis a perfect night. The warriors will love being near the water. That will put the loudest noise away from us in the courtyard. The stable lads are busy readying for the onslaught of horses. Most will be kept in the meadow but Black Lightning and Quade and Logan's stallions will be brought in and brushed down. I have extra lads there to ensure they're treated well. Brodie and Nicol are helping get the lads ready. Gillie's with Brin, who said he'd take care of Black Lightning. He loves his uncle's horse. Gillie will be excited to see the victors come riding in. He's a good lad. Puts me in mind of Loki and Kenzie."

"Perfect," Aunt Jennie said. "I've arranged for extra help in the kitchens for Cook. Meat pies and bread for all, lots of ale. I borrowed some from the abbey. They were more than happy to help us feed the lads who put an end to Simon de La Porte. Word reached the monks that he had plans to go after the coffers of the abbey. They sent over fifty huge loaves of bread, thank goodness. I'll go warn Cook."

Uncle Aedan helped Kyla mount her horse. "Nervous, lass? You're sure you can handle the horse?"

"Aye, I feel better being down here to greet them. I hope Papa is all right, and Finlay and Jamie and Jake. 'Twas Connor's first battle. And Sorcha and Molly were there, too, and there are so many I worry about."

"I trust their laird's judgment. If they weren't battle ready, they wouldn't have been allowed along. They'll be here soon. I can feel the vibrations of the horses. I'm quite certain there are more than fifty, so it must by your sire. I promised your mother I'd keep you here until I determined it was indeed your clan and not the Buchans."

"My thanks, Uncle Aedan." She stared out over the moors, the spires of Lochluin Abbey pointing toward the heavens as a backdrop to the rows and rows of galloping horses that had just crested over the ridge. Banners waved in the air and the sound of Ramsay and Grant whoops echoed over the hills. Kyla lifted her face to the wind of the Highlands, saying one last quick prayer for all to be whole. The rippling sound of the banners called to her so she opened her eyes to see her clan riding toward her, hoots and hollers becoming louder the closer they came. She glanced at her uncle as her eyes filled with tears that she fought to swipe away so she could see clearly.

Jamie and Jake carried the banners on either side of her father. They were all smiling and sitting with their heads held high as they slowed their horses. She found Connor off to the side and swiped another tear away so she could locate Finlay, but there was no sign of him. Her heart leaped into her throat and her face broke out in a sweat even though she knew Jamie wouldn't be smiling like that if his best friend had been hurt.

Her father pulled his horse closer to Jake's, and the horse behind him came forward, the rider grabbing the Grant flag from Jamie, and whooped as his horse took the lead.

Uncle Aedan slapped her horse's flank and she took off toward Finlay, who was now leading the group, his eyes on her and only her.

He was magnificent, and as soon as he came abreast of her horse, he reached over and scooped her up off her mount, tossing the flag back to Jamie as he rode off the path away from others, clutching her to his chest.

He stopped his horse and she stared at him, sobbing. "I love you, Finlay. You are well?"

"Aye, my sweet. And I love you. Do me the honor of becoming my wife?"

She nodded, her throat full of tears that kept her speechless. She threw her arms around him and mumbled, "Aye," as soon as she was able. He cupped her cheeks gently so as not to hurt her and kissed her. The crowd around them cheering as they passed by them, their tongues dueling in a fury as he tasted her, telling her how much he loved her in his own special way.

When he ended the kiss, breathless, she whispered, "My sire? Please. I need to see my sire."

He moved her in front of him and turned his horse toward the stables.

☾

Maddie stood just outside the stable, searching the chaos descending on Cameron land as her husband's warriors brought their horses outside the gates and celebrated their victory. Her heart burst with happiness when Finlay broke apart from the others and scooped Kyla onto his lap, kissing her for everyone's entertainment. She was so happy her daughter had found love, and she hoped it would be a good love like the one she herself had found with Alex.

Her gaze drifted past each of her sons to check on them before finally coming to rest on her husband. She caught his gaze and relief swept through her, but she knew him well enough to sense something was off. He rode his horse well, but it struck her that he wasn't carrying a flag. Had he given one to his sons because he wanted to give them the honor as lairds...or because he was weakened from battle? The closer they came, the more she fretted.

Aye, her husband, the wonderful Alexander Grant, was proud of their sons and all they'd accomplished, but his countenance told her two things. First, he was pleased with the outcome of the battle. She knew without asking that the tyranny of Buchan and de La Porte had come to an end. Second, he struggled. He'd not shown his sons how he struggled, but she could see it in his face, in his hands. At the moment, he fought to stay upright on his horse. She glanced at Brodie, the man who'd acted as his second many times, to see if he'd noticed. He nodded to her, mouthing the words, "I'll get him."

Alex rode in a direct path toward the stables, followed fast by Robbie and Connor. Jake and Jamie drew the attention away from their sire, running another circle back around the warriors and Finlay, waving the flags and calling the warriors into another invigorating round of celebration.

Brodie had already made his way to the stables, and as soon as he dismounted, Maddie grabbed his elbow and said, "Bring him to the stall at the end." She raced to the cupboards, pulling out Cameron plaids, and made a bed in the corner of the stall as fast as she could. She would not allow her husband to drop in front of his men.

When she finished, she made it back in time to see Robbie standing next to Black Lightning, appearing to clasp his brother's shoulders while he was actually supporting him. Brodie stood in front of Alex to catch him when his knees buckled as his feet hit the ground. They managed to fake a walk with him until he was inside the stables, and then Brodie called all the lads out to give them instructions. They were each given different directions.

The stables were empty except for Brodie, Robbie, Connor, and

Maddie. Alex caught her gaze as soon as he stepped inside. "Wife, I've come home to you this time."

A tear trickled down her cheek as she leaned forward to kiss him. "And I thank the Lord for that. Alex, if you do not mind, I'd like to sleep here in the stables this eve so we can hear what goes on around us."

He nodded and took a step forward, saying nothing. The glint in his eye told her that he knew exactly why she'd made the suggestion. She'd never allow him to be embarrassed in front of his men. The last experience had been difficult enough for him. This time, he'd come home from the battle with his pride intact.

She was leading him down the passageway to the spot she'd set up when she heard Connor say something. She spun around as her youngest son pushed Robbie aside and then lifted Alex up to carry him down the rest of the passageway.

"Do not put him down alone, lad," Brodie said. "He's too tall. We'll help you."

His brothers helped Connor get him onto the plaids on the straw. Alex was able to say, "Many thanks, all," before he rested his head down on the pillow Maddie had made from the blankets and closed his eyes.

Each of his brothers clasped his shoulder and said, "Well done, Alex." They turned and left.

Connor knelt next to him and said, "You made us all proud, Papa. Now 'tis time to rest." He clasped his father's hand, then kissed his mother's cheek and whispered, "If you need aught, come and get me, Mama. He's just exhausted. He fought hard."

"I know. Thank you, Connor."

"We'll keep everyone away." He reached up to a top cupboard and pulled another blanket down. "Here's another one to cover yourself with, Mama. 'Twill be cool tonight."

When they'd both gone, Maddie lay down next to her husband, her arm over his shoulder. "Alex?"

"What, love?" He opened his eyes and smiled. "Lass, 'tis done. How's our daughter?"

"She's happy now. Quite bruised and she has a sprained ankle, but she'll heal. She told me Finlay asked you for her hand in marriage. She wishes to marry him as soon as possible. What say you?"

He reached over to brush a stray hair back from her face. "I will accept. What say you?"

"Finlay is a fine lad, and she loves him. If you're happy, I'm happy."

"I told him I'd think on it. Besides, the lad saved my life."

"He did? Finlay?"

"Aye, I was fighting in Buchan's great hall and had my back to Buchan. He came at me with his sword. Finlay warned me. That was when I finished the bastard. I'll talk to them both on the morrow."

"What about you? Do you have a wound I should know about? Anything I should tell your sisters?"

His hand rested on her cheek. "Nay, I just need sleep. I'm not as strong as I used to be, but please don't reveal any of my secrets. This spot is perfect. I'll awaken on the morrow to tell you how much I love you and how proud I am of our children...all of them."

His eyelids drifted closed again, and Maddie sighed and kissed his forehead. "I will be waiting for that."

His eyes flew open again and he said, "Och, I forgot to tell you. 'Tis finished. Both." He closed his eyes and began a light snore in a matter of minutes.

She lay on her side, watching this man who had brought her such joy over the years, saying a prayer of thanks to the Lord for bringing him home safely. He'd gained some streaks of gray in his dark hair and some creases around his eyes, but he was still the most handsome man she'd ever met. Her love for him had only grown stronger over the years.

Then something suddenly occurred to her. She kissed his cheek and said, "I'll be right back."

He never moved.

She raced down the passageway of the stables, checking her pockets to make sure she hadn't lost her treasures while she searched each stall for Black Lightning. She almost passed him, but she heard his soft, breathy nicker as she strode by him.

She stopped and turned to her husband's dear horse, opening the gate and stepping inside with him. He tossed his head in a greeting and gave her another soft whinny as though he knew Alex was sleeping.

She stepped forward and rubbed his muzzle, rummaging through her pocket for him. "Did you think I forgot you, my sweet?" She pulled out an apple and held it out for the dear animal. He took it without hesitation so she stepped to his side and rubbed his withers, a movement that often calmed him. "Many thanks to you, my friend, for bringing your master home."

She fixed his dark forelock as she often did, but then laughed when he nudged her arm. "You know I have another, but you must finish chewing the first before you'll get it."

When he finished the first, he nudged her again and she pulled the second apple out, holding it in front of his muzzle. He took it and she leaned in to kiss his forehead. "You did a fine job of bringing your master home tonight, Black Lightning. It could not have been easy keeping him on your back." She gave him a small hug around his shoulders and whispered, "Such a fine job that I promise to return with another treat on the morrow."

She opened the gate and closed it, blowing him a kiss as she padded back down the passageway.

When she passed the door leading outside, she heard Kyla's sobs.

Now what had happened?

CHAPTER TWENTY-ONE

⚘

KYLA SAID, "FINLAY, I NEED to see my papa. Take me to him, please?"

Finlay tugged on the reins and headed toward the stables. Her sire had taken his horse directly there, and she could see he was having trouble dismounting, but Uncle Brodie and Uncle Robbie and Connor had all joined him.

No one else stopped to pay them any mind since Jake and Jamie had called the crowd back out again, hollering and celebrating, raising a ruckus while her father struggled to walk.

Tears streaked down her face as she came closer, but her uncles and brother managed to get her sire inside the stables quickly, keeping everyone else outside. Gillie raced over to Finlay and Kyla, and helped her dismount. "My lord, Cameron land is grand and they make the best meat pies ever!"

Kyla patted his shoulder. "They do, but what about my sire? Where did they take him?"

Gillie pivoted his head to glance over his shoulder. "I know not, but he was hale when I saw him. Finlay, did you get de La Porte? Did you kill him? I hate him."

Finlay filled Gillie in on the details, keeping his hand wrapped around Kyla's waist from behind to help support her weight. Gillie liked to talk, and she didn't wish to draw his attention to her father's condition. Her father disliked wagging tongues, especially when it came to his personal business.

Aunt Brenna stood by the doorway, waiting, after Uncle Brodie and Uncle Robbie came out and headed to the keep. When Connor exited a few moments later, he spoke to Aunt Brenna and then ran to join Jake and Jamie.

She tugged on Finlay's arm, trying to give him a hint that she needed to see her papa. *Now.*

Finlay said, "Gillie, you better do your job with the horses. Whatever Brodie and my sire told you to do. They could use your help."

The lad grinned and scurried off toward the bevy of beasts roaming the area.

But before Kyla could slip into the barn, Finlay's sire walked up and hugged him. "I assume all went well and the threat is gone."

"Aye, Papa. Alex took Buchan out and I settled with Simon de La Porte, but we wish to put it all behind us now. I've asked Kyla to marry me and she's accepted. We just wait for her sire's approval."

His father did his best to hug Kyla without taking her off balance. "Naught could please me more. Your mother always believed you two belonged together."

"She did?" Finlay asked.

"Aye. 'Twas why she wanted you to go that day. She said Kyla could be in trouble and she would feel better if you were there to watch over her." He shrugged his shoulders. "I know not why she felt that way, but she did. Your mother would be pleased. If you hear aught about waiting to wed because your mother recently passed, please ignore it. Your mother would like to see you two happy together." He clapped Finlay on the back and headed into the courtyard.

His father took a few steps before Finlay stopped him. "Papa, how did Mama know Kyla was going? Even I didn't know she'd be traveling with us when I left."

His father shrugged his shoulders again and smiled. "Sometimes, we don't understand everything, lad. Just accept it." He continued on his way.

Kyla brought his attention back to her father. "Finlay, my sire." She pointed in that direction and he helped her over to speak to her aunt.

"Aunt Brenna? How is my father?"

"Lass, do not be upset, but he was verra tired, so your mother made a bed for him in the stables. She's checking him for wounds. Why do you not wait here until your mama returns?"

She nodded and leaned into Finlay, tears coming fast. Though she was relieved that everyone else seemed hale, she worried about her sire. She sobbed into her love's chest, praying that all was well.

Finlay asked, "Have you seen many injuries, Brenna? I've not heard of anything serious yet."

"Aunt Jennie just left to see to the wounds in the hall. Mostly sword wounds, possibly a couple of broken bones. Naught that should be fatal. Bethia is coming down to tend the horses. Still, the Ramsays have not arrived yet. Most of the Menzie and Drummond warriors headed directly home."

Just then, Kyla's mother opened the door and stepped outside.

"How is he, Maddie?" Aunt Brenna asked.

"He's verra tired. He told me he has no wounds, but he needs rest. His strength is not what it should be. In fact, Connor carried him down the passageway. I'm surprised he made it home on his horse. I'm grateful that Black Lightning is so in touch with Alex." She paused, a frown on her face. "Kyla, why do you cry?"

"I was worried about Papa. And I wished to ask him if he would accept Finlay. He asked me to be his wife and I accepted. I wish to marry on the morrow."

Finlay jerked his head around. "Truly? The morrow?"

"Aye. I do not wish to wait. Almost everyone is here. I wish for us to be married in the abbey."

Her mother embraced Finlay first and then kissed her daughter's forehead. "I asked your sire before he fell asleep, and he said he would approve. He tells me you saved his life, Finlay?"

"You did? How?" Kyla asked, shocked.

He nodded, a sheepish expression on his face. "Glenn of Buchan came at him from behind. I just warned him to watch his back. He still moves unlike anyone I know. 'Tis as though his sword is an extension of his arm. He spun around and took Glenn of Buchan out with one blow."

"Why do you not go down to the loch and celebrate?" Maddie asked. "Finlay looks as though he could use the bath, and you could sit and watch the celebration."

Finlay's face lit up. "They're celebrating in the loch?"

"Aye," Aunt Brenna said. "And in the courtyard. Uncle Aedan thought the men would enjoy relaxing in the late summer water. 'Tis actually quite warm. There's ale and food there, too."

Finlay glanced at Kyla. "Och, I'm going in, and you're going with me." He scooped her up in his arms and ran toward the loch.

Her condition must have suddenly dawned on him, for he slowed and a terrible look crossed his face. "I'm so sorry. I must be hurting you. But I wanted to go in the water. I do need a bath. I thought it would be fun."

"You are so gentle, Finlay. I'm not worried unless I have to walk. You didn't hurt me, not even a wee bit."

"Good." He smirked and his eyes sparkled. "Then you're going in with me."

She squealed as he took off across the meadow. "You are daft. I have breeches on because of my leg."

He continued to run until he reached the edge of the water. There were a number of plaids strewn about on the grassy slope, along with a multitude of expectant male gazes from the water. Finlay grinned and said, "Mayhap you're about to get your first lesson in male anatomy."

"Finlay!" She covered her eyes. "Not here."

He threw his head back and laughed as soon as the taunting began from the water. Then he yelled, "*My* male parts are all the lass needs." He took a different path around the loch. "We're going down to this end by ourselves."

The other lads continued to call out to her.

"Kyla, come back."

"Kyla, we love you."

"Kyla, marry me. I'll carry you into the loch."

Much to her dismay, her face turned a bright red. She squealed as she saw a couple of bare backsides as the lads ran into the water, yelling and shouting, having a good time.

"Finlay, nay! Slow down. I'll watch you swim."

He slowed but did not stop. "Do you need to put weight on your ankle to swim?"

She thought for a moment before answering. "You're right. I don't. I'll be able to swim on my own. Just be careful of my hip. 'Tis the only other place that's quite sore."

He stood at the water's edge, ignoring the chorus of well-wishers at the other end of the loch. "Get ready." She screeched again and grabbed his neck. "One-two-three. Here we go." He took off at a dead run and tossed her into the air. She landed in the deeper water with a loud splash, squealing all the way down until she went under.

She came up sputtering, brushing her hair out of her eyes. "It's cold."

He went underwater and popped up in front of her. "Then allow me to warm you." His voice had taken on a husky sound that sent shivers of desire through her. "I promise not to let go of you, and I'll be careful not to touch your hip."

A chorus of Ramsay war whoops rent the air along with the pounding of more horses' hooves, causing the men at the other end of the loch to run out and grab their plaids so they could greet the archers and the Ramsay warriors who'd just arrived.

"The Ramsays have arrived. They'd planned to stop at the abbey. Don't look." Finlay covered her eyes while the warriors climbed out of the water. When he dropped his hand, he whispered, "Now we're truly alone."

He kissed her, a kiss that heated her all the way to her toes. She parted her lips, allowing his tongue inside to tease her, tantalize her, and leave her wanting more. She touched her tongue to his and he groaned, tugging her closer so their bodies fit together perfectly. His arms dropped to her bottom and he caressed her round globes, lifting her so she could wrap her legs around his waist.

"Do you know how it pleases me that you're all mine?" he rasped, panting as though he'd run from the abbey.

Kyla wanted more. "Kiss me again, Finlay."

He ravaged her mouth, taking possession of her as though he'd never get the chance to kiss her again. Her hands wrapped around his neck, setting his hands free, so he brought them around front to caress her breasts. The tunic she had on was wet, and his warm touch through the soaked fabric set her body on fire. He teased her nipples, plucking them and pulling on them until she wished to scream.

"Were we not outside where all could see, I'd have your clothing off in a few seconds and you'd find my tongue on your beautiful breasts, teasing your nipples until you begged me to stop."

"Don't stop, it feels too good." While she'd often wondered what it would feel like to be with a man, she'd never expected it to be like this. That she would be so involved with her mate that she would care for nothing else, hear nothing around her. She wanted him to finish what he had started because she was searching for the edge, the finish she'd heard so much about.

Instead, they were interrupted by the sounds of running feet. "Lasses at that end, lads down here," someone called out to the new arrivals. Connor, Gavin and Gregor were on a dead run headed straight for them, having apparently decided to go to the lasses' end of the loch.

Finlay lifted his head, and together they scanned the shore. Sorcha and Cailean were headed down the length of the loch, Sorcha screaming and Cailean chasing her, yelling, "'Tis a good thing you practiced sprinting all your life." Molly and Tormod followed with Jamie and Gracie, both couples running hand-in-hand. Aline had stayed behind at Grant Castle, but Jake came up behind the others, joining in the fun.

Splash after splash continued through the night.

Kyla had never laughed so hard in all her life.

Just when they thought everyone who meant to join them had, another couple came hauling down the side of the loch, one carrying the other, one cursing and the other laughing.

Uncle Logan leaped into the water, never letting go of Aunt Gwyneth until they both went under with a squeal.

Her *clann* was everything to her.

☾

Alex woke up just after dawn. He rubbed his eyes and checked his surroundings, the truth of all that had transpired settling over him. His wife was still asleep, and he propped his head on his elbow to watch her until she stirred. "You always did want to make love on a mound in the stables, did you not?" he said, stroking her hair.

She sat up and said, "You are better, husband? You did have me worried a bit."

"It pleases me to wake up and know the matter with Buchan and de La Porte is at an end. We're all safe, and we can return to our normal lives."

"With one exception."

He frowned. "What is that?"

"Your daughter wishes to marry Finlay right away. She and your sisters agree the abbey is a perfect place for a wedding. What do you think?"

He shrugged his shoulder and said, "Sounds wonderful to me, as long as it's a few hours away. I just need to find a leine that fits me. I have an extra plaid, though 'tis not my best."

"So you agree?"

"On one condition."

"What?"

He leaned down and nibbled his wife's ear. "I need to make sweet love to my wife first."

Maddie smiled and removed her gown, tossing it off to the side, then lay back down and reached for him. "Agreed."

☾

The next morning, Kyla managed to make it down the stairs with Elizabeth's help, hoping to see Finlay, but the hall was nearly empty. Uncle Logan came over to her right away. "I'll help her, Elizabeth. Why not see what you can find for her in the kitchens?"

Elizabeth smiled and hurried off to find some food.

"Uncle Logan? Is aught wrong?"

Her uncle settled her into a chair by the hearth and propped her sprained ankle up on a stool for her. "How do you feel, lass?" He sat down on the chair next to her.

"Better. Aunt Brenna gave me something for the pain. It comes and goes, but after all I've been through, 'tis not much to handle. I'll not let it slow me down. I wish to marry Finlay this day."

He smiled and kissed her cheek. "I heard that, and I'm happy for you and Finlay. Are you sure 'tis not too soon for you? Mayhap you should wait until you're feeling better."

"Nay," she stared at her hands in her lap. "Truthfully, I've never been so sure of aught in my life. I think we are well suited. After what happened, I'd rather not waste any time."

"You went through a terrible trauma, and it will affect you for a while. You are a strong lass and I believe in you so I will gladly attend your wedding. I think Finlay is a fine man." He waited, gazing into her eyes before he continued. "I have something to tell you, so I'll just say it. Davina is at Lochluin Abbey. She wanted me to tell you she is there with her daughter, and they are both well."

"I'm so glad to hear she's safe! I wished to ask about her. Finlay told me there was no sign of her or the babe in the tower." Davina's uncertain fate had left her unsettled, and she was relieved to hear she'd made it to the abbey after all.

"If you'd like, I'll take you there."

"Now?"

"Right now. 'Tis probably the only chance you'll have if you're to marry later."

"Then aye, I'd like to go."

He stood up and held his hand out to her. "Come."

Elizabeth emerged from the kitchens with a plate of pastries. "Cook only has these ready. She's busy preparing for the wedding."

"Perfect." Kyla took one and thanked her sister. "Tell Mama I'm going off with Uncle Logan, but I'll return in less than an hour."

"Aye, Elizabeth," Uncle Logan added. "'Twill be no longer. We all have things to do."

They left the hall, and he helped her mount before climbing on the horse behind her.

As they rode toward the abbey, Kyla couldn't help but think about how much poor Davina had suffered. Now she'd lost her father, too—he'd become nearly daft, for certes, but the man was still her sire. They arrived before she knew it, and Uncle Logan helped her down. She greeted the abbess, and the woman led them to a small room for visitors.

A few moments later, Davina entered, carrying her daughter on her hip. Uncle Logan kissed Kyla's cheek and left, closing the door behind him.

Kyla stared at her for a moment, so grateful to see her alive and well, then limped over and wrapped her arms around her. "I'm sorry for all your troubles. Finlay told me about what your sire expected of you."

Davina wiped a tear from her eye and moved over to sit in a chair by the window, settling her daughter on her lap. Kyla sat in the chair beside her.

"You are walking?" Davina asked.

"Aye. A wee bit. My aunts have advised me not to walk much, and one of them fashioned a crutch for me, but I'm not handling it well. As you can see, I am healing. With time, *all* my wounds should heal." She stared at the strong woman in front of her. "Will yours? Your wounds are much deeper than mine."

Davina kissed her daughter's forehead as the wee one played with the ribbons on her mother's gown. "I know not. A part of me will miss my sire. He had his faults, but he was my only family.

Our clan has deteriorated over the years, 'tis why the battle was so quick."

"Is there no one for you? An aunt or uncle? Cousin?"

"Nay. I think this is the best place for me." Her gaze followed her daughter's movements as she chewed on anything she could manage to get into her mouth. "I adore Raina, and I'm pleased we are here." As if on cue, Raina turned to smile at Kyla, two wee teeth sticking out of her lower gums.

"You know you will always be welcome at Clan Grant."

"My thanks, but I'd prefer to stay here. I've had enough men in my life for a while. I can live a simple life here. I'll learn to cook with the nuns, and sew and garden, but mostly, I'll be free to spend my time with Raina."

Kyla nodded. "I understand."

The babe began to cry.

"Och, wee one. 'Tis all right. We'll be just fine here. I'll raise you to be a sweet lass, and we'll never be bothered by another man." Tears slid down her cheeks. "I think Ranulf would have been a good father, that is, until my sire planted all those foolish ideas in his head. But I'll never know."

Davina swiped at her tears. "Because of my daughter, I am in a better place. I will pray for you, and pray that someday you will be blessed with a child as I have been. She has changed my life."

"Mayhap someday you'll find a man you could be happy with. Not all men are abusers."

Davina stood and moved to stare out the window. "It wasn't meant to be. Raina and I, we'll not know such happiness. But at least she'll never be forced to endure the horrors I've known. We'll be happy together here." She turned back to Kyla. "I thank you for being one of the few people that ever cared about us."

She nodded to Kyla and left the room.

CHAPTER TWENTY-TWO

FINLAY GREETED HIS SIRE AND his brother when they came into the chamber the Camerons had given them. "Papa, Fergus. I'm so glad you're here to share this day with Kyla and me."

Fergus clasped his brother's shoulder. "I still feel I acted poorly, brother. I should have trusted you, but I was so upset over losing Mama that I lost sight of that. I'm proud of how you carried yourself in the battle."

"Thank you," Finlay said, clapping him on the back. "Papa, I need to tell you something, and I'd like Fergus to hear it, too."

They all sat at the table near the hearth.

"I met Uncle Geordie."

His father was shocked. "Fergus told me Gillie mentioned his name. But how? How would you know it was him?"

"When I awoke in the Buchan keep, Uncle Geordie was sitting there waiting for me to awaken. He and some of the other men had joined Buchan and de La Porte after being promised payment in gold coins. Uncle Georgie said it was strictly business. He was there when we first visited the keep on our mission of peace. I never saw him, but he recognized me and told Buchan I'd be a hell of a warrior. De La Porte sent the note to lure Kyla and me back. They wanted Kyla as a hostage and they wanted me to train Buchan's men."

"Geordie helped them in this?"

He nodded, "Aye. He was paid for doing so. But I tell you this because after Kyla and I were beaten, he came to me again. He was the one who suggested I turn traitor and appeal to the Buchan, agree to fight with him."

His father stood up. "He did what? I'll kill my brother."

"Papa, please sit down and listen to the whole story. You, too, Fergus." They both sat, and though he was doubtful they believed him, he told them the whole story, from the seer to the messages she'd received from his mama to what Uncle Geordie had done for him in the end.

"You expect us to believe the seer was in contact with Mama?" Fergus said, his voice full of disbelief.

"I didn't believe her at first either, but there was no denying she knew things she had no way of knowing. And if I hadn't followed her advice, the battle might have unfolded very differently."

"I don't know what to think," his sire said. "That my brother caused this whole disaster to unfold, or that he helped you. I'll have to give it much thought."

"No one else needs to know. Alex does not know, and I would prefer it if we kept it between us. I've already spoken to Gillie. He doesn't know what Geordie said to me, but he did see him. He won't say aught to anyone. What I'd like you to remember is that Mama was watching over me. Whether you both believe it or not, I do. I knew she was there with me. And Papa, as others have said, Buchan was the cause of this whole debacle, not Uncle Geordie."

"Did you see him after the battle? Did he survive?"

"I know not, Papa. I searched the entire keep while the others searched the grounds outside. The last time I saw him was before the Grants arrived, when he helped Kyla and me escape. I hope he made it out before the battle."

His father stood up. "What's done is done. Now we move forward and you will marry Kyla. I am verra happy for you. Mayhap someday you'll give me grandbairns."

"I hope so, and when I do, Mama will watch over them, too."

"That I believe," Fergus said, nodding.

☾

Kyla sat in the great hall, wiping her hands for the tenth time down the fabric of her gown. More than anything, she wished to twirl her hair with her fingers, but her aunts kept their eyes on her. They had worked very hard on her hair, now intertwined with ribbons. Aunt Jennie had found one of her gowns she'd worn to court and adjusted it to fit Kyla's slim figure. The particular gown they'd chosen covered her bruises better than any other. All the aunts and her mother had spent a few hours fussing over all the details, adding new ribbons and extra beadwork to make it special.

She wore the same color her mother had worn at her wedding, a soft blue that matched her eyes. Her aunts had decided to use silver ribbons and beadwork to go with her nearly black hair, a reminder to all that she was Alex's daughter. A dark blue velvet overskirt had been added to the lower part of the gown.

She had cried tears of joy when she'd tried it on. Her mother's pearls, the same ones that she'd sent to her sire as a signal, adorned her neck.

Aunt Brenna set her hands on Kyla's shoulders and turned her toward the door at the end of the hall. Her mother and father had just entered the door opposite them. Jake, Jamie, and Connor followed them, along with Uncle Aedan.

Elizabeth and Maeve, who'd been sitting by the hearth, hurried over to their parents. "Mama, you're so pretty," Maeve whispered.

"Papa," Elizabeth cried, "you look splendid."

Uncle Aedan laughed. "Aye, he does, but 'twas a challenge finding leines large enough for your brother and your nephews, Jennie."

Her mother leaned down and kissed her youngest daughters before sending them over to Aunt Jennie. "Go along with your aunties. I'll follow soon. This moment is for your sister and her father. Her brothers will lead them."

After much rustling and arranging, the others left. Her mother kissed her on the cheek and said, "You are a stunning bride, daughter."

"Even with all my bruises, Mama?"

She kissed her forehead. "Even with your bruises. I hardly noticed them. You've chosen a fine man, and I wish you nothing but happiness."

Jake kissed Kyla on the cheek before he left to escort their mother to the abbey.

Jamie and Connor stood on either side of their father. Kyla stared at Connor. "Oh my, Papa."

Her sire lifted his brow in question.

"Connor looks exactly like you, and he's the same height."

Connor gave them all a mischievous grin, and her sire rolled his eyes.

Her father glanced at his sons and pointed to the door. "Go check if Gillie and Kenzie have the horses ready."

For the first time since the battle, she was alone with her sire. She pushed on the crutch Aunt Jennie had fixed for her, but her father took it and tossed it off to the side. "I'll support my daughter."

Tears began to flow as soon as her gaze lifted to his.

"Why do you cry on your wedding day, lassie?" His thumb wiped her tears from her face.

"Oh, Papa." He'd just called her lassie, sending her heart into her belly. "I was so worried about you, and I know I was the cause of much of this trouble. I had hoped to help, and I did the very opposite. I just wanted our *clann* to stay the same forever. I tried to take over for both of you because you were wounded and Mama was so worried. I want you and Mama hale and hearty, and for everything to stay the same forever."

He kissed her cheek. "Life is forever changing. You must accept that. Look at the fine young man you've found. He's been there all along—you just needed to find him for yourself."

"Aye. I do love him so. I cry out of guilt *and* gratefulness."

"Buchan would have caused trouble one way or another. You just helped bring it to a conclusion a wee bit faster. Please do not think on it any longer. I slept much better last eve knowing that blight on our land was gone. And now, since I can no longer carry you on my chest, it pleases me to give you to a man I know will protect you. But if you ever sneak off again like that, I'll be chasing you next time." He grinned as he said it.

She giggled. "I promise, never again. You stay at home with Mama." Her hand reached up to brush a piece of lint from his leine. "You look so handsome in your finery, though I know you don't have your best plaid."

"This day is for you. You've chosen a fine man." He held his arm out to her. "Shall we go, my wee princess?"

She smiled and took his arm, happy they'd had this moment together. Jamie and Connor held the doors as they exited the Cameron keep. Kenzie and Gillie fussed over the horses, their eyes on her father, both clearly eager to please. Connor settled her on her horse and fixed her skirts the best he could, which sent Jamie and the two lads into gales of laughter.

"You're just like a lass, Connor," Kenzie said in delight.

Loki had been leaning against a tree keeping an eye on Kenzie and Gillie. He came over and said, "I'll do it, Connor. Hell, know you naught about women?" When he finished, he kissed Kyla's cheek and said, "And that's how you do it, lads."

Kenzie and Gillie laughed so hard everyone else started chuckling with them. Then Alex cleared his throat, and the two lads jumped to attention.

"Aye, my laird."

"Aye, my laird."

Kenzie and Gillie were getting along together even better than she and Finlay had expected.

Loki gave them direction. "Take the reins of the horses. Connor and Jamie will lead with their steeds."

Her father sat atop Black Lightning, looking as regal as any king. Her horse was a beautiful white mare. Her cousins Lily, Sorcha, and Bethia had braided the horse's mane and tail with silver ribbons and had even woven in a small bouquet of bluebells above her forelock. They'd attempted to do the same to Black Lightning, but her sire had balked.

They rode toward the abbey, a much longer ride than it was to the Grant chapel from the castle.

The sun sat high in the blue sky and shone down on the abbey, but an even more impressive sight was the rows and rows of warriors arranged before the abbey. As they got closer, two lines of warriors created a path for them to follow. The guards were all on horseback with their swords held high in the air as a tribute to their lairds. They did not lower their weapons until all had passed them by. Her father held her hand and nodded to his warriors.

At this point, Kyla had eyes only for Finlay, who was also mounted and had ridden out to greet them. He awaited them with his father and brother, all on horseback, at the end of the warrior lines, and he and his family escorted them the rest of the way to the abbey.

Lines of nuns stood along the walkway in front of the church. Several priests were present, too, their cassocks billowing in the wind. This was the abbey's way of showing respect and appreciation to the Grants, Ramsays, Menzies, and Camerons, who had saved them from de La Porte's planned attack.

The Cameron guards had spread out around the two buildings

of the abbey, demonstrating their dedication to always protecting the church.

At the end of their procession, Connor helped Kyla down and her sire leaned over to kiss her. "You've chosen well," he whispered in her ear. Then he stepped back to be with her mother.

Kyla could hear her mother's sobs, a bit stronger than she expected, but when she took Finlay's arm and moved to the front of the abbey to stand in front of the priest, she discovered why.

A gray-haired man pushed himself out of a chair to stand in front of them. Though he struggled a little to get to his feet, a young lad in vestments assisted him.

The man straightened his robe and nodded to them. "Good evening, Kyla and Finlay. My name is Father MacGregor, and since I performed the ceremony at the marriage of your parents, Kyla, nothing could please me more in my old age than to preside over your wedding." He took a moment to greet her parents with a nod. Kyla glanced over her shoulder to smile at them.

Finlay squeezed her hand, bringing her attention back to him, the tall, handsome Highlander who'd stolen her heart in such a short time. He was such a rugged warrior, yet so gentle with her. His bright smile and twinkling eyes lit up her heart, reminding her of his quick wit, and how easily he could send her into gales of laughter.

Soon after he held her hand, his thumb reached around to caress the inside of her wrist, their small intimacy she'd never, ever forget.

Father MacGregor wrapped the Grant plaid over their hands as he continued in Gaelic, and all she could do was say many, many prayers of thanks as she stood in front of Lochluin Abbey, all her *clann* behind her.

When Father told Finlay to kiss the bride, she had to keep herself from leaping into his arms with joy. She and Finlay were husband and wife.

CHAPTER TWENTY-THREE

FINLAY DIDN'T THINK HE COULD be any happier. The festivities began in the courtyard of the Cameron keep, but he and Kyla moved inside, mostly because of her injury. It was too difficult for her to stand on the uneven cobblestones, even with his support.

"I wish I could dance with everyone else." She gave a wistful look at the group of dancers in the middle of the hall.

Finlay kissed her on the cheek and said, "I'll be right back. I'll get you a goblet of wine."

He found her brothers chatting off to the side and explained his plan, hoping he could enlist their help to find proper materials. Fortunately, they liked his idea and took off to get him what he needed. He grabbed two goblets of wine, but he made several stops along the way to the dais. He finally made it back at about the same time as her brothers. The three of them descended on Kyla with expressions that drew the attention of many of the guests.

She peered at the four of them. "Finlay, what did you do?" she immediately said. She knew him too well.

"Naught," he cried. "I just want you to enjoy our wedding."

"So what have you planned?"

Her brothers unfolded the piece of cloth they'd brought in, which was used as part of a tent, and set it on the floor in front of her. Her mother and sire watched, their eyes full of glee.

"Finlay? Explain, please," Kyla said.

"We just wish to dance with our sister," Jake said, answering for him.

Finlay moved behind the dais, scooped her up, and then sat her down in the middle of the makeshift tarp. "Now don't move. Give us a chance to get you stabilized."

The look of fear on her face disappeared as soon as they picked her up, each brother holding onto one corner of the tarp. Finlay had a sturdy hold on the fourth. Her hands rested on the fabric as if that would steady her. He'd advised her brothers not to be too rough, but Jamie and Connor had mischievous looks on their faces.

Jake took over with instructions. "Let's step away from each other first so we can get her centered in the fabric."

Finlay had specifically chosen the corner in front of her so he could see her face. They each stepped back until the material was taut, lifting her into the air so she was level with them. Her squeal caught everyone's attention, so the crowd stepped back to give them room. They motioned for the pipers and the fiddlers to continue with their music.

"Move in a circle," Jake instructed. They started a slow circle, but as soon as they saw how much she was moving, they stepped up their pace, now bouncing her a bit.

Before he knew it, other warriors had moved in to grab a piece of the tarp—Cailean, Gavin, Gregor…they just kept coming.

Her fear seemed to swell up again. "Finlay?"

"Don't worry. If anyone lets go, you'll not fall. 'Tis for your own protection."

"Take one step in, then one step back," Jake said, guiding their movements. He was ever a leader, even now.

The musicians decided to make their music match the event going on in the center of the room. When the men stepped forward, they dropped their volume. When they stepped back, the music moved toward a crescendo—as did Kyla.

That began their pattern. They followed Jake's instructions and moved in together, then moved out. But Finlay had to laugh. Every time they took a step back, the snapping of the fabric tossed Kyla into the air a bit higher.

Her squeals of laughter carried throughout the hall, drawing more and more attention to her. Finlay laughed with her each time she bounced into the air and landed with a squeal.

Jake continued his instructions, and before he knew it, they'd carried her to every corner of the room, bouncing her and twirling her at his discretion. Her father's booming laughter echoed to the rafters. He'd never heard their laird laugh so hard before.

It was all great fun until he saw a slight change in Kyla's expression. She did her best to hide her pain, to endure this discomfort so as not to halt their fun, but he never wished to see her in pain again.

Finlay halted them and motioned for the group to set her down. He scooped her up and carried her toward the tower passageway. He yelled, "Garderobe. Give us some privacy."

The crowd laughed and applauded as he carried her off. She waved to all of their friends and family and guards, a phony smile still plastered to her face.

Once they were alone in the passageway, he leaned against the wall. "What happened? I could see the pain in your face."

She did her best not to give in to tears, but she wrapped her arms around his neck and said, "Naught, 'tis fine. I…"

Just then, Gracie and Lily fell in behind them. "Follow me," Gracie said.

Kyla said, "Nay, please. I don't think I can handle any more. I just need some quiet for a moment."

Lily set a hand on her shoulder. "We know. Gracie and I both know what you've been through, how it feels to be held captive and then thrown back into your normal life when you feel aught but normal. Besides, your body has been bruised and you were tortured. We know what you need. Trust us."

"Follow me, Finlay," Gracie said.

Finlay hoped they knew what they were doing because they'd described exactly how he felt too. He and his wife had been through so much. Celebrating their freedom was special, but he wished for some time alone with her, even if just to hold her close.

They followed Gracie outside. At one point, she stopped them and said, "Hush. We're going by the kitchens, but we're almost there."

Finlay thought his arms were about to break, but he didn't stop. He'd been through worse than carrying his wee bride down a path on Cameron land. Up ahead, he saw an isolated cottage standing in the middle of a forest.

Once inside, he set Kyla down in a chair and the two of them froze. "Where are we?" Kyla asked.

"Your home for your first two nights together." Gracie explained. "This is Aunt Jennie and Uncle Aedan's getaway, the place they go when they wish to be alone. They allowed Jamie and me to use it for our first night together after the battle. We understand the need to be away from everyone. We all love our *clann*, but you need time to settle after all you've been through."

"We left two baskets of food, some ale and wine," Lily said. "Uncle Aedan likes to sleep under the stars." She pointed to the ceiling, which was wide open to the night sky. "Is it not beautiful? He has this contraption set up over the bed so you can use the ladder outside and pull a covering over the hole in the ceiling. There's a small stream not far to the east if you want fresh water."

Finlay glanced around. The place seemed perfect—it would be heaven with just the two of them alone together.

Kyla grasped his hand and said "I love it. 'Tis beautiful with the candles and the flowers. I couldn't have asked for anything nicer."

"Jamie and I will keep everyone away," Gracie said, "but we are all exhausted from the trials we've been through. I doubt the festivities will go verra late. No one got much sleep last night."

They all exchanged hugs, and before Finlay knew it, he and Kyla were alone together. Finally alone.

A fire crackled in the hearth, so he picked Kyla up and sat down in a chair next to the table where the food sat, closer to the fire because dusk was falling and the night air had turned cooler.

She closed her eyes and rested her head on his shoulder.

"Now will you tell me what hurts?"

She took a deep breath and sighed. "I'm sore in spots. Mostly my hip and my ankle. I took some of Aunt Jennie's potion for the pain, and she promised it wouldn't make me sleepy. I wasn't in too much pain—I'd just had enough. I was afraid my ankle would get caught underneath me, and I just wanted to be alone with you." She lifted her head and kissed him quickly before setting her head down again. "I think Gracie and Lily are correct, do you?"

He thought for a moment, rubbing his hand up and down the side of her leg. "Aye, I have to agree with them. 'Twas fun to see so many of us together, to know the fear was behind us, to know we'd won. But then 'twas as if my insides crashed, begging me to take myself away from it all. To…unwind. Every muscle in my body felt tight, like they needed to be released, relaxed." He kissed her forehead. "With you and no one else."

"Do you think we were rash to marry so quickly?"

"Nay. I've never been more certain about aught in my life. We belong together. Allow me to show you." His mouth descended on hers and he kissed her, gently, tenderly at first, before he allowed his need to take over. She returned his passion, teasing him with her tongue, making soft sounds that called him to do more.

He stopped and leaned his forehead against hers. "I've never wanted aught more than I want you. I want to lay you down on that bed, taste every inch of you, and make slow passionate love to you. I want to show you why we belong together, how good 'twill be between us, but I wish to do it so badly that I fear my need will frighten you. Promise me you'll tell me to slow down whenever you feel the need?"

"Aye."

He kissed her again, his hands roaming down her cheeks, across the delicate bone above her chest, down her belly, and then back up to cup her breasts. He teased her nipples through the fabric, please to see she was as responsive to his touch as she'd been before. He wanted this night to be perfect for her, but he was afraid she would tire easily. He followed his hands with his lips, trailing down her neck, nibbling on her earlobe until she gasped, then kissed her neck.

Kyla sat up and pushed his hands away. "Enough."

Hell, what had he done wrong?

CHAPTER TWENTY-FOUR

$\mathcal{L}$

KYLA BOLTED OFF HIS LAP, turned around to present her back to him and balanced herself with her hand on the desk. "First, please remember I have bruises." She glanced over her shoulder at him, hoping not to see any disappointment in his expression.

"I'll bet mine are bigger." His eyes widened and she giggled. "Seriously, lass. You are beautiful to me. Nothing could make you less so."

She turned, cupped his face and said, "I love you. Now, untie these ribbons and get me out of this gown, if you please. And then take me to that bed and do as you promised. You're torturing me and I need more. Please?"

He grinned, but her Finlay loved to tease. Before he stood behind her to untie her buttons, he leaned down to kiss her neck and whispered in her ear, "I cannot wait to feel your bare skin in my hands, in my mouth."

She shivered and she jerked her thumb toward her ribbons. "Undo me."

He laughed. "I have you at my mercy, my dear." He leaned over her and caressed her breasts from behind her, lifting them and flicking his thumbs across her nipples. "My, but they are bountiful, are they not?"

"Oh," she moaned as she leaned back against him. She felt his arousal behind her and decided to tease him in return. She rubbed her bottom against his hardness until he groaned.

"Finlay?" Her thumb pointed again. "My ribbons, if you please."

He set her away from him, but in a position so she could lean against the table. "Aye, my lady."

As soon as he had the ribbons undone, he helped her lift the fabric over her shoulders and she folded it over the back of the chair. Facing him, she put her thumb under the band on her shift, ready to drop it, but she stopped. The expression on his face gave her a dizzying sense of power. She'd thought to tear her chemise off in a hurry and throw it on the ground, but after seeing his expression, she decided to tease him a bit more.

"I can tease, also."

He growled and his gaze followed her hand. She dragged the edge down so it rested on the top of her breast, then continued to inch it down more slowly. His gaze never left her chest, seemingly transfixed. "Is this what you wished for, my lord?" She did a last flick of her wrist and freed one breast, her nipple popping out and standing erect as if waiting for his attention.

He groaned and his head fell to her breast, licking across the underside and up to her nipple. His hand tugged at the other side of her chemise, freeing her other breast so he could cup it with one hand while his mouth and tongue took care of the other one. When he rolled his tongue in a circle around the areola and his teeth nipped at the tender peak, she nearly screamed, gripping his hair and pulling him closer until he took the full mound in his mouth to suckle her.

Her hands shoved against his shoulders. "Your turn," she said.

He smirked and dropped his plaid to the floor. His leine came next, and when she saw him in all his glory, she licked her lips. She beckoned him toward her and kissed each bruise still on his body, then treated his nipples the same way he had hers.

"Where did you learn that?" he rasped, gripping her hips to keep her balanced and pull her closer.

"You just taught me," she whispered. Her hand fell down between them and stopped above his arousal. "May I touch you?"

"Aye, but be careful," he panted.

"Why?"

"If you tease me too much, I'll lose myself in your hand and that will put an early stop to things."

She gripped his erection lightly, enjoying how he groaned and squirmed, his hands on her shoulders. When she started moving her hand back and forth, he stilled her movement and said,

"Enough." He lifted her and set her down on the bed, pulling the covers back before he settled himself on his elbows over her, leaning down to kiss her cheek. "I don't know how much longer I can hold out."

His hands kneaded her breasts, his lips feathered her neck.

"Then don't stop. Finish this."

"I'll hurt you."

"I don't care. Just do it."

He settled his knee between her thighs, nudging her apart so he could tease her entrance with his tip. His finger found her curls and touched her where she'd never been touched before. She'd never known that part of her could feel this way...

Moaning with need, she spread her legs without realizing it. He thrust his fingers inside her and groaned again. "Damn, but you are so slick for me. I love your passion, my sweet."

"Finlay?"

"Relax and wait for it. I'm sorry that this will hurt, but I promise it will get better."

He gripped her hips and thrust inside her. She tensed at the pinch inside her. It did hurt, but it was nothing compared to what she'd been through, and it was already subsiding.

"Are you done?"

"Nay, lass. Just beginning." His finger caressed her bud until she opened for him again. He plunged in again. "Forgive me, tell me when it improves."

A sheen of sweat coated his forehead, and she could tell it was torture for him to wait. She found she did not wish to wait either. "I don't want you to wait, 'tis not that bad."

She spread her legs, and he drove into her again. He pulled back and said, "All right?"

"Aye, do not stop again."

☾

He groaned and buried himself in her tight sheath, then pulled back and thrust again. A small moan came from the back of her throat, and he took that as a good sign. Increasing his rhythm, he pulsed against her again and again until he could feel her need building. Intense pleasure blasted through him, their moans both so loud he couldn't tell whose was whose. He let her set the rhythm until his need hit him so hard that he pounded against her a few times before pulling back enough to tease her nub and force her over the edge.

Her grip on his shoulders tightened and her body clenched, sending him into a burning frenzy to finish this for her, hitting her where she needed it most until she screamed and he followed, his body shaking with a raging orgasm as her body clenched tight around him, her spasms taking every last bit from him.

He was spent, barely able to speak and hold himself above her, and his head fell to her neck. His panting almost matched hers.

"I had no idea. That was wonderful." She laughed and wrapped her arm around his shoulder. "No wonder my cousins are always so happy."

He chuckled and rolled off her, taking her with him.

When their breathing finally calmed, she whispered, "Did I please you?"

"Och, aye."

She fell asleep with her head on his chest, her legs sprawled across his.

C

The next morning, Kyla awakened to find her husband leaning on his elbow staring at her. She smiled, wrapping her arms around his neck, and kissed him. He'd made slow love to her sometime in the middle of the night, and all she could remember was that she'd never been so satisfied.

"You have not changed your mind? I was so randy last night I feared you'd run back to your mama this morn."

"Nay," she chortled. "How could you think such a thing?"

"Good, because Gillie already came to the door. Your parents are requesting our presence this morning in the hall. Some of your extended family are heading home, and they wish to see us first."

She bolted out of bed. "But I'm a mess. I cannot go up there like this."

"There's a tub filled with water that I believe is still warm enough for you, compliments of Jamie and Gracie, who sent buckets of water with the lads."

"Oh, good. I'll just be a moment."

An hour later, they found their way to the front door of the keep.

She managed to use her crutch well enough that Finlay didn't have to carry her. As soon as Finlay held the door for her and she stepped into the great hall, cheers greeted them from the group gathered inside. She blushed, knowing all too well what they were all thinking, but she didn't care. Her parents were seated by the hearth, so she greeted them first.

"Before breakfast, come to the solar for a moment with Uncle Logan," Kyla's sire said.

They followed him into the solar, Finlay with a hand on her hip to keep her balanced.

The door closed behind Finlay, and she found a chair, then stared at the two men. "What is it?"

Her father nodded to Uncle Logan.

Uncle Logan asked, "Did either of you hear aught about someone named Bearchun?"

"I did," Finlay said. "He asked me what I knew of the Ramsay lasses."

"And you said?"

"Naught. 'Tis exactly the word I used. Naught. I didn't recognize him, but then he told me his name."

Kyla said, "He's the one who kidnapped Jennet and Brigid."

"I thought so, but he left and I was in no position to follow him."

"It helps me to know he could still be alive. And now I know he's looking for me. I'll find him first." Uncle Logan paced, his hands twined together behind his back.

"Were there survivors?" Finlay asked.

"Not many," her father said. "But there are always some who run when they see which way the battle is turning, especially if they've been brought in as mercenaries. He may have gotten away."

Her sire paused for a moment, then asked, "What did you learn from Davina? Logan tells me you visited her at the abbey."

"I did speak with her. She's a woman who has had a most difficult life. I feel sorry for her, Papa. But she's pleased to be at the abbey, and says she'd not interested in having another man in her life." Finlay reached for her hand and squeezed it. "I think 'tis right for her," Kyla continued. "She may change her mind someday, and I told her she'd be welcome at Clan Grant."

"I'm glad to hear that, and if she came, I would welcome her." Her father stood. "No more questions. The rest of this morn is for everyone's entertainment, but we've kept this group to our immediate *clann*. Join us in the hall."

Uncle Logan got up to help her, then led her and Finlay to a couple of chairs in the middle of the hall.

"What is this about, Uncle?" She glanced around the hall and the entire group stared back at her and Finlay. There were all sorts of puzzling expressions—excitement, anticipation, eagerness…

Uncle Logan stood in front of them, and she could hear her sire's deep chuckle behind her. "We need answers, lass."

"Answers?" She glanced at Finlay and then at her brothers off to the side.

Connor stood up and said, "Aye. We have many questions, and we have wagers, besides."

Uncle Micheil pointed at the group of lads seated at the same table as Connor. They were the guards who'd been on the mission to Edinburgh, along with David, Micheil's son, and Jake and Jamie. "Rumors and tales have been floating around. The lads were actively involved in this, and they need to know what's true and what's a tall tale. We can't answer them, and truth be told, there are many of us who would like answers of our own. So the lads are each allowed one question, and you're to answer truthfully. We've all agreed to do the same. Do you and Finlay agree to this?"

She glanced at her husband and shrugged her shoulders. He laughed and said, "Sure. As long as it's about the battle and not about last night. Because I'm sworn to secrecy…"

Kyla swatted him while everyone laughed and teased them.

Uncle Logan stood up and said, "I'm the moderator. No questions until it's your turn."

After everyone agreed, he pointed to Jake. "You get first question and you must direct it to one or the other."

Jake stood. "Kyla, did you really stick a dagger in Simon de La Porte?"

Kyla said, "True. In his leg."

Jamie raised his hand. Logan said, "Go ahead, Jamie. You're next."

He stood before delivering his question. "Kyla, did you throw your dagger and hit de La Porte?"

Kyla shook her head, and the table of lads jumped out of their chairs, each pointing at the others, yelling about who was right and who was wrong, who'd won the wager.

Finlay stood up and held his hands out, halting the ruckus. Then he said, "It wasn't her dagger she threw, it was Simon's."

That set the group into a round of bellowing, stomping, and slapping one another on the back. Finlay pulled Kyla to her feet, helping her balance, and whispered in her ear. "Tell them exactly what you did. 'Tis part of the glory of winning a battle. They want to hear your tales."

Once the group settled, she said, "Aye, he tried to force me to do something I didn't wish to do, so I stuck my dagger into his thigh, which made him jump back screeching, and I noticed a table covered with his weapons, so I grabbed a dagger and flung it across the chamber, catching him in his shoulder."

Dead silence followed as everyone present stared at her in awe.

Connor raised his hand.

Uncle Logan gave him the floor.

He stood up and asked, "Did my sister truly spit in Simon de La Porte's face?"

Kyla couldn't have been more astonished. Apparently, they'd had quite a conversation in their absence. "Where did you hear all of this?" Who had been around to witness that happening?

Gillie stood up and raised his hand. "I just told them what I heard from the Buchan guards."

Finlay laughed and said, "Well done, Gillie."

The lad sat back down and Uncle Logan pointed to her. "Truth, niece? Did you spit on him?"

She rolled her eyes and said, "Aye." Then she pointed to her black eye. "Got me this."

The table of lads erupted again.

Jake nodded to both of his brothers, marched up to Kyla, and knelt in front of her. He dropped a bouquet of bluebells at her feet, and Jamie followed him with a bouquet that he held up for all to see. Gracie clapped and broke into hysterical laughter as he dropped a bouquet of purple thistles at Kyla's feet.

Jake and Jamie both stood back, waiting for the last one.

Connor came forward, shaking his head. "I lost all my wagers, Kyla, but you deserve these." He knelt in front of her and handed her a bouquet of primroses.

The three stood back and bowed, saying in unison, "We salute you."

The entire hall broke out in applause and Kyla couldn't stop her own laughter. She stood with Finlay's help and managed to hug each of her brothers before they sat down. As soon as she sat down again, her sire stood. A respectful silence fell over the hall as he strode over, stood to the side of her, and leaned down to plant a kiss on the top of her head. Then he squeezed her shoulder before he announced, "'Tis my lassie."

Uncle Logan calmed everyone down and said, "We have a few more." He looked over the crowd and pointed to David.

David stood and asked, "Finlay, did you truly force your way up to see Kyla by holding a dagger to Simon de La Porte's throat and then take eight of his men out by yourself? What happened next?"

Finlay stood and said, "True. Gillie informed me that Kyla had been beaten, so I beat the wall in my cell with a stool until Simon came down. He and one of his men came into my cell. I took care of the man, then grabbed de La Porte and twisted his own dagger to his throat and made him take me to see Kyla. Once I saw her, he told me he'd have his guard cut her throat if I didn't drop my dagger. I dropped it, then fought off as many of his men as I could. Don't remember it all." He glanced over at his wee friend. "Gillie, eight? Truly? I don't remember."

Gillie stood up and demonstrated how Finlay had fought, sending the wagering group into gales of laughter again.

"Next," Uncle Logan said, scanning the room.

Torrian raised his hand.

"Go ahead, Torrian."

"Finlay, did you really slice de La Porte's arm off with one stroke?" The other lads shouted out over this one.

"Not true." Silence followed. Finlay said, "It took two strokes, and then..." He mimicked a man's arm falling off. The entire hall exploded over his answer.

"Am I allowed a question?" Finlay asked.

Logan said, "Go right ahead."

He stood up and asked, "Did I really see someone shoot a dagger from atop the curtain wall that struck one of the enemies right between the eyes?" He scanned the group and waited. He heard a couple of comments from the table of lads.

Gavin said, "I saw that."

Gregor said, "I did, too."

They all waited, but no one stood up to claim the act as their own.

Logan said, "You all agreed to stay and participate. Someone has to stand up. I've never seen a dead eye like that. I'll bend on my knee in front of whoever threw that dagger."

Kyla guessed who it was, but it wasn't for her to say.

After a few moments, Maggie stood, her face a deep red.

Uncle Logan's eyes widened and he whispered, "Maggie?"

She nodded, her eyes downcast.

Her father ran over to her and hugged her.

"That's my lass. I'm so proud!"

CHAPTER TWENTY-FIVE

☙

FINLAY STOOD WITH HIS ARM around his wife, waving to another group as they left for home. Earlier that afternoon, the remaining Ramsays, Menzies, and Drummonds had all taken their leave. Kyla's mother had requested that they stay one more day, though she had not said why. Alex had sent a large group of the Grants home with Jake and Jamie. Finlay's family had chosen to go back to Grant land with the others. Connor, Maeve, and Elizabeth remained. They were more than happy to stay on with their Cameron cousins.

Aunt Jennie came flying out of the kitchens, a basket in her hands. "For you, Kyla. Take your husband back to the cottage and spend the evening together. You're not far from the loch and can take a cold swim, if you'd like." Then she leaned over to whisper. "I think your mother wanted your sire to have another day of rest before they tackled the trip home. I know she feels better with either Aunt Brenna or me near when he's not at his best. He'll be fine on the morrow. I'm taking the wee lassies for a picnic and Uncle Aedan is taking the lads out to check our land. So here's your supper."

Finlay couldn't have been more pleased. "My thanks, Jennie."

Kyla peeked under the linen to see what was in the basket. The aroma of fresh bread and berries floated in an enticing cloud of steam. "Aunt Jennie, it smells wonderful. Thank you."

"And there are meat pies packed underneath. We don't expect you until the morrow. I'll make excuses for you."

Kyla kissed her aunt, then said her goodbyes to her parents seated by the hearth.

Once they'd arrived back in their cottage, Kyla removed her boots and sat on the bed.

"Tired, lass?" Finlay asked. He couldn't ignore the dark circles under her eyes. He had kept her awake most of the night. "Why not take a brief nap? Then I promise to make you smile later. It will be a night you'll never forget." He whipped off his leine, leaving himself with only his plaid on. He struck a muscular pose and said, "I'm sure you want more of this."

She laughed and fell back on the bed. He helped her position her foot so it was elevated as Aunt Jennie had suggested, then fell into bed beside her. They were in a perfect position to look up at the sky above. They hadn't replaced the covering over Uncle Aedan's lookout in the ceiling.

He stared at the blue sky. "I love this view. Mayhap once it's dark, we'll take the time to look at the stars. I was too busy looking at you last night."

She laughed again, grabbing ahold of his hand. He set his other hand behind his head.

She sighed. "I suppose I am a wee bit tired. 'Twas a tiring day."

"Aye, 'twas just the day that was tiring. All that time in captivity was wonderful because I was so relaxed and slept like a lamb. Did you not do the same?"

"Oh, Finlay. I love you." Giggling, she rolled onto her side toward him, adjusting her foot. "I guess we did have an exhausting sennight or two."

He rolled his eyes and caught her gaze. Her eyes then closed, so he allowed his to flutter shut, too.

The next time he awakened, it was dark because he'd only left one candle lit in the wall sconce.

Her voice came to him, a whisper full of awe. "Can you believe how beautiful it is?"

He tugged her over and she rested her head on his shoulder as he wrapped his arms around her. "Aye, 'tis a wonderful view. We don't have many clear nights in the Highlands, but there's not a cloud up above."

"Finlay, do you think your mother is watching us?"

He tried to think of a way to convince her. "Aye, I truly do."

"How do you know?"

He struggled with his words, but he didn't have to wait long. He pointed at one section of the night sky.

"That's how I know. 'Tis my mother telling me she's happy."

A shooting star blazed a trail across the darkness, telling him all would be well.

EPILOGUE

ॐ

THE CAVALCADE OF HORSES TRAVELED toward Ramsay land in the early evening, having finally taken their leave from Cameron land two days ago.

"Push it, Torrian. I want to be back on Ramsay land by dark. We'll not keep the bairns and the women sleeping in the night air again. We can make it," Quade shouted across the horses.

Logan nodded to his brother, indicating his agreement. One of Lily's twins had started with a cough last eve. It was time to be back in their own castle. The Buchan fiasco was finally behind them.

He glanced over the column of the riders, checking his family's formation. Torrian rode in front with his wife and children, Maule at the back with Lily and the twins. Quade and Brenna rode near the front with Bethia while Gwyneth rode near the back with Brigid, Maggie next to her. Jennet and Sorcha were in the middle with Cailean assigned to protect them.

Over a hundred guards traveled with them, some in the lead, some at the rear, but most at the periphery as protection.

He kept Molly, Tormod, Gavin, and Gregor at precise archer locations near the outside of the group, able to check for anything in the trees and shoot in a second but still protected by the guards.

No one would get near Logan Ramsay's close family.

He wouldn't calm until they were safe within their own curtain wall.

As he galloped up the side of the procession, Gwyneth called to him, "Logan, relax. We're almost there."

How he wished he could. He hated having all the people he

loved most in one open place. Aye, there were plenty of guards, but there was too much at stake. He should have split them up, but at this point, they were almost at their destination. He'd breathe a sigh of relief as soon as they were on Ramsay land, where another fifty guards should be awaiting them for escort.

A chill ran up the back of his neck.

He turned his head from side to side, scanning the area for any movement, any creaking of a branch, but he saw nothing.

☾

He sat not far from the convoy of Ramsays, huddled up in the tallest tree he could climb and behind the thickest leaf cover possible.

Bearchun stuck his head through the branches for just a moment before ducking back behind his cover.

They were all there. A slow smile crept across his scarred face. He rubbed his eye out of habit, grateful the sword that had cut him in battle had missed his eye socket, instead leaving a gash across his cheek and forehead, almost completely scabbed over. No one else would feel the same, but he'd been grateful the wound had been to his face because he couldn't see the blood. Having the injury out of his line of sight prevented him from passing out cold whenever he saw the red fluid flowing, the malady he'd gained from the wee Ramsay witch. Once she'd cursed him, the condition had worsened.

He'd make them pay.

The Grants and Ramsays had ruined everything *again*. He'd given Sorcha up for the chance to fight with the renowned Simon de La Porte, the grand spitter as Bearchun had liked to think of him. The bastard hadn't carried through on the number of mercenaries as promised, and their measly three hundred men had been massacred by the mighty Grant/Ramsay force of over five hundred. He'd heard one swear he'd counted seven hundred.

Hogwash.

Either way, they'd cost him the gold coins Buchan had promised him. Buchan and de La Porte were both dead, along with the majority of their guards. Dead men can't pay. He'd returned a few days after the battle to scour Buchan's castle in search of his bounty, but Grant guards had still covered the area, making a true search impossible. The two clans had cost him nearly everything again. He needed coin to get to London. One way or another, he'd get that bounty out of the clan that had caused all his trouble—the Ramsays.

They were not invincible. This would require careful planning, but he could do it. There would be no rush this time. He'd do it his way—there was no need to follow MacNiven's or de La Porte's or Buchan's plan.

His way.

He knew how to bring them down. Sweet Sorcha was never out of her husband's sight, so he had to abandon her, especially since her husband was a maniacal beast.

Then there was the one called Jennet. He'd never go near that wee witch again. He crossed himself, breaking out in a cold sweat at the thought of the power she wielded.

The wee one's friend Brigid cried too much, so she was out of the question.

He'd given this careful thought and decided who the perfect target would be—the one who'd been in the chamber when he'd kidnapped the other two. She'd never made a movement or a sound, frozen in fear. She was Quade and Brenna Ramsay's first born, riding near the front of the group.

That's who he'd grab this time, and the power would finally be his.

☾

The parade of horses finally crossed into Ramsay land, and Logan couldn't be happier. Yet something did not feel right.

"Molly, you see aught?"

His eldest daughter shook her head, but he recognized the expression on her face.

"Headache?"

She lifted her gaze and turned her head so the others wouldn't see the tears misting her eyes. "Aye, my head began to hurt when we crossed into Ramsay land."

He leaned over and kissed her forehead. "Go on home and rest. You've been through too much. I'll check everything."

Tormod motioned for her to move ahead of him.

Molly's headache was not a good sign. She had visions of the future, oft preceded by terrible pain in her head. Logan shouted, "Cailean? See anyone?"

"Nay, there's no one there that I could see."

Maule held up the end of the Ramsay family line. "Did you see anyone, Maule?"

Kyle shook his head. He waited until Lily and the rest were far enough ahead of him to not be overheard. Kyle rode over to Logan. "Why? What is it?"

Logan's gaze narrowed as he scanned the area behind them one more time, stopping at the forest in the distance.

"I'm not sure."

He glanced in the opposite direction, not finding anything, but unable to shake the feeling in his gut.

Kyle asked, "Logan?"

Logan turned his head back to Kyle. "I can't explain it, but I smell something foul."

~ THE END ~

NOVELS BY KEIRA MONTCLAIR

DEAR READER,

Thank you for reading Kyla and Finlay's story. Finlay and Fergus were always wee favorites of mine back in Jennie's story when they tried to help their sire heal from battle.

Losing Inga was difficult, but if I were true to medieval times, there would be many more who would never have survived long enough to make it to the second series. Her battle with ovarian cancer would have just been identified as a growth in her belly back then.

My next story will be Bethia's story. Expect to see more in the future of the group of cousins that began in this novel: David, Braden, Roddy, Gavin, Gregor, and Connor. These six will grow together and who knows what will happen? You can also expect to see Maggie's story not too far down the road.

Too many stories, too little time…

Want to help an author? Tell your friends about your favorite books, and leave a review on Amazon and/or Goodreads. I will be grateful.

To sign up for my newsletter: **www.keiramontclair.com**
My Facebook page: **www.facebook.com/KeiraMontclair**
My Pinterest page: **www.pinterest.com/KeiraMontclair**

Happy reading!

Keira Montclair

ABOUT THE AUTHOR

KEIRA MONTCLAIR IS THE PEN name of an author who lives in Florida with her husband. She loves to write fast-paced, emotional romance, especially with children as secondary characters in her stories.

She has worked as a registered nurse in pediatrics and recovery room nursing. Teaching is another of her loves, and she has taught both high school mathematics and practical nursing.

Now she loves to spend her time writing, but there isn't enough time to write everything she wants! Her Highlander Clan Grant series, comprising of eight standalone novels, is a reader favorite. Her third series, The Highland Clan, set twenty years after the Clan Grant series, focuses on the Grant/Ramsay descendants. She also has a contemporary series set in The Finger Lakes of Western New York.

Her newest series is The Soulmate Chronicles, historical romance with a touch of paranormal.

www.ingramcontent.com/pod-product-compliance
Lightning Source LLC
Chambersburg PA
CBHW071907220626
47052CB00002B/242

9 781947 213029